DEAL WITH THE DEVIL
BOOK FOUR

DANCE
with the
DEVIL

CARIN HART

For those of you who want a tatted motorcycle man with a soft touch and a fierce bite...

FOREWORD

Thank you for checking out *Dance with the Devil*!

At the end of *Dragonfly,* it was revealed that Genevieve, Damien's beloved younger sister, had gone missing. She disappeared with an unnamed member of the Dragonflies' former rival/current ally, the Sinners Syndicate. That man is Carlos 'Cross' da Silva, the official tattooist for the Sinners, and a minor character that's appeared in both *The Devil's Bargain* and *The Devil's Playground.* This book explains what happened to Genevieve and Cross: starting with their first meeting to the moment they were taken captive by the next big bad of the series —and the aftermath of a traumatic few weeks following being kept in a cage.

Because of the nature of the book, as well as the hero's backstory, it has some heavier themes, though it does end with a happily-ever-after (no matter how it might seem otherwise). It also sets the stage for the finale, *Ride with the Devil*, coming in early 2025!

Dance with the Devil includes: instalove; insta-obsession; murder (on-page); body mutilation; captivity; forced sex acts (the hero and heroine together, forced to be by the villains); dubcon; mentions of childhood sexual abuse (the hero by his stepfather); childhood trauma (including the hero losing his family in a fire); grief; disordered eating; denying food; insomnia; homophobia/slurs; unprotected sex; discussions of abortion (amid a possible pregnancy), guns, drugs, and sex work.

xoxo,

Carin

mariposa

ONE
THE PLAYGROUND

GENEVIEVE

If my brother knew I was here, he would kill me.

Well, no. Not me. He loves me, and would forgive me almost anything.

But Christopher? He doesn't have a prayer.

My best friend is nibbling on his thumb nail as he stands on the edge of the dance floor. Slender, if a little lanky, the low-cut silky blouse he has on is so different from the suit he normally wears, but it's perfect for a night out at the club. Though, if the slight furrows in his brow are any sign, he's wishing that he'd managed to talk me into going to an establishment on the East End of Springfield rather than the West Side.

Silly Christopher. The East End is Dragonfly territory. What would the fun be in that? The Libellula Family owns the drug trade in this city, plus the counterfeiting ring, and there are plenty of nightclubs where I'd be welcomed in on sight despite the fact that I don't have the trademark dragonfly inked on my arm. After all, as Genevieve Libellula, my name is all it takes.

But that's the East End. On the West Side, no one knows who I am. That's how Damien prefers it, and my overprotective older brother has gone to great trouble over the years to keep me away from his rival's territory. From giving orders that I can't leave the three-floor manor where I live with him, his new wife, and our cousin, Vin, to insisting that I only agree to dance on stages far from this part of Springfield, I've been coddled and shielded from the brutality of his criminal empire since he became my guardian when I was only ten.

Damien is fifteen years my senior. Sometimes, he seems to forget that I'm not ten anymore. You'd think that after we hosted his fortieth birthday dinner a month ago, he'd realize that I'm firmly in my mid-twenties, but that's never going to happen. If I leave it up to him, I'll be seventy-five instead of twenty-five, and that man will still think I'm too delicate and innocent to know the truth about what it's like to run a Family in a crime-filled hotspot like Springfield.

Not only am I nowhere near as innocent as Dame thinks—except in one way, and that's part of the reason why I'm here tonight—but I'm *fascinated* by the darker side of my brother's career. I always have been. I know better than to think he'll ever let me help him run the Family, but if I can prove to him that I'm not the little girl he's convinced I am...

Step one: realize that there is life beyond ballet and doing what Damien tells me.

Ignoring my brother's stubborn insistence that I be a mafia princess instead of a co-runner of the Family is easy. When there's never been any repercussions to defying him, I got into the habit of blowing Dame off when I was a rebellious teen. Scaling back on ballet was harder, but as I got older, I had to admit that I wouldn't be able to dance forever, even if I wanted to. My body doesn't bounce back like it used to, and my marathon training sessions while I'm preparing for an upcoming performance suck way more now than when I was younger.

I still stretch and dance and perform as much as ever. Only I also sneak out of my bedroom a handful of times a month so that, for a night at a time at least, I can just be 'Gen' instead of Genevieve Libellula.

Of course, whenever I try, all it takes is one look at Christopher's guarded body language to know that I can never forget for a moment what my last name is—or the identity of my brother.

Christopher is my best friend. He's also Damien's admin, which is a fancy way of saying that he runs my brother's calendar, keeping track of all of the meetings he has—both legitimate and not—as well as doing all kinds of odds and ends for the head Dragonfly. I got him the job when we were eighteen, and he's spent the last seven years making himself indispensable to Damien.

But despite my blonde hair, I'm not a ditzy idiot. Christopher is my best friend, but Damien is his boss. When I sneak out, I'm pretty sure my brother has no clue what I'm doing—in order for him to, he'd have to have figured out there's a blind spot for his cameras near my room, and that the tree growing outside my window makes it possible for me to shimmy down and slip away sight unseen—but I have no illusions about why Christopher offers to join me on my adventures.

He's not just my wingman. He's my chaperone.

Tonight, his leather pants are so tight, they're basically plastered to his ass. That shirt leaves little to the imagination. Knowing him as well as I do, I'd put money down that he has at least one weapon tucked out of sight *somewhere*, and if anyone threatens me, he'll handle it since God knows Dame would definitely kill him if he doesn't.

Christopher has come a long way from the shy eight-year-old boy who was teased for taking ballet lessons before I punched Lindsay Chant in the lip to get her to leave him alone. We've been fast friends since the day I protected him, and if he has this silly idea that I need *him* to protect *me*, I'm happy to let him... so long as he lets me have my fun, too.

I don't like to think of it as blackmail. It's such a dirty word for the agreement between Christopher and me. But we've been sneaking out to be wild teens since before

Damien hired him on, so as far as I'm concerned his loyalty is to me first. Will he ever admit to Damien that he follows me all over Springfield—including Sinners Syndicate turf? If he had to, I'm sure he would. But since this is a case of 'what Damien doesn't know, won't hurt him'...

I'm staring out at the dance floor, working up the nerve to go out there and shuck my training, letting the music move me, when someone near the bar catches my eye.

I grab Christopher's arm. "Hey. Is that her?"

He cocks his head, raising his voice over the noise as he asks, "Where?"

I don't want to point, so I tug on him, guiding him until he's staring in the same direction as me. "There. The Playground uniform. Waitress... she's got a serving tray in front of her."

"You mean the redhead that I've been dying to fuck? Yeah, that's her. That's Jessie."

My gaze goes from the blonde waitress I was staring at to the other one. Ah. So that's who *Christopher's* been watching.

As a Dragonfly, he'll run his gaze over the crowd, searching out any threats.

As a man, he has his eyes set on his next target.

I let go of him. "That's not who I meant, but— hang on, Jessie's a chick?"

Christopher is bi. I shouldn't be surprised that the Jessie he mentioned a few times these last couple of weeks is a woman. Unlike me, he's definitely *not* stuck with his V-card. Lately, though, he's been dating mainly guys. There was Sal. Ben. Tony was around for a couple of weeks before he ghosted Christopher, and then he had a fling with one of the newer Dragonflies that didn't last. As far as I know, he's been single for a bit now.

No wonder he didn't really push back against me earlier when I told him that we could go out tonight because Damien would be spending most of the evening in the basement gym, 'training' Savannah—and I say 'training' because while he's definitely teaching his wife self defense techniques, I made the mistake of opening the door to the basement the other night and discovering that that's not *all* they do down there. They're definitely going to be too distracted to come up to the third floor and check to see if I'm there. And since Christopher would be cruising for a little action of his own...

It's been a while since he's been hung up on a woman. Part of me wonders if that's because, if he dated more girls, Damien could remember that Christopher might one day hit on me. I know better. That'll *never* happen. We're best friends, and as much as I want something like Damien and Savannah have—except, maybe, for the whole stabbing meet-cute thing that my brother still refuses to elaborate on—it's not going to be with Christopher.

But I want him to be happy, too, so I give the redhead a once-over. Her hair is a fiery if unnatural shade, wild and wavy, and it's styled around a striking face. Add that to the tits she has on display and the sassy way she cocks out her hip to rest her empty serving tray on it, and I nod.

"She's hot," I tell him.

"Hell yeah, she is. Nice, too. Last time I came by, she comped me a free drink."

I poke him in his upper arm. "You came by without me?"

He winces, more from the accusation in my tone than the fact that my fingernail did any damage. "Sorry, Gen. But that was a night when your brother was home and you thought he'd check on you. Tony texted me and invited me to hang out at the Playground. He was such a good lay, I thought I'd give him another chance."

I roll my eyes. I should've guessed. No wonder he didn't tell me. After how pissed Christopher was after Tony ghosted him and how he ranted to me about the disrespect, I would've given him an earful if I knew he gave Tony a second chance.

"And? You make up with Tony before he disappeared on you again?"

Because if he has his eye on Jessie, Tony's no longer a focus for Christopher. He might change lovers as frequently as I change my underwear, but he's loyal.

"Never happened. He was a no-show. So I flirted with my waitress a bit, and she gave me the drink. I meant to get her number, but I got a call and had to head out before I could. But I see she's here tonight. Maybe that's a sign I should... wait. I was talking about Jessie. Who were you talking about?"

"Me? Oh. Yeah. The blonde next to her."

"What about her?"

"Is that the girl? The one who was with Kieran when he got killed?"

Christopher glances over at me. "And how do you know about that?"

Is he serious? "Because you told me that Dame lost one of his enforcers after the thick idiot tried to steal a Sinners' girlfriend from him."

There's more to the story than that. Between Christopher and what I overheard at Damien's dinner party—when he was too busy keeping an eye on Savannah's introduction to the Family to notice I was eavesdropping on some of his soldiers as usual—it seems like one of my brother's top killers went rogue, kidnapping his ex-girlfriend after she moved on with a member of the Sinners Syndicate.

That man ended up shooting Kieran to get her back, and he put the word out that he'd do the same to anyone else who hurt her. I was curious when I heard that—like me—she was purposely kept out of the life, instead working as a waitress at the Devil's Playground.

Makes sense. From what I learned, her husband is the second command to the Devil of Springfield himself, and he also manages the Playground. I haven't seen him prowling around the crowded club just yet, but when I noticed the pretty blonde and she looked a bit familiar, I had to wonder if that was her.

It made me wonder other things, too. What would it

be like to be so loved by a man that he'd do anything to keep you safe? To make you his? Not because he's your brother and he thinks he still has to take care of you after all this time, but because you're the one woman he can't live without?

I have no idea, but here's hoping that one day I'll find out.

For now, I'm content to needle and tease my best friend while, if only for a couple of hours, I can shed the mantle of who I am, and who I'm supposed to be.

Christopher flushes as he realizes I'm right. "Oh. Yeah. I did say that, didn't I?"

"Don't worry," I tell him, going up on my tiptoes so I can throw both my arms around his neck, laying my head on his shoulder. "I didn't let Damien know that, after a gin and tonic or two, you gossip like a schoolgirl."

"Thanks, Gen," is his dry response. "I appreciate it."

I kiss his cheek, then let him go. The blonde waitress has disappeared into the crowd, serving the tables that border the edges of the dance floor. I decide I'm bored with the topic of whether that was Nicolette Williams or not, instead focusing on the redhead who still has Christopher's attention.

I tap my chin. I'm not sure if it's because of the obvious dye job influencing me or not, but... "She looks like she might be feisty. You sure you want to take her on for size?"

"If she'll have me, *definitely*."

From across the floor, I watch as Jessie suddenly

flips her empty serving tray up, then swings it out, smacking one of the male club-goers in the back of his head after he boldly grabbed her tit as he 'danced' by her.

The man spins on his heels, looming over her, but the much smaller Jessie tilts her head back, jutting her chin as she says something to him.

As though summoned by the commotion, two guys in black suits appear just as suddenly behind her. She angrily waves them off, her body language making it clear she's more than willing to handle the handsy customer on her own.

I bump Christopher with my hip. "My fucking God, she's going to eat you alive."

Christopher's dark eyes light up. "If there is a God, I hope she will."

"Then what are you waiting for?" One of the suits leans down, saying something to Jessie. She reluctantly nods, and the guy grabs the customer by the arm, muscling him away from the bar. Jessie tosses her hair over her shoulder, slams her tray on the countertop, and leans over to talk to the bartender. Christopher is watching her every move as if hypnotized. I nudge him. "Go say hi."

"She just got groped, Gen. I don't think she'll want to be hit on right now."

"Or maybe she'll appreciate a good guy who won't cop a feel because she's working the dance floor," I point out.

Christopher narrows his gaze, looking as if he's seeing

me for the first time. "You're trying to get rid of me, aren't you?"

I give him my most innocent expression. "Me? Why would you say that?"

"Because I know you, Genevieve—"

"Ooh. Full name. I'm in trouble." I pause for a moment, thinking it over. "I call you Christopher all the time. Does that mean, if I shortened you to 'Chris', that's when you're in trouble?"

Christopher exhales, pinching the bridge of his nose.

I grin. "You've been hanging around my brother too much. When I get on his last nerve, Dame makes the same exact face you just did."

"Forget it. I know what you're up to." He glances at the bar again—and takes a step closer when he notices that Jessie is still hanging around there. "And there's nothing I can do about it right now. Fuck it. I need a drink."

Huh. That's a new record. We've only been at the Playground for about ten minutes. Usually Christopher makes it at least a half an hour before he has his first gin and tonic in hand. Too worried that I'll get into trouble—and then *he'll* get into trouble with my brother—he stays sober while we have these secret nights out. He's my ride, after all, but I consider it a success if I work the uptight Christopher enough for him to have two drinks before he inevitably announces it's time to leave.

But if he wants an excuse to go to the bar...

"Ooh. Get me a piña colada if you're heading that way."

His lips purse a little, like he's trying to hide his smile. "Virgin, right?"

And... that's what I get for poking at him earlier.

"Haha," I say dryly. "Very funny."

I don't drink alcohol. That's a leftover from my hardcore ballet days. I still audition. I still train and practice and dance every day. But now that I'm responsible for myself, instead of studying under Madame Durand, I don't freak out about gaining ounces like I used to. I'll splurge with a mocktail, but even I can't bring myself to indulge in actual alcohol—and Christopher knows it.

More than that, he encourages it because we both know I'm already enough of a handful without booze. Add it and who knows what kind of trouble I could get into.

Still, as much as I tease Christopher, he gets his back whenever he can. He's happy to swap lovers frequently, nowhere near ready to settle down at twenty-five. And then there's me. I've kissed guys before, but that's as far as it's gone, and Christopher knows that, too.

He also knows how much it irks me that, between my family and my career, I've missed out on so many life experiences normal people my age have had which is why, in his way, he enables me sneaking out so that I at least have *some* of them.

But that doesn't stop him from saying, "Stay here. I'll be right back."

"Take your time. I'm going to go dance on the floor for a bit."

"Gen—"

I roll my eyes. "I know. Don't draw attention to myself. It's an upbeat dance song, Christopher, not a piece by Tchaikovsky. I'm not about to do pirouettes and arabesques in the middle of the dance floor. No one will even notice me."

He raises his eyebrows.

"What?"

He sighs. "Did you happen to look in a mirror before you snuck out of your bedroom earlier?"

I was in my studio which is wall-to-wall mirror from floor to ceiling. "Obviously."

Christopher opens his mouth, thinks about it for a moment, then shakes his head. "Never mind. Just... dance by yourself, okay? Until I'm back with the drinks. Can you do that?"

"Be careful," is the answer I give him. "You're starting to sound like Damien."

"I mean it. Just because there's a truce—"

I wave him off. The entire ride over to the West Side of Springfield earlier tonight, I had to hear Christopher's lecture about how dangerous it would be if anyone from the Sinners Syndicate realized that Damien Libellula's sister was on their territory. I heard that before the recent truce. I've heard it after.

It's just a nightclub. I'll be fine.

Christopher hesitates, as though he wants to push the subject, but a quick glance over his shoulder reveals that Jessie has moved behind the bar now.

He's my best friend—but he's also a guy.

"Behave," is the last thing he says before he starts pushing his way through the crowd, moving like a great white shark who has its prey in sight.

Behave?

I scoff.

Now why would I do that?

mariposa

TWO
BUTTERFLY

GENEVIEVE

The Devil's Playground is packed tonight. Not so surprising considering its rep, though this is only the second time I've been inside; as daring as I am, even I couldn't risk it before, back when the Sinners were my brother's enemies. Hell, it took months after the Dragonflies and the Sinners Syndicate agreed to a truce last summer to convince Christopher to let me check it out the first time a few weeks ago.

I'd heard rumors about the girls who service customers upstairs, and the money that passes hands in the casino at the back of the club. Christopher didn't think it was the place for me, but I wore him down, and proved that I came him for one reason: to dance.

And if I found someone I wanted to dance with...

I didn't that night. After Christopher's warning, I

doubt I will tonight, either, but as a dancer to my core, it was inevitable that I'd find my way to the dance floor eventually after I spent the last few minutes watching the club-goers dance and grind and sway and, okay, I'm pretty sure those two over there might actually be screwing each other…

I pause in the middle of the throng of people dancing around me and, yup, that's exactly what they're doing. The woman moans in time to the beat of the techno song blaring through the speakers, while the guy moves his hips completely out of sync to the music.

She seems to be enjoying herself, though I can't help but shake my head. If you're going to fuck in public like that, at least do it with a little rhythm.

Now, I like to think that I'm not a prude. Between my dad bringing home hookers when I was too young to really get it to spending my pre-teen years with a Damien in his mid-twenties, I knew about sex early on. And, true, my dad died before he could try to pimp me out—as if Dame would let him—and Damien started bringing his dates to hotels once he realized that curious Gen was eavesdropping outside his bedroom door, but, once again, I can blame two things for my virgin-at-twenty-five state: ballet, and my brother.

So preoccupied with my dance career, there was no time for boyfriends. And even when I found a dancer who filled out his tights *and* actually liked pussy, there was Damien, effectively cockblocking me. Same thing happened whenever he brought me out of the manor for

Family events. If anyone in the East End so much as looked at me like a woman and not a little girl, he was standing between me and them, fingering the hilt of his stiletto in a not-so-subtle warning.

No one wanted to fuck me bad enough to test Damien. Dragonflies knew that, in the Family, to betray him was a death sentence. Going after his beloved baby sister? That clearly counted.

I'd hoped that settling down with Savannah would make him realize that he has his own life to live, and so do I. I mean, the first time I met my new sister-in-law, he already had her on her knees. He doesn't shy away from sex, and he has to realize that, by now, I'm really fucking curious about it.

Even if I did threaten to have to wash my eyes out with bleach to forget what I walked in on, but can you blame me? I've seen dicks before. From porn to changing in the same room as Christopher and a couple of other male dancers, but when it's your *brother*'s?

Ew. Gross.

No, thanks.

Since I'm not so curious that watching someone thrust on one-and-threes instead of two-and-fours sounds appealing, I do actually what I came out on the floor to do: I dance. As soon as I noticed that Christopher took a seat at the bar, leaning in to flirt with the redhead, I knew it would be a while until he came back with my piña colada. Might as well work up a thirst for it.

I love this song. It's electric, and though I'm trained in

ballet, I'd taken every single type of dance class offered in my youth. Even if I didn't, dancing can be instinctive. Your body knows what to do, and without any inhibitions or care, you just let yourself do it.

This is a solo, not a duo, and I turn away whenever someone tries to join in. Christopher told me to be careful, and maybe he's just a bug in my ear, but tonight is about letting loose. Being free. It isn't often that I'm allowed out of my prison on the third floor of the manor, and almost never that I can leave without Damien there to watch over me.

I stop paying attention to everything around me. It's just the music. It's just the dance. What begins as a sway and a bop becomes a little more theatrical until, as the music slows just before it crashes into a new beat, I'm twirling in the middle of the dance floor.

It was a triple pirouette. Nothing elaborate, even if it's out of place in a mafia-owned nightclub, but sometimes twenty years of training takes over and I mix ballet in with other types of dance.

I'm not trying to show-off. In fact, I'm in my own little world as I throw one arm up over my head, grasping the crook of my elbow with my other hand, shaking my hips in time to the music. I take a step with my left foot, turning so that I can do a quick check in on Christopher's progress with the gorgeous waitress when I notice that someone is watching *me*.

I grew up on a stage. If the eyes of the crowd aren't on me while I'm performing, I'm doing something wrong.

I'm used to it—but when I catch his stare, I do something I *never* do.

I lose my footing and stumble.

It's not my fault. Not really. I stopped dancing as I took him in, but another couple behind me kept moving. One of them bumped into my back, and though I right myself immediately, regaining my balance, the stumble brings me even closer to the man who was watching me dance.

And, oh, what a man.

He's about my age, or maybe it's just his pretty face that makes him seem younger. Because, yeah, he's *pretty*. Not in a girlish way, though. His features are undeniably masculine, with a chiseled jaw, full lips, and a pair of cheekbones so sharp, they remind me of blades. His hair is as dark as his eyes, and it's cut longer than most men I know. Dragonflies all seem to have the same high and tight haircut that Damien favors. This guy looks like he once wore his hair long, but decided for a change. The front pieces are carelessly tousled, with the back a little shaggy. It's styled perfectly to suit him, and I find him incredibly attractive.

And that's just his face.

Beneath the neon of the Playground, his tanned skin is enticing, and that's just counting the parts of it I can see. Even dressed, it's clear that he is covered in tattoos. The only parts that aren't are his face itself and his hands.

I know I'm staring, but now it's his neck that fascinates me. Up the sides of his neck and covering the hollow of his throat, all I see are flames created from ink.

Holy shit, that's cool.

I'm staring, but so is he. I figure that gives me license to gobble him up with my gaze a little longer.

He has a can in one unmarred hand; I recognize it as an energy drink brand that many dancers in my local company guzzle for the high amount of caffeine in it. He's holding his phone in the other hand. I get the vibe he just picked up a drink from the bar and was cutting his way through the floor to head out. The door is behind me, and he has on a weathered leather jacket over a plain black t-shirt that's tight enough to highlight the muscles on his chest.

In his mass of beautiful hair, he has a stick pen tucked behind his ear. Palming his phone, he reaches up, grabbing the pen between his pointer finger and his thumb.

And then he says the last thing I ever expected he would:

"Dance for me."

This stranger's voice is a deliciously deep grumble. To be honest, I'm almost so shocked that he's speaking to me, I barely make out what it is that he said.

When I think I did, I ask, "You want to dance?"

Christopher told me not to, but Christopher is busy with Jessie. And even if it is just one dance, I have this strange feeling like I'll regret it if I say no.

And then he does.

"No." He shakes his head. "I want you to dance for me."

Oh. I must have misheard him then. Fair enough. It's loud, and I'm distracted.

Hm.

Dance for him? That's not weird, is it? Considering what the girls upstairs do for money, having this beautiful stranger ask me to dance for him could be intriguing—or he could be a perv.

I really hope he's not a perv.

I also don't normally like people telling me what to do. I get enough of that in my real life. From demanding dance teachers to my controlling older brother, and even Christopher, it bothers me when I don't get to choose my own actions. Most everyone who knows me figures that out before long, then they just let me do what I want anyway.

But this guy... it's a good thing I'll never see him again because it would be a bad idea to set a precedent, letting him think that I'm the type of woman to simply obey, and yet...

Instead of quipping that people spend hundreds of dollars to watch me perform, I ask, "Just dance?"

If this guy says he expects me to strip or give him a lap dance—

"Just dance. I saw you before. It's like you're floating on air. I want to watch again, if that's okay."

"In that case, sure. I love to dance."

He gestures for me to follow him. We don't touch, but

as I move at his heels, the tiny hairs on my arms seem to stand on end. Like there's a spark passing between us, an undeniable chemistry that I might be imagining.

Does that stop me? Not even a little. In fact, I move until I'm right behind him, humming a bit as something woodsy and earthy with a hint of... motor oil? Maybe motor oil... the rich smells clinging to his hair and his leather jacket have me ready to follow him anywhere.

Okay. Let's be real. If this man wanted me to dance in the alley behind the Playground, I would've gone with him without a doubt. But that's not where he brings me. Instead, he guides me to the edge of the dance floor, right where a side booth rises up about a step higher than floor level.

He slides into a seat, dropping his phone on the table, setting his unopened energy drink on the top. With the pen twirling between two fingers, he uses his free hand to grab one, two, three paper napkins from the holder before placing the small stack in front of him.

Then, with a look of pure concentration, he pops his chin in his hand and waits.

He wants me to dance? I dance. Ignoring the upbeat music, I listen to the music in my heart—a rapid rhythm that started the first moment I looked in this beautiful stranger's eyes—and I move in time to a song only I can hear.

I forget about Christopher. I forget about how I was supposed to keep from drawing attention to myself. I dance because I love it, and I dance because I've always blossomed under the attention of anyone who appreciates what I can do.

At one point, I peek over at him. It's a little frustrating to see that he's bowed over the napkin, pen scratching away at it, but I tell myself that it doesn't matter. I came to the club to have a good time, and even if he's not impressed by my skill, at least I'm enjoying myself.

Minutes go by. I allow myself to be swallowed up by the crowd because if the stranger has had his fill of watching me, then I'll perform for me alone.

It's his turn to follow me. I've barely gone out of his sight before he's tossing the pen down, sliding back out of the booth, maneuvering his way so that he can stand right in front of me before I'm gone.

He lifts up the napkin. He's not handing it to me, showing me the white square instead, and I focus on what he's drawn in the middle.

It's a butterfly.

I stop dancing, marveling over the unique design. How did he do it? Using the black ink from his pen, multiple different shading techniques, and some impressive skill, he's captured a butterfly in flight—and he's showing it to me.

"You drew that?"

He jerks his head. A nod.

"You're an artist," I breathe out. My fingers ghost against the edge of the napkin, barely touching it. "It's beautiful."

Oh, mama. *He's* beautiful, and he smells so damn good.

"It's what I do," he says, taking the napkin back. He disappears it into his pocket before I can ask for it. "I'm a tattooist."

Know what? That makes a lot of sense. If he's responsible for all the ink I can see—and what I can only imagine is hidden beneath his shirt—then he's a walking advertisement for his craft, and he's excellent at it.

And then he says, "I own Sinners & Saints on Third," and I'm slapped back to reality.

The truce is too new. My knee-jerk reaction to anything Sinners Syndicate is to flinch because they were my brother's enemies for so long. It doesn't matter that the Sinners's leader—Lincoln Crewes, the Devil of Springfield—was a friend of Dame's when he was younger. For years, a war was brewing between both of our gangs, and Damien drummed it into my head so damn often, I still think *run* when someone flashes the devil horns and tail in front of me.

You don't get to use 'Sinners' in any business unless you have an in with the Sinners Syndicate. It's like how, on the East End, Dragonfly-vetted businesses have a decal on their window. That doesn't mean that he's part of the syndicate, just that Devil is allowing him to represent his crew.

I mentally cross my fingers, then ask, "You cater to the Sinners Syndicate?"

For a moment, his face hardens. It doesn't make him

any less gorgeous, though it's a hint of danger that shouldn't be half as alluring as it is.

I get it. I know what I look like. Petite and blonde and deceptively innocent, in another life, I might've been a sorority girl instead of a mafia princess. I shouldn't be casually mentioning one of the two powerful gangs in Springfield.

I shouldn't even *know* about them.

I do, though, and when I don't back down under the weight of his stare, he nods.

He shoves up his worn leather jacket, revealing a full tattoo sleeve covering his arm. There's so much to take in. I catch a handful of names written in black script, an immaculate drawing of the virgin Mary, interwoven details that connect different elements together... but there, in the middle of it all, is a four-inch-tall red-skinned devil.

There's my answer. He doesn't just ink Sinners.

He *is* a Sinner.

Shit.

His dark eyes run over me, then drop to his ink-covered arm. He pulls his sleeve down, busying himself with straightening out the seam. I get the feeling that showing me his tattoo was a test, and that I somehow failed.

He clears his throat, ducking his chin a little. A long strand of hair falls forward into his face, and he leaves it there as he searches mine.

"What about you?" he asks. "Any ink?"

My dress is sleeveless. The skirt reaches mid-thigh, and since it's May, I'm not wearing any tights or hose. Unless I'm hiding a tattoo underneath it, it's clear that I don't have anything decorating my skin.

"Not yet," I tell him, a hint of a dare in my voice.

"Virgin skin," he rasps. "My favorite. Here." He reaches into his back pocket, pulling out a metal rectangle. He presses a button, a lid pops open, and I see he has a couple of business cards in there. He plucks one out, snaps the cardholder closed, then offers the card to me. "You decide to mark up that pretty skin you've got, butterfly, you come to me. I'll take care of you."

Accepting the card, I give him a curious look. "Butterfly?"

"Yeah. Butterfly."

I think of the napkin with the beautiful butterfly in flight, and how he drew it as I danced. Was he inspired by *me*?

And if so, why does the slight brushing of our fingers together as he gives me the card have butterflies taking flight in my belly?

I glance down at his card. It has the name of his tattoo parlor embossed in black ink in the center—Sinners & Saints, just like he said—as well as an address. Beneath that, it has a single name: Cross da Silva.

I tap it with my fingernail. "Cross. Is that your name?"

"Sure is."

"Cool. I'm Genevieve."

"You got a last name, Genevieve?"

I could lie. If I really believed that this was a chance meeting that I'd forget about by the time I'm climbing the tree later tonight to let myself back into my room... I'd give him one of a hundred different fictitious names I've used over the years. In Springfield, it's not a good idea to use my surname unless I know I'm on friendly turf.

But that's the thing. I don't want it to be a chance meeting that means nothing. Something about this Cross... I want to see him again.

And that means I might as well be honest from the jump.

"Libellula. My name is Genevieve Libellula."

He sucks in a breath, whistling it out through his teeth. "So not a butterfly, then. A Dragonfly."

Not quite.

A small smile plays on my lips. I show him my naked arm, missing my brother's mark. When you're accepted in the Family, you get Damien's dragonfly inked on your skin. I was born into his family, and he's made it clear that while I'll always be a Libellula, I'll never be a Dragonfly.

"Hey," I tell him, "I'm a virgin, remember?"

Though if my last name and my older brother don't scare Cross off, maybe I won't be for much longer.

mariposa

THREE
FASCINATION

GENEVIEVE

SIX WEEKS LATER

As I flip idly through the book of tattoo designs I snagged from Cross's waiting room, it hits me that I'm playing a dangerous game. I know I am, but I can't stop myself from rolling the dice anyway and taking my turn.

That's exactly what I did earlier today. I made it obvious to Damien and Savannah that I planned on having breakfast, a stretch, and then returning to my studio to train after the stress of the last couple of weeks... where I pointedly turned on the music before convincing Christopher to pick me up and drop me off on the West Side to steal a few hours away with Cross.

After I tapped on the front door of Sinners & Saints, the tattoo parlor he owns, he invited me in before he flipped the garish neon sign from 'open' to 'closed' so that we could do exactly what we've been doing since I first met him at the Devil's Playground: hang out and talk and... well. That's about all.

Not for a lack of trying on my part, either. Which is probably why I'm still drawn to him like a moth to a flame, completely aware that I'm risking everything by getting closer and closer, but unable to stay away regardless.

Damien's bound to catch on to my obsession eventually. When I only snuck out with Christopher once every few weeks, it was easy to pick a night when the darker side of the Dragonflies kept him occupied; instead of the dinners and the public meets where I was allowed out with my brother as my chaperone, those nights when he conducted other business in the shadows, convinced I was locked away on the third floor. Then came Savannah, and he focused on keeping his wife inside of the manor with him while I crawled out of my window every chance I got.

If I'm not seeing Cross every day, I'm staying up all night, talking to him through text or over the phone. I get antsy if I go too long without hearing the way his deep voice rasps, "Butterfly," and I know what I'm risking by being so reckless... but I'm already in too deep to stop.

Especially since, two weeks ago, I thought it was all over...

The sneaking around. The thrill of dashing to the back of the manor where Cross would be waiting for me on his motorcycle on the nights when I couldn't ask Christopher to bring me. Pulling on the helmet he picked up just for me, both for safety reasons and because I insisted—something that Cross completely agreed with —that I should keep my face covered whenever we were on the East End of Springfield together.

My brother owns the entire territory. All it would take is one of his men to see me out with Cross for Damien to hear about it. It wouldn't matter that I refused to be microchipped like Orion, Savannah's cat; or, for that matter, Savannah herself. I'd have a tracker in my arm and my butt back in my room before I could blink.

That's why I refused to say anything about my budding relationship with the Sinner. I couldn't stand the idea of overprotective Damien butting his nose in before I can even figure out what is brewing between Cross and me—but when I nearly killed Orion two weeks ago and desperately needed a ride to bring the unconscious cat to a vet, I had no choice.

The clinic we went to first was closed. Damien was suddenly missing. My big cousin, Vin, wanted to figure out what was going on with Dame, and as panicked as Savannah was over Orion's state, she was determined to track down her husband.

That left me with the cat. I was worried about my brother, too, obviously, but Orion... what happened to him was my fault. Both because I believed Dr. Liz when she told me that the shot was to help the poor orange-and-white cat with his shitting problems, then when I administered the injection without second-guessing why a human doc would care so much about a feline patient.

I trusted her. When I tweaked my chronic ankle injury about two months ago, she was the one who helped me with it. Especially since she already knew about Orion's constipation issues because I'd foolishly asked her for advice about him being all stopped up, it made sense when she said her vet friend suggested the meds for Savannah's cat.

Of course, I know better now. The doctor was working with a rival gangster—Jimmy Winter—and using me as a pawn in her own twisted plan that would end with Damien's new wife dead and Dr. Liz taking Savannah's place. Only Jimmy Winter wanted *Damien* dead, and if it wasn't for Savannah and Vin charging across town to save the day, that might've happened.

Not that I'm supposed to know about any of that. Damien came back to the East End beat to hell, and Vin had a pair of bullet holes in him that he's still recovering from. Following Dame's lead, Savannah blew past all of my questions about what happened, though I'll give her credit. Once Damien was safe and sound, she was only concerned with how Orion was.

The answer: sedated, but alive. The vet I eventually got him in to see assured me that, within a few more hours, he'd be thirsty and lethargic, but he should recover quickly. He did, and Savannah was so incredibly elated, she purposely neglected to ask any questions about the friend I called to go to the vet with me.

Vin couldn't ask, either. He was getting patched up by a Sinner doctor since Savannah killed ours—and, yup, that's something else Damien didn't want me to know—and by the time he was home again, so much had happened, he forgot to badger me about the 'he' I mentioned.

Forgot or, knowing Vin, he's just biding his time. He probably didn't want to set Damien off on the heels of my brother being drugged, tied up, and worked over by a rival, and with all Dragonflies on high alert after such a close call, he's being careful while also dealing with his own recovery. Doesn't matter that the rival—like Dr. Liz—is dead now. Damien has a reputation to protect. Vin's his bodyguard, and there's no limit to what my cousin will do to protect Damien in every way that counts.

Dangerous, Gen. It's a dangerous game...

So, yeah. I didn't have to admit that I've been spending all of the time I can with a stranger to them because none of my family actually pushed me to tell them why Cross da Silva—a member of the Sinners Syndicate, and the tattooist who is very quickly leaving his mark on my heart—floored his motorcycle across town to hold my hand as I turned into a nervous wreck inside the vet's office. They weren't affiliated with the Dragonflies—at least, they didn't have the trademark symbol on their window or front door—and even if they were, that wouldn't have stopped me from leaning on Cross.

Friends. I sigh, both in appreciation of the floral design he drew in his book and frustration that I'm head over heels for a man who clearly thinks of me more like a little sister than a prospective lover. I learned that Cross is older than he appears—thirty to my twenty-five—and even if he insists the slight age gap doesn't bother him, I'm not so sure about that.

I made it clear that I was into him. He made it clear that we can be friends. No more. No less. He's someone I could trust to drop everything if I called him, even after knowing him for barely more than a month, and he proved it that day—but despite the heated look he gets in his eyes sometime when I glance over at him and see him staring, he's putting up shields between us.

Friends...

I want more than that. Of course I do. From the moment he showed me that napkin and I saw the beautiful butterfly he drew for me, I've wanted to experience my first *everythings* with this man in particular.

Christopher thinks I'm being impulsive. He's not wrong. I've spent my whole life being coddled by my older brother. I found serenity in my dancing, and fascination in the world outside my gilded cage bars, and with Cross... there's something there, something I struggle to understand or deny. I see him and I *want*. I want things I've never had, and even if this quiet friendship is all he can offer me, I'll take it.

But if there's one thing I've learned as a Libellula? It's that, with the right amount of grit, determination, and ruthlessness, I can have it all.

Damien wanted Springfield. He has it. He claimed Savannah. She wears his dragonfly on his skin and the leaves of an enforcer on the back of her arm.

I want a relationship—*any* relationship—with my sensitive artist.

And nothing is going to stop me from having that.

Not even the man who is sitting on his rolling stool, head bowed over the iPad resting in the crook of his elbow, the long, white pencil moving while he's completely oblivious to the way that I'm paying far more attention to how he loses himself in his drawing than to most of the designs in the book on my lap.

I know what he's doing, besides driving me crazy with his nearness. I asked him after we exchanged numbers and started to text, what was up with the way he first met me and instantly asked me to dance for him.

He called me his muse. That my graceful dancing inspired him to draw that butterfly, and the pale blue color of my eyes led him to create a sleeve for a customer based on a galaxy design, complete with a bright gold nebula of stars the same shade as my hair...

Almost as soon as I sat down before, after we caught up—Cross asking after Orion, me using my new friendship to learn more about the state of the truce between the Sinners Syndicate and the Libellula Family than I ever would've if I only had my brother to rely on—he gestured for me to get comfortable, then grabbed his Apple pencil to sketch.

I tried to peek at what he was drawing, laughing when Cross tilted the screen back so I couldn't. It's another little game we play. In my experience, as soon as he's done, he'll be more than happy to show me, but not until the perfectionist that he is finishes it down to every detail.

Cross is quiet. That's one thing I learned. He seems like a sensitive soul, and when his dark eyes don't have that heated look, I can't ignore the sadness that lurks there.

I want to know what made him so sad.

I want to know everything about him.

I'm an open book. When Cross asks me about my ambitions, my experiences, my past, and my relation-ships—with Christopher, who I'm pretty sure he's jealous of, and with Damien, who he seems smartly wary of—I'm so flattered that he cares about me... about Genevieve... about his butterfly... that I tell him everything.

You know what I've learned about Cross in the last month and a half?

He's been a Sinner since the syndicate formed, mainly because he went to high school with Royce McIn-tyre—a highly ranked Sinner, and the mafia fixer who killed Kieran Alfieri for what he did to Nicolette Williams, the pretty blonde waitress I recognized at the Devil's Playground. Nicknamed 'Rolls', he's Cross's oldest friend, and really *only* friend, and I'm irrationally pleased that Cross is hesitant to introduce the two of us, not because I'm related to the head Dragonfly, but because he considers Rolls too handsome for his own good.

Please. The man is married. I have no interest in going after someone else's husband, and though Cross is careful with what he shares, I pointedly asked him if he was single right before I coyly convinced him to exchange numbers with me.

I'd have to get over my silly crush if he wasn't. He seemed curious when I pushed the topic, finally admitting that he doesn't really do relationships and hasn't had one in a while. That was his way of reminding me that we're destined to be friends, but poor Cross. He didn't know how determined I could be just yet. By confirming he was single, that just gave me the go ahead to continue this forbidden friendship while hoping it grows into something more.

So I know about Rolls. I know about Cross's loyalty to the Sinners, and how he doesn't just cater to the syndicate: he's the official tattooist for them. I know that he's as lonely as I am, and whatever happens, we both honestly did need a friend.

His family is gone. I learned that one, too, and wasn't that an 'open mouth, insert foot' moment? I mean, how was I supposed to know that the flames on his neck and his throat are a memento to the brother, sister, and mother he lost in an house fire when he was a kid?

Then again, when Cross humors me, shoving up his sleeves so that I can dissect the art on his arm, and I saw that he has three names scrawled in script on his left one... that should've been a sign that he cared enough about three someones once.

Jealous and as emotional as ever, my first instinct was to think that they were previous lovers who earned their spot on his skin. Yeah. I was wrong about that, and Cross reminded me that not only does he purposely avoid committed relationships, but he often counsels his clients not to get a permanent tattoo for someone who isn't a permanent fixture in your life.

Right. Message received, and that's about when I stopped treating him as a future conquest, finally seeing my sensitive artist with the sad eyes as something even more precious: a true friend I can rely on.

From texting late at night to sending him videos I took of me dancing in my studio, receiving a piece of art inspired by me in return... it's been a little more than six weeks since I bumped into him, but I can't shake the feeling that I've known him so much longer.

Then again, maybe it's because—for the first time in forever—I can forget that I'm Damien Libellula's baby sister when I'm with him.

My heritage doesn't faze Cross one bit. In fact, when I first texted him the night after we met, asking if he'd like to meet for coffee somewhere since that's what I figured dating was like, right? Getting coffee... when I invited him out and he didn't hesitate to offer to pick me up on his motorcycle, I couldn't help myself.

We didn't get coffee. He suggested a twenty-four-hour

diner on Sinner turf, and as I dipped one of my disco fries into the gravy, I had to ask, "Aren't you afraid of my brother?"

Cross had a plate of pancakes drenched in syrup in front of him. He thought about it for a moment, nibbled on a piece of the pancake, then shook his head. "I'm not afraid of that," was his answer, and I've been intrigued ever since.

He's clearly not afraid of Devil; he's a loyal Sinner, but not a die-hard like my brother's enforcers are. My being related to Damien doesn't bother him at all. And yet... *I'm not afraid of* that.

So what *is* he afraid of?

I don't know, but like everything else when it comes to this enigmatic man, I won't stop until I find out.

Our silence is strangely companionable. At home, I nearly always have music playing; if not out loud, then it runs like a loop in my head. But Cross uses the quiet to concentrate, and I find myself so drawn to the slope of his nose, the edge of his jaw, and the muscles flexing on his tatted arm as he gives all of his attention to his drawing that I can sneakily watching him without him realizing all while enjoying the quiet.

He lives above his studio, but the two of us hang out downstairs on the rare chance that my brother tracks me down. I have the same excuse at the ready that I always do: Cross offered to give me my first tattoo. That's why I always grab one of the design books when we're spending time together in his space, even though

I've told him I'm not ready to get rid of my virgin skin status.

As for the other virgin state I'm in...

I shift in my seat, crossing my legs, squeezing my thighs together beneath my sundress as I appreciate his masculine beauty.

In fact, I get so distracted by him that I barely notice it as he swivels in his chair, the iPad nestled on his lap, as he reaches beneath his desk for something.

Seconds later, I hear something crack. A sharp noise, followed by a *psst* sound, and I can't stop my lips from twitching upward as I flip the design book closed.

I know something else about Cross that I've picked up on over the last six weeks. It became pretty obvious when he was always there to answer a call or a text, no matter the hour, or how he enjoys driving through Springfield in the middle of the night on his bike, but Cross, like, *never* sleeps. He's an insomniac, and I blame the can he just grabbed from the mini fridge beneath his desk for his inability to shut down.

"What flavor is it today?" I ask, tapping my fingernails on the cover of the design book.

Cross brushes his hair out of his face so that he can look at the flavor printed on the bottom of the energy drink can he's holding. "I had a peach mango earlier, but this one is fruit punch."

"You keep drinking those, your heart is going to explode," I tease.

He shrugs, contemplates the can for another moment, then takes a swig.

I shake my head. "You're addicted to those things."

"There are worse things to be addicted to," Cross points out.

My brother is responsible for the entire drug trade in Springfield. Trust me, I know.

And, yet, when I look at Cross da Silva, I know one thing about *myself*: I could easily become addicted to him—and if settling for friendship with him is all I have to look forward to, beggars can't be choosers.

mariposa

CROSS

When I look at Genevieve, I see flames.

That should scare the shit out of me. My only experience with fire is a fucking tragedy. I wasn't even home the night that my childhood home burned down to the ground and my entire family died, but I saw the ashes after. I smelled it on the late autumn air, the char and the death and the *burn,* even hours after the Springfield Fire Department got the blaze under control. It's clung to me since, following me doggedly through the years—

As the report swiftly revealed that my mother, my younger sister, and my younger brother all died of smoke inhalation before the fire consumed them. That it was arson—and that my sick bastard of a stepfather was the one who spilled the gasoline and lit the match.

As I went through the motions of foster care because I didn't have anyone else, eventually aging out before I found a new family with the gang of brawlers, gamblers, and gun runners that would eventually become the Sinners Syndicate.

As I rose up through the ranks, joining the inner circle under the Devil of Springfield himself as the official tattoo artist for the syndicate... the smoke and the dust and phantoms of my past followed me every goddamn step I've taken for nearly twenty years, but never fire. Never a spark.

Never any heat.

Until Genevieve Libellula danced her way into my life.

I'm fucking obsessed with this one. *Addicted.* She's all I think about, her pretty blue eyes, her impish smile, her forwardness, her sass... I love it all. She's life personified, and when I'm in her orbit, I don't feel as I'm simply existing. I come alive, too, when before only my art made me feel that way.

Now it's all Genevieve. My muse and my secret weakness in one, I knew from that first dance that it would be far too easy to fall in love with her. Even so, I never expected that it would happen so fast. I told myself it was innocent at first, swapping numbers with her, that I wouldn't *have* to call her.

She could be my Madonna. The woman on a pedestal that inspires me to create, but virginal in a way that meant I couldn't sully her with my dirty hands. Then, during one of our first conversations—that she initiated, and I was helpless to continue—Genevieve coyly admitted that she isn't just virginal. She's an honest-to-God *virgin*.

And I knew from that moment on that I couldn't have her. Maybe if she was broken like me, we could heal the cracks in each other. But she's nothing like the Sinner I am. She's kind. Smart. Thoughtful. Ambitious, too; she doesn't just dance because she likes it, but because it's her calling.

Genevieve doesn't know what it's like to struggle. To have had to rely on free lunch during her school days, secretly pissed when a more well-off classmate would swipe part of the only meal he'd get that day right from the tray. I had three foster families before one stuck, but they kicked my ass out the door on my eighteenth birthday.

She lives in a fucking *mansion* with her older brother on the East End.

She doesn't rub it in, though. Because her brother got his money the same way I do—through the syndicates that run Springfield—she believes we're on the same level. A secret criminal fling, made all the more exciting because, up until last summer, the Sinners and the Dragonflies were kill-on-sight rivals.

Genevieve thinks that I'm hesitant to start any kind of relationship with her because her brother runs the Libellula Family and I owe my loyalty to Devil. While I'll do what the Devil of Springfield says because he's my boss, that's not enough to stop me from pursuing my butterfly the way I want to.

Knowing that I'll only destroy her if I do? That has me lying through my teeth as I tell her that I just want to be friends.

Friends? I've never wanted to tuck a friend of mine under me, fucking them until they scream my name, feasting on their virgin pussy with the masculine sense of satisfaction that I got there first. I don't jerk off to the thoughts of my friends in the shower, or stay up all night drawing their faces over and over again until I make fire work for me this time, burning my paper obsession as if I could cut her out of my heart.

Six weeks. It's been six weeks and Genevieve Libellula has managed to worm her way under my hard exterior, burrowing so deep, I don't think I can ever get her out again.

I need to put an end to this. Eventually, we'll get caught. I don't know Damien personally, just by reputation. Rolls, on the other hand, has to deal with the Dragonflies a lot, especially after shit went down between that enforcer dickhead and Rolls's wife, Nicolette. He'd be the first to tell me that Damien is just as dangerous as Devil. Don't let the expensive suits and debonair act fool you. Devil looks like what he is: a brawler who got his name when he hacked a guy's head right off the stump for threatening Ava.

Damien looks like a CEO, but prefers the intimacy of a close kill courtesy of a blade he wears at all times. And that's if he doesn't send one of his league of trained killers, his enforcers, after any of his enemies.

How much do you want to bet that he'd consider the worthless Sinner panting like a dog after his younger sister an enemy worthy of disappearing?

Genevieve doesn't see that. She thinks sneaking around is another aspect that makes our 'friendship' thrilling. Smart enough to know that it would be a bad idea to tell Damien we're hanging out—especially after he nearly got assassinated by a new rival moving in on Springfield territory a couple of weeks back—she just thinks her brother would try to forbid her from leaving her bedroom again.

Me? I'm expecting a bullet between my eyes, or a stiletto through my ribs.

Does that stop me, though? Does that stop me from riding my bike across town so that I can watch my dainty dancer shimmy down a tree, dancing out of the sight of her brother's cameras, all before she throws her arms around me, then hops on the back of my motorcycle?

Does that stop me from looking at Genevieve now, sitting in my studio like she owns the place—like she *belongs* here—and fantasizing about taking her hand, leading her upstairs to my private apartment, and admitting that I'd give anything to kiss her.

To fuck her? I'd welcome Damien's fury, knowing I got to have her at least once...

I can't. I know I can't. Genevieve is twenty-five, but she's a young twenty-five. I'm an old thirty, even if everyone thinks I look younger. Those five years seem like an eternity between us, just like the miles between the West Side of Springfield and the East End are too big a chasm for my bike to cross.

I'm damaged goods. I always have been. Quiet and sensitive when I was much younger, I was easy pickings for my stepfather. I was nine the first time he snuck into my bedroom, telling me that my mother had a late night shift, and as the next oldest in the house, it was my responsibility to give him what he wanted.

We lived in a narrow three-bedroom house in the poorer part of Springfield. Chad was right. I was the oldest. When I was nine, Rafe was seven. Ana Lucia was only six. They shared a room the same way Chad and my mother did. I had the smallest one, but before Chad came around, I was the man of the house. When he moved in, I still got to keep a room for myself. I thought I was so grown, but at nine... I didn't know what sex was. When my tiny prick got hard, I was curious about it, but I didn't understand.

Thanks to that fucking bastard shoving his much bigger cock into my hand that first night, I learned pretty damn quickly what he meant.

If I told my mother what her husband was doing while she was at work, he'd kill me. If I refused to let him use me however he wanted, he'd sneak into my siblings' room and wake one of them up instead. He wasn't partic-ular. He fucked my mom when she was home. He forced me to suck his cock when she wasn't. He was a predator who'd target *anyone*—and even then, I knew I had to protect Ana Lucia and Rafe.

For three years, I did. But I got older. I got bigger. He started eyeing Ana Lucia a little closer... and I punched him the next time he tried to get me to touch him.

Not because I was jealous. Fuck no. It was because I'd finally had enough.

Chad beat me so bad, I had to kick him in the nuts to escape him otherwise he would've killed me that night.

Instead? While I slept in an alley, blocks away from my home, the sick fuck tried to burn the whole place down.

That was almost twenty years ago. Eighteen to be exact, and I've dealt with the remorse and the survivor's guilt every single day of my life. I didn't want a heart, didn't want to love, didn't want to have strong feelings for another person because it only ends up in flames.

And when I look at Genevieve, that's all I see.

I should tell her to go. I should block her number, let my butterfly free before I inevitably break her.

I don't.

As Genevieve conversationally mentions that she forgot to eat lunch before she came over, I don't shut her down. I don't offer her one of the granola bars I keep in the studio for a quick sugar boost during longer ink sessions, and despite my initial reaction to take the opportunity to invite her upstairs after all, I warn my wayward cock to get itself under control.

She wants to eat, and I know what that means: she wants to go out.

I doubt Genevieve has any clue I'm aware what she's doing. When I was just as straightforward as she was, telling her I don't do relationships after she boldly offered herself up to me for one, she decided to be a little sneakier.

Dates. She tries to get me to go on dates. Riding around town on my bike, Genevieve wearing the helmet I bought even before I picked her up for the first time. Because, yup, part of me already knew I had it bad and the helmet proved it, but she kissed me on the cheek when she saw it so, fuck it, I don't regret the impulsive purchase at all.

Dinners. Late night snacks. Breakfasts when she could sneak away... she has this idea that, if we sit down for a meal together, *we* are together. It's funny, too, because Genevieve rarely eats more than a few bites of her food. She thinks I don't noticed *that*, either, but I notice *everything* about this woman.

If Genevieve wants food, I'm getting her some food.

"What about you?" she asks. "You hungry?"

Whenever I'm near this woman, I'm starved—but it's not for a meal.

It's for her laugh. It's for her fire. It's for her sunshine and brightness.

Fucking hell, it's for her *taste*.

But I can't tell her that, so I shrug instead. "I could eat."

She checks her phone. "I've got another hour or two before our cook serves dinner. If I don't come down, Dame will just think I'm really focusing on my new choreography."

"New choreography?" I ask. I love watching Genevieve dance, and hearing her talk about her career reminds me why I'm throwing up the admittedly weak walls I already have. She has something more important than her crush on me: her professional career. "What's that about?"

Her features light up. She's always so pleased when I show an interest in her job, just like I can't help but crumble under her praise whenever I show her another finished sketch.

"I'm practicing a new piece," she gushes. "The Performing Arts Center in Union City is hosting open auditions in the middle of June. It's been a while since I had a show to do, and this one is my favorite. *Black Swan*."

Maybe that's for the best. Between the audition next month and rehearsal, she won't have as much time for me.

And, no, I'm not bitter about that at all.

Keeping my features impassive, I say, "I hope I'm not distracting you."

"You're not," she says quickly. "But," and I see a flirty twist to her lips as she climbs up off of the stool, inching her way closer to my desk, "what about me? Am I a distraction, Cross?"

Yes.

I pretend not to understand. "I'm not quite finished with my sketch yet," I tell her, grabbing the folded cover of my iPad, flipping it so it hides the drawing of Genevieve sitting in my studio, looking at my book of designs. "But that's cool. Let's eat."

"We don't have to go out. If you're expecting a client or something, we can order in." Her pretty blue eyes sparkle. "We can take the food upstairs."

Bringing Genevieve up to my private apartment, in the same space where I keep my bed? That's a temptation that I don't think even I can resist.

"Nah. I'm feeling tacos. What about you?"

"Tacos are good," she agrees. "But if you don't want to go out with me..."

I never want to come between Genevieve and her family.

I never want to derail her career.

I never want to singe her with the fire I've never been able to escape...

But not want to spend time with her, here or outside?

"You know where I keep your helmet, butterfly. I'll go get my keys."

WE'RE BEING FOLLOWED.

I noticed the nondescript black car tailing my bike about four streetlights back. They were on my ass, and I just thought it was another asshole driver who didn't want to share the road.

So I took a turn that would add five minutes to our trip, but I wanted to see if they would take the bait. Two right turns and a left later, and I had my answer. They were definitely following us.

Shit.

This is my fault. So desperate to prove to Genevieve that I was different than her brother... from the moment we met at the Playground, she's told me that one of the things that she likes most about me is how I'm sensitive. I'm not brutal and ruthless like the other gangsters she knows, and that's including both her older brother and cousin. She's convinced herself that I'm an acceptable Sinner because my speciality is in ink and because I have a soft touch when it comes to my art.

And I let her. I let her believe that since I knew I'd lose her if she knew the truth. That, despite my quiet nature and my sad eyes, I'm as much of a morally gray villain as any of the criminals walking around Springfield with a devil or a dragonfly on their skin.

I could protect her. In a way I couldn't protect my family when I was a boy, if anyone came after Genevieve, *I* could protect her now. That didn't mean I was reckless; with her safety, I would *never* be. I just refused to keep her locked up when she's with me the same way her brother does. If Genevieve wanted to explore Springfield on the backseat of my bike, I was confident in my abilities to keep her safe.

Besides, the taco place was only fifteen minutes away. Less if I speed, which I wouldn't normally do with such precious cargo clinging to my waist. But as soon as I caught on to our tail, I floored it.

They matched our pace, even after I started weaving around other cars.

In retrospect, maybe I shouldn't have painted a pale pink version of that fateful butterfly onto the white helmet I bought for Genevieve. She was so pleased when she saw I personalized it, as though part of her had suspected that I treat every girl I've ever been with the same way I do her.

Not even close. I didn't even know how to pick out a women's helmet since this is the first one I've ever bought, and I was lucky that Nic let me use her head as a guide to see if it would fit before I offered it to Genevieve.

Luckily, their heads are about the same shape and it worked. It fit Genevieve perfectly, both concealing her face when she didn't want anyone to know she was sneaking out of the East End and adding protection to her in case something happened to my bike.

I've never crashed before. I'm a good driver because, despite the shit I've gone through, it's not like I want to die. I just wish my family *hadn't*. With Genevieve clinging to me tightly… I'm doubly as careful.

But the helmet that'll cradle her head in case something *does* happen has a downside: anyone who knows she's the gorgeous face beneath the butterfly will be able to track us through Springfield.

My bike's not so unique. It's a basic Kawasaki cruiser, and my helmet is a dinged-up black, standard issue motorcycle helmet. There are more than enough bikers in the Sinners Syndicate that I could blend in with the traffic.

I could.

Genevieve can't.

It would be pointless to try to tell her to lose the helmet. Whoever is following us is already on our ass, and turning the afternoon drive into something more dangerous than it already might be is a stupid fucking idea.

I can't grab my piece, either. To reach my concealed carry pistol from my ankle holster, I'd have to risk tipping over my bike or slowing down enough for them to catch up. I didn't want Genevieve to know that I carry around her, either, but if the choice is between letting something happen to her or blowing up my 'nice guy' persona in front of her, I know what I'll have to do.

I never get the chance.

So concerned with the black car following us, I never see the white van come barreling toward us from my left side. Ignoring the red light, it plows right through it the second I push my bike into the next intersection.

A split second before it makes contact, I have a moment of sudden clarity.

The black car wasn't following us, I realize. It was *herding* us.

Without meaning to, I went exactly where they

wanted me to go: the run-down section of the West Side where it only comes to life at night. During the day, it's a ghost town, and no one is there to witness it as the van sideswipes us, I lose control of my bike, and the damn thing skids out from beneath me.

Genevieve screams. That's all I hear before the motor-cycle lands on its side, bouncing on the asphalt. I'm still clutching the handlebars. Genevieve is still clutching me. My leather jacket tears as we hit the ground. If my thick bomber is toast, the light sweater Genevieve pulled on over her sundress doesn't have a chance.

And that's if she survives the crash.

Considering the side of my helmet slams into the road, my head rattling around inside of it before my vision goes black, I don't even know if *I* will.

mariposa

FIVE
TRAPPED

GENEVIEVE

I remember a crash.

I remember a scream.

I remember thinking I was dead, and hoping that Damien doesn't blame himself for his wayward sister dying on the back of Sinner's motorcycle—or that he doesn't use that reality to put his hard-won truce in jeopardy, either.

I don't know all of the details. Just that, for years, the Dragonflies and the Sinners Syndicate were at odds, close to coming to blows and heading toward all-out war, until my brother somehow managed to convince the Devil of Springfield to agree to a truce. The Dragonflies would continue running the drug trade and our counterfeiting ring, the Sinners would get their guns, their girls, and the gambling at their private casino, tucked away in the back room of the Playground. At the same time, both gangs would work together if necessary, the same way Damien and Devil met up to discuss how to take down Jimmy Winter before the white-haired freak got killed going up against my brother.

As much as I'm sure Dame prefers to think otherwise, I'm not *that* naive. I know that Jimmy Winter isn't the only threat to the Family. When he died two weeks ago, Damien expected repercussions.

He expected them.

My mistake was in forgetting that, if someone really wanted to hurt Damien, I was the perfect target. Well, me or Savannah, but Savannah went ahead and changed up her style before dying her hair from a rich black color to a mahogany shade that suited her much better. Me? I thought that the helmet Cross gave me would be enough to hide my identity, and whether it did or didn't, one thing's for sure: my head is aching, my body feels like I've been hit by a fucking truck, my leg is on fire, but I'm *alive*. Considering my last memories consist of that scream and a horrifying crash, the helmet probably is to thank for that.

I'm alive—and when I try to make sense of my state and my garbled memories, I'm shocked that I am.

I was riding with Cross when we were sideswiped. He lost control of his motorcycle, we hit the asphalt. And then...

And then...

"Genevieve?"

Cross?

I... I know that voice. It's a struggle to open my eyes when my eyelids seem to weigh a hundred pounds each, but the amount of concern he slips into the three syllables of my name he whispered... I swallow, whimpering when I realize how dry my mouth is, and force my eyes open a crack.

The second I do, I wince and I recoil.

"Genevieve!"

It's more of a strangled shout, like he's trying to be quiet for some reason.

I shake my head, not ready to speak just yet.

The light... it's so damn bright. It sends a shooting sensation, stabbing straight through to my brain, and I have to flutter my eyelids in a vain attempt to get used to it. As my senses start to come online again, I realize I'm sprawled out on my back, something bumpy and uncomfortable beneath me. I don't like it. I feel super vulnerable all of a sudden, and I struggle to pull myself into a sitting position before something hard and craggy is behind me.

I quirk open one eye when I can, then the next. It's still super bright, but I can manage, and when I get my first glimpse of where I am, I almost wish I couldn't.

It's not familiar, as in I have no fucking idea where I am, but the slate grey cinderblock walls are the staples of too many basements I've seen. We're surrounded by three of them, with the fourth wall made of glass that reveals a hallway made up of, you guessed it, more cinderblock and scorchingly bright fluorescent lights.

In one corner of the cage, there's an open *toilet*, right next to a sink mounted to the cinderblock, a metal pipe beneath it disappearing in the only break in the wall I can find.

In the other?

There's Cross.

One he sees I'm up, he surges toward me. I notice his leather jacket he was wearing earlier is gone, and except for a blossoming bruise along his jaw where the helmet must've smashed into his face on impact, he seems no worse for the wear after having been through a motor-cycle crash.

He reaches the cot—because, holy shit, I'm sitting on a thin cot with a scratchy dark brown blanket on it—before dropping one knee on top of it, holding his arms out to me.

"Genevieve."

Cross.

I clutch his closest arm, pulling him onto the cot and nearly flopping into his lap in my panic to get close to him. I hate that I'm the epitome of a damsel in distress, but while he looks deceptively calm, my heart feels like it's about to beat its way out of my chest.

Digging my nails into his tatted arm, I rasp out, "What's going on? Where are we? Are you okay?"

He purses his lips, murmuring a hush under his breath. "There are cameras," he adds, lips thinned now. "Someone's watching. They could be listening."

Oh, God.

I didn't notice. How did I not notice them? Though that makes sense why Cross was standing in the far corner. Directly beneath one of the two cameras pointing down on the cot, it's probably one of the two spots that might possibly be out of the camera's range.

On the plus side, that means the toilet might not be caught on camera. But that also means I'm admitting that someone tossed me into a room smaller than my walk-in closet at home, and they expect me to *use* that toilet at some point.

No. I don't know what's going on, but I don't care.

I have to get out of here.

"Where's my phone?" Stupid question, but it's the first thing that pops in my mind. I want out of here and my instinct is to call my brother or Christopher... only my purse is gone. Cross's jacket is gone. So is my sweater. I'm in the dress and shoes I was wearing earlier, Cross is in his t-shirt and jeans and boots, and that's about all.

He shakes his head. "They rolled us, butterfly. My phone and wallet are gone, too."

That's fine. *Fine.* We'll get out of here, then worry about finding some good samaritan to lend us their phones. Wait. Do I know Damien's number? Shit. He told me that, when he was a kid, they didn't have cell phones like we did when I was the same age. He knows the phone numbers by heart of everyone he's in constant contact with, but me?

I think there's a six in it. Maybe a four?

Fuck.

That's fine. I'll walk. I have my shoes. I just have to make it to the East End of Springfield, and there's bound to be a Dragonfly who'll trip over themselves to deliver me to my brother—

"Not like it matters," Cross adds. "I tried busting down the door. It looks like glass, but that shit won't break."

What? No. Glass breaks. Everyone knows that. Glass breaks, and I'm not sure what he tried, but I'm desperate.

I get up.

"I'm gonna try. I'm a ballerina, right? A dancer. Maybe... maybe I can do it."

I flex my right leg, cursing when pain radiates up it.

"Genevieve," he hisses out on a breath at the same time as I notice the red marks covering the entire side of my flesh. "Your leg."

Well, that explains the burning sensation. "Road rash," I grit out once the pain subsides enough that I can. "Must've been when I hit the ground."

A muscle ticks in his cheek. "I'm so fucking sorry. I—"

Nope. "You have nothing to be sorry about."

"Of course—"

I hold up my hand. "Look. Unless you want to confess that the last six weeks have been some kind of long con, that you knew who I was from the beginning, and that you're working with one of my brother's enemies to trap me down here, I don't want to hear it."

Cross frowns. "Butterfly? How hard did you hit your head in the crash?"

I exhale. Until his visibly confused reaction, I wasn't

sure if there was a grain of truth in my wild accusation. I mean, technically that would explain a lot of things. His insistence that we keep our relationship casual, only friends, while also being there whenever I need him. It could be that Cross is a good guy who doesn't want to take advantage of me, or he could be a villain hiding in plain sight.

I want so badly to believe that he's on my side, but after tonight...

I shake my head. "My head's fine. My leg hurts like a bitch, but as long as it doesn't get infected, it'll heal."

"Unless you break it by kicking that thick glass door."

True, but it's worth the risk—

—and I believe that up until the moment I rear back with my left leg, mule kick the glass, and absolutely nothing happens except I feel the impact of the kick as a painful vibration that reaches all the way up to my hip.

Cross is smart enough not to say 'I told you so', or to point out that anyone on the other side of the camera would've probably gotten a kick out of seeing my failed one. He just stands there patiently, waiting for me to come to the same conclusion he must have while I was still unconscious.

"We're stuck here," I say after a moment.

"Yes."

Why isn't he freaking out? He can't have anything to do with this.... right? "You don't get it, Cross. We're *trapped*."

"I know, butterfly."

Then why doesn't he *care*? If he's not involved, then he's an innocent bystander, because—

"Cross... *crap*. I should be the one apologizing. This is all *my* fault."

Okay. My words coupled with my rising panic, that definitely shakes him up a little. Losing that annoyingly calm look on his face, he frowns. "What?"

"My fault," I repeat. "Whoever did this... they had to be targeting me."

His expression snaps back to that deceptively calm one from before. Right. He already guessed that, didn't he?

A hysterical bubble rises up in my throat. "What do they want with me? What are they going to do?"

"It doesn't matter." His eyes flash. "They can't touch you. I'll make sure of it. I'll protect you."

"Cross, I—"

He cradles my cheeks. "Listen to me, butterfly. Can you do that?"

Over the roar in my head? Over the realization that this is happening? That someone followed us, that they purposely ran us off the road, did something to us to knock us out so that they could lock me and Cross in this *cage*?

But if this is my fault like I expect it is, then Cross really is an innocent bystander. He's already tried to break out himself, and when he figured out he couldn't— and neither could I—his first instinct is to promise that he'll protect me.

Listen to him? I'll try. I nod, forcing myself to focus on Cross's face. The slope of his nose. The sharp edge of his jawline. His fiercely dark eyes.

I shudder out a breath.

He strokes the underside of my jaw. "Okay. We have running water. That means we can piss if we have to, and we have something to drink. That gives us a couple of days at least to figure out what the fuck is going on. That's all we need. You know why?"

I haven't a clue. "No," I whisper.

Cross bows his head, pressing his forehead against mine. I'm pretty sure he does it because he's trying to keep anyone from seeing his lips move or reading them if they can, but I need the connection at this moment.

I need *him*.

"You're Genevieve fucking Libellula. If there's one thing I know for sure, no matter why they targeted us, it's that your brother will come for you."

"Damien will come for me," I whisper back.

"That's right. I'm a Sinner. My guys won't leave me here to rot, either. They'll find us. Doesn't matter that they can't track us through microchips or any shit like that. I know Tanner. If they were dumb enough to bring our phones anywhere near this place, he'll definitely find us. We just have to make it until then."

I nod.

We can do this.

Right?

mariposa

SIX

QUIET

GENEVIEVE

Our third day in the cell, Cross is once again up already by the time I accept I just can't stay asleep any longer myself.

It's my stupid empty stomach that forces me awake. After close to two days of nothing but water, I've never been so hungry—and considering my job, that's saying something. As a professional ballerina, I spent most of my life eating less calories than I should so that I could stay as small as possible. It's a downside to the career I chose, and I've seen too many of my colleagues go down the road of EDs and injuries because they didn't have enough nutrients to prevent one.

I was lucky enough to be born with a slimmer frame. Hours of training gave me the muscle I needed to perform, but if my bones were any heavier, I'd have aged out of ballet years ago. This past year's recurring ankle injury is just another sign that I've probably pushed my body to its limits, but when it came to my diet, I never overdid it like so many other dancers. I skipped meals whenever Madame Durand pinched my side and told me I was getting too chubby for my leotard, but I drew the line at starving myself.

Skipping dinner and cutting my portions in half is one thing; it wasn't healthy, and I stopped doing that after I left Madame's studio, auditioning as part of a local company for theaters in Springfield, Riverside, and other nearby cities. But neither of us have had anything to eat since breakfast two days ago, and the gnawing hunger is really getting to me.

It hurts, but when I force myself up, resting on my elbows, searching for Cross, I see that he climbed out of the cot. He's sitting on the floor, back up against the cinderblock wall, head bowed. The longish front strands of his hair are falling into his face, hiding it from me, though when he hears the cot squeak and glances up, I can't miss his wince.

He's hurting just as much as I am.

Keeping my voice low so that I don't make it worse, I murmur, "Still bad?"

"It's getting better."

He's lying to me. Another way for him to protect me, I figure, but if I hadn't caught him rubbing his temples last night, I don't think he would've even let me know how much his head is killing him right now.

That's the caffeine withdrawal. It was one thing, teasing him when all I ever saw him down were energy drinks. It only took until yesterday morning for the caffeine withdrawal to kick in. Pair that with no food and Cross did his best to hide how miserable he was until he slipped up and I finally caught on.

There was nothing we could do about it, and if there really is someone watching us on the other side of that camera, they have a front-row seat to see how their actions are affecting us. I mean, we're prisoners. That much is a given.

I just wish I knew *why*.

It doesn't matter that I can pretty much guess. Damien might have done his best to keep me shielded from the criminal side of his Family, but a nosy younger sister can't truly be kept ignorant when she's as curious and insatiable as I was.

Now look at me. All I wanted was for Damien to realize that I wasn't a little girl, that I grew up, that I finally found a man who I thought could make me happy... and now we're both stuck behind a glass wall like we're animals in a zoo, hungry and hurting and pretending like everything is going to be all right.

That's why I let Cross have his lie.

His head doesn't hurt? Okay. I don't see him wince when the overly bright light flashes a certain way? Sure. That wasn't his stomach rumbling? Well, maybe he's right. It could've been mine.

"Did you at least get some sleep?"

I'm prepared for him to lie about that, too. It wouldn't be such a surprise. I knew before we woke up together in this cage that Cross suffered from insomnia. With the bright lights on around the clock, making it impossible to tell how much time is passing, or for either of us to fall asleep without pulling the blanket up and over our heads and hoping for the best, I knew he'd struggle a lot more than me when it came to getting a couple of hours down.

But something happened that first night. When going to sleep seemed a much better option than spending another minute longer thinking about hungry I was—especially since the hunger's only gotten so much worse since then—I curled up on the cot and regretted every fucking decision I ever made that led me to being trapped in a cage of cinderblock walls with a glass door.

It's my fault. No one's had to tell me otherwise. Being Genevieve Libellula... that's why I'm here. And Cross... I wouldn't be surprised if his slight indifference turned to hate that my family name is the reason he got captured with me.

But that night... he didn't just sit on the floor, his back against the wall, keeping his distance like he's done since I woke up. Instead, he climbed onto the cot next to me, wrapping me up in his arms, and holding me tight as he promised again that he'd keep me safe.

That he'd do anything to make sure I got out of here.

Was it his fervent promises that lulled me enough that I actually succumbed to sleep? Or was it his possessive hold, squeezing me to him, making me feel like he actually gave a shit?

I needed him to care then. I needed to know I had someone on my side.

So I slept curled up in the arms of the man who insisted we could only ever be friends, and when I woke up later and found him sleeping peacefully, still clinging to me, I thought that I might have found something to cling to myself.

Cross da Silva.

We slept the same way last night; if we could even call that last night when neither of us have any idea what time is. Between Cross's headache and the hunger pangs growing so much worse on our second day, I escaped this nightmare by falling into a fitful sleep that I only managed because he was there with me.

He was gone again this morning. I don't realize how much I've come to rely on the warmth of his body against mine until I woke up just now and he was sitting on the other side of our cage. Now he's standing up, pacing the lengths of the cell, unable to stay still.

"I slept enough," he says at last.

Really? Cross has lost some of the color he had yesterday. I frown. "Okay. But did you sleep well?"

A tiny spark finds its way to his dull dark eyes. "Yeah. Because I got to hold you."

That... that's not a lie.

I offer him a weak smile. "You telling me that we

finally figured out a cure for your insomnia? Toss your ass in a cell and you'll finally sleep?"

He pauses in his pacing. After giving me a scrutinizing look, he heads over to the cot, dropping down into a low crouch in front of me. "I'd go a hundred fucking years without another hour of sleep if it meant I could break you out of here."

A lump lodges in my throat. "I know."

"And it's not this hellhole. I promise you that. It's you, butterfly. Holding you in my arms... keeping you close? It's such a goddamn dream, I can't help but fall asleep because I know that it won't last. You and me..." Cross shudders out a breath. "If I had the chance, I would've done everything differently. In case this ends badly... I want you to know that."

I reach out, cupping his cheek. Last night, he was so warm. Today? There's a chill to his skin that wasn't there before. "We're going to get out of here, Cross."

We have to. For God's sake, I'm a Libellula. My brother will come for me," I remind myself. "He has the entire East End to command. They'll find me, and they'll save me.

We just have to survive long enough for that to happen—and on day three of no food, that's looking less likely than ever.

He leans into my hand. "That's one thing I love about you, Genevieve. You don't know how to quit. Even when you should."

I give him a half-smile. "You should talk to my old

ballet teacher. Madame Durand would tell you in great detail how I quit on her to pursue my own career in dance."

"This Madame Durand live in Springfield?" Cross asks, a dark look flashing across his features.

"Last I checked, her studio is still on the East End. Why?"

"Now I have even more motivation to get us both out of here. So you can show her how much of a fucking amazing dancer you are, and she can kiss your ass."

I laugh. It's more of a huffing sound than anything, hot air that escapes me because we're still careful to keep our voices low in case someone is listening in on us, but I laugh for the first time since I realized we've been taken captive.

Cross's expression softens. He turns his head, just quick enough for his lips to brush against the palm of my hand, before he's pulling back, out of my reach.

He rests on his heels, gaze roving over my face. "Know what? You're right, butterfly. No glass jar is gonna hold you. We'll get out of here."

I hope *he's* right.

Considering I know I was full of complete shit when I told him the same thing, I doubt it—but it's only day three. I haven't lost my hope yet.

At least, not *all* of it.

We're not alone. I know that much. As if the cameras seemingly tracking our every move aren't enough to figure that out, I hear footsteps over our head sometimes. They travel down the hall, purposely avoiding our cell.

I know there are more down here, too. If you jam your face up against the glass, angling your head just right, you can kinda see the dip in the cinderblock next to us, plus the reflection on the thick glass door.

There's a keypad out there, too. It explains why the glass door keeping us trapped in here doesn't have any visible locks on it. Our first 'night' in the cell, before I broke down and sobbed, Cross holding me tight and telling me we just had to make it through until the next morning, we searched every inch of the room.

My first impression was of the toilet and the sink. Cross was the one who pointed out the cameras. On closer inspection, there's a small vent near the ceiling— providing us fresh air so we don't eventually suffocate— and the glass door is on some sliding mechanism. I broke the nails on each of my pointer fingers, trying to see if the mechanism had some give to it until I had to admit that we were well and truly trapped in here.

But that leads us to even more questions:

Who trapped us? Why?

And how many other people are down here?

Three days in, and we still don't have an answer to any of the ones that matter.

We tried screaming to see if that caught anyone's attention. The footsteps make me think that, despite the thick glass and the dense cinderblock, the room isn't soundproofed. I can definitely confirm that the whole damn square seems to echo when I finally gave in to Mother Nature and squatted over the toilet. Cross turned his back; as a gentlemanly Sinner, he gave me privacy after I confessed I had to pee but I didn't want to do it with an audience. Poor guy. He thought I meant him, not the cameras, and while I quickly corrected him, he still stood with his back to me, trying his best to block both cameras.

But no matter how loud we screamed or as often as we got up and kicked the glass just to make us feel better, the response was the same: *silence*.

No one has come for us. If there are other prisoners in this unfamiliar place, they're keeping quiet. If they're as hungry and uncomfortable as we are, I get it.

Leaning up against Cross after he joins me on the cot again, resting my head on his shoulder, for the first time in my life, Genevieve Libellula has absolutely nothing to say.

mariposa

SEVEN

EAT

GENEVIEVE

I smell garlic.

At first, I think I'm imagining it. When the hunger finally seemed to fade a little a couple of hours ago, I knew that was a bad sign. My body has started to accept that I won't be eating soon, and instead of giving me signals to grab some food, it's probably starting to catabolize my muscles for fuel. Then I caught a whiff of garlic and convinced myself that my nose was playing tricks on me.

I didn't ask Cross if he smelled it, too. He's already so worried about me. If I admit that my senses are failing and there's nothing he can do about it... no. I ignored it, even as my stomach rumbled, and sat on the cot, preserving my energy.

And that's when I heard the footsteps.

Cross cocks his head. "They're getting closer, aren't they?"

He's right. "Someone's coming." I know better than to hope after three long days, but I feel it pushing against my chest anyway. "Do you think it's someone coming to let us go?"

I can tell how much it hurts him to have to dash my hopes like this, but if there's one thing I can expect from Cross, it's that he won't lie to me. "If it was someone on our side, I'm pretty sure the footsteps would be louder, or we wouldn't hear them at all."

True. "Then who do you think it is?"

He doesn't answer. He just motions for me to stay on the cot while he eases himself to his feet, positioning his body between the glass door and me.

The footsteps get a tiny bit louder, but there's a leisureliness to the rhythm that tells me Cross is right about this, too: whoever is coming, they're not here to save us.

Though they are here to finally *feed* us.

It's two men. Both of them have white skin and dark hair, and that's where the similarities end. The man on the left is at least a head taller than the one on the right. He has his hair pulled back in a low ponytail, with his face narrow and thin, his expression almost bored; he has that strung-out look a lot of older addicts have. The other man is thicker, though I wouldn't say fat, and he's about the same age: late thirties, early forties. Though, like his friend, it could be a history of drug abuse that ages him, because the way his round face pinches a little, he looks like he might be on Breeze right now.

The second guy immediately gives me the creeps, and not just because I'm pretty sure he's high. I can't really say why except for how bright his eyes get when he peeks through the glass and his gaze settles on me. He makes me feel dirty, and yeah. I haven't showered in days. But this is a slimy, sleazy, oily sensation slicking my skin as he looks me over, darting his tongue out, playing with the corner of his mouth.

Ew.

I scoot a little, ducking behind Cross. Not even the steaming pile of white noodles he's holding on the plate in his hand is enough to entice me to sit there and let this creep eye-fuck me like that.

The shorter guy peers at Cross next. He nods. "So you're Carlos da Silva."

Carlos? Who is—

Oh, holy hell. I mean, Jesus fucking Christ, Gen. Did you really think that his birth name was 'Cross'? Of course he has a real name... and after six weeks, I probably should've known that.

Damien would have. There isn't anyone he would've gotten into bed with—or thought about doing so—without knowing every single detail about them first, down to their blood type and shoe size.

These guys know more about Cross than I do. They know his real name—and they know mine, too.

"And Genevieve Libellula," he says, gaze back on me again, "the Dragonfly princess."

I fist my hands into the scratchy material of the blanket beneath me. I fucking *hate* it when people treat me like a mafia princess. Actually calling me one? I already didn't like these two, but now I loathe the second man in particular.

The other man nods his head. So preoccupied by the plate of pasta his friend had, I didn't notice that the taller idiot has a gun in his hand.

He waves it now, moving over to the keypad. He presses four buttons—I hear four beeps—and, for the first time since we've been in here, the glass door opens with a hiss, sliding just enough to allow the shorter man through.

"Go on," the tall guy says. "I got your back. Bring in the tray."

"Gotcha, Noah. Hold the door."

The shorter man turns slightly to fit his thicker bulk in through the gap. A quick daring look at Cross has him taking a few pointed steps back before the shorter guy drops the plate on the cot next to me. Some of the alfredo sauce splashes onto my wrinkled sundress, but I ignore the white dots on the pale pink material, raising my eyebrows at the sloppy plate of noodles instead.

"Bon appétit, sweetheart."

Ooh. My skin crawls as he leers at me, using a sickly sweet tone to call me 'sweetheart'. But when he gestures with his chin at the fork that toppled to the edge of the plate, I realize he's serious.

He really thinks I'm just gonna scarf this down.

Well. At least I know why they kept us hungry for so long. My hunger returning with a vengeance, I almost *do*.

But then my brain kicks in and I wrinkle my nose. "How do I know this is safe?"

I want to eat it. My mouth is watering. Do I care that alfredo sauce has always been a no-no food for me? I can just hear Madame's derisive sneer that I would dare have, heaven forbid, *heavy cream*, but the tantalizing aroma of garlic drowns her out. I'm not sixteen anymore. I'm twenty-five, I have a womanly figure now, and if I want some alfredo, I'm gonna have some alfredo.

But though I can drown out Madame, my brother's drawn-out sigh and dry, "You ate a meal prepared for you by the enemy, Gen?," is enough to have me swallowing the saliva in my mouth as I look wistfully down at the plate of pasta before shaking my head.

The taller man smirks, voice carrying through the glass. "You owe me twenty, Mickey. I told you that the princess here would look down her nose at anything we offer."

Right. So Noah sucks, too.

Doesn't matter. "Sorry, but I can't do it."

"You will."

No.

"If the boss wanted you dead, you'd be dead," Mickey says, nodding at the plate. "Now eat."

I push the tray away from me. It takes every ounce of strength I have to do that as I give the two men a defiant Libellula shrug. "Pass."

Mickey sucks in a breath. "You can eat it off the plate, or you can eat it off the floor, but you're gonna eat it." He pointedly meets Cross's quiet stare. "Both of you."

When we don't respond, Mickey makes a move to knock the plate off of the cot, onto the floor. Shit. He's *serious*. He'll really expect us to lick the pasta up off the floor—

"Here," Cross rumbles. "Give it to me. You want us to eat? Fuck it. I'll go first."

"Not very gentleman-like of you," Mickey snorts, taking a step back as Cross snatches the plate. "Shouldn't it be ladies first?"

"Not unless you did something to the food. In that case, I'll be the one to test it."

"You got a death wish, da Silva?"

"No. But if it's laced or poisoned, it's better that I find out over Genevieve." He swirls his fork in the pasta, gathering up the noodles then plopping them into his open mouth. He chews, swallows, then adds, "Not that I think it is. Like you said. If your boss wanted us dead, we wouldn't have survived the motorcycle crash."

The taller man laughs. "You're smarter than you look, pretty boy."

Cross doesn't respond. He just sets the fork down on the plate, then offers it to me.

I hesitate.

He nods. "We don't know when we'll eat again. Go on. Have some."

"Listen to the Sinner, princess," Noah says mockingly. "Be a good girl and, if you're lucky, we'll come back with breakfast."

"Or maybe we won't," adds Mickey. "Haven's gone. Dumb bitch got relocated right before we got the orders to move you in. With the compound down to a ghost crew and only two visitors, maybe we forget."

I know what he's implying. If I refuse to eat, I'll be punished. If I *do* eat, they'll know they can control me.

Cross has already shown them that they can use me to control *him*.

I guess you could say the same about me. I'm not going to let him go hungry because I'm too stubborn to save my own skin.

Damien would tell me to do whatever it took to survive. Now that Cross tasted the food first without any obvious adverse reactions, I might as well take a bite or two.

So I do, and once the two hired men get what they wanted, they each smirk at us, then Noah lets Mickey out of the cage, leaving Cross and me behind with a mound of woefully under-seasoned fettuccine alfredo.

I set the plate down. My stomach is roiling, unwilling to eat another noodle, and I ignore how uneasy it is by focusing on something else.

Cross.

"So," I ask, breaking the awkward silence. "Your name is Carlos?"

"It was," he says flatly, a clear signal that he doesn't want me to push the topic without actually having to shut me down with his words.

It isn't often he takes that tone with me. In fact, when you consider how often I badger him with my questions, trying to get to know him, I can only remember one distinct time that he did: when I asked him about the flames on his neck and discovered his family died in a house fire.

He's hungry, I tell myself. The promise of the food is probably twisting both of our stomachs, plus the realization that this wasn't some big misunderstanding. They know our names. They know who we are. They took us on purpose, and it doesn't look like they're going to let us go anytime soon.

He's hungry—and I've lost my appetite.

I push the plate toward him. "You should have some more."

"I'll eat when you've had enough, butterfly."

"I'm full—"

He thins his lips, looking absolutely beautiful in his utter defiance. "When you've had enough. If that means I don't eat, I don't eat. But I won't take a spoonful out of your mouth. Understand?"

I gulp.

His expression softens. Running his thumb under my chin, he lowers his voice. "Eat, Genevieve. I've been hungry before. I'll survive. But you've gotta let me make sure you do. Okay?"

I nod. "Okay."

"That's my butterfly."

And though the noodles taste like goddamn dirt in my mouth as I chew them, I take another bite because it's the only thing he's asked of me.

Starve my savior. I swallow roughly.

It's the least I can do.

mariposa

EIGHT

VISITOR

CROSS

Part of me can't help but wonder if it would've been better for the both of us if the crash was meant to take us out.

I woke up before Genevieve did after the fact. Not surprisingly. Whatever they gave us to make us docile and easy to transport from Springfield to wherever the hell we are now, it had to have been a strong dose. I've got a good fifty pounds on Genevieve easy, plus I don't sleep. Ever. They're lucky that I knocked out as long as I did, but I expected that Genevieve would be unconscious a lot longer than I was.

What I didn't expect? Was how full of rage I'd be when I came to and found her sprawled next to me on a tiny cot, laid out like a broken doll.

I told her that I tried to bust the door down so we

could escape. That might've been a bit of an understatement. After seeing the rough way they treated her, I saw fucking *red*. I threw my body at the glass, kicked it, even risked my hand by punching it, but nothing I did made any impact.

I got control of myself by the time she was waking up, but surprise, surprise: I managed to get it all wrong then, too. In my bid to keep her calm and promise that I'll keep her safe, I somehow managed to make Genevieve think that I had something to do with this. Luckily, she realized that I couldn't almost immediately after she made her accusation, but that still cut me to the core.

I would never hurt her. *Never*. And no matter what I have to do to prove that to her, I will.

In return, she trusts me to hold her while she sleeps, and if it wasn't for the fact that we're being trapped by some unknown villain, treated like trash by his goons, I might've marveled over the fact that Genevieve was right: in the most unlikely and unfortunate of circumstances, I found a cure to the insomnia that's plagued me almost my whole life.

Who knew it would take a blonde ballerina believing in me and my promises enough to allow me the pleasure to hold her close to chase away the demons that constantly keep me awake?

I don't look forward to what'll happen when we get out of here. Not leaving isn't an option. Whatever it takes, I will make sure that Genevieve is safe long enough for either her brother's Family or my syndicate to find us and burn the world down for taking us prisoner, no matter who the target was.

Genevieve believes it has to be her. As much as I hate to admit it, I have to agree that they came after her because of her last name. A man like Damien Libellula doesn't accrue as much power as he does without making formidable enemies. He only just survived an attempt on his life two weeks ago. Is Genevieve's abduction retaliation for that?

Or is something more sinister at play?

I got nabbed for a reason, too. They know my name and my affiliation. If I had any doubts that this was syndicate-related—whether mine or Genevieve's Family—they're gone now. Whoever is running the show wants a pet Sinner and Dragonfly, and he has them.

What is he going to do with us? I haven't a goddamn clue, and as awful as those first couple of days in our cage were—without food to sustain us, and my caffeine withdrawals a bitch to get through—I should've known that it would only get worse when our captor decided we were worth feeding after all.

He has a reason to keep us alive. I don't know what it is, but as long as he has one, I thought we were okay. At the very least, I thought Genevieve was untouchable.

I was *wrong*.

IF WE COUNT EVERY TIME WE SLEEP MORE THAN AN HOUR OR so at a time as another full night, it's day six in our cage. By now, I've picked up enough on the routine to figure out some details to help us survive.

Food. We get fed twice, a meal we consider 'breakfast' and one that's 'dinner'. It's never anything too elaborate. Mac and cheese. A cold hamburger from a fast food joint. A stale croissant from one of those coffee chains you find on every damn corner in Springfield. Pasta. We wash it down with sink water, and wait for one of the goons to pick up the plates.

The plates are always plastic, as though they're worried we might smash a ceramic one and use the shard to go for their jugular. And if I thought about snapping one of the plates in half and seeing if that might make a good weapon, it's pointless when the plates are too flimsy to break.

The goons. Turns out, there are at least *three* of them. Mickey is the squat one with a bit of a belly. Noah has the ponytail, mustache, and the gap between his teeth. Then there's the bald guy who's at least a head taller than both of them, who looms in the hallway as the other two take care of serving us the food.

He's the one who gives me a bad vibe. Even as a kid, I learned to listen to my gut. I knew Chad was trouble the first time my mother brought him home, and I got the same unsettled feeling when Twig came to me to get his Sinners brand. When I saw Devil blow him away for disrespecting Ava the way Twig did, I knew my gut got it right...

I can only imagine what *this* guy is capable of, and I watch him closer than I do the other ones when they open our cage.

That, I realize too late, was a mistake. So concerned with the quiet, glaring bald guy, I completely missed the way Mickey started looking at Genevieve the way she did that first plate of pasta they brought us.

Like he's *starving* for her.

By the time I caught on, I began moving in front of Genevieve so that he didn't get to ogle her. That worked for two days, but on the third?

He doesn't follow the routine.

First of all, the goons only come by our cage twice a day. Other than that, they leave us the hell alone. We had 'breakfast' already—a stack of dry pancakes we were forced to choke down—and only about an hour ago, Noah and the big, bald guy stood there as we used our hands to pick at a couple of pieces of oily fried chicken.

Genevieve barely ate a wing, then declared herself too full to continue. Before Noah barked at her to finish, I tore into the chicken breast myself. That satisfied the prick enough, and they disappeared down the hall.

We'd only just finished doing our best to wash the grease away without any soap when a heavy footstep echoed down the hall.

Genevieve's eyes widen, both in curiosity and in fear.

I rise up from the cot in time to see Mickey fiddling

with the keypad outside our cell. The door slides open, he steps inside, and almost immediately it closes behind him.

And he's alone. No backup. No help.

This is our chance.

I have every intention of doing something. Bum-rushing him, using my shoulder to knock him down, maybe even throttling him if I could get my hands around his thick neck first. Something. I would do *anything* to save Genevieve, and this seems like it might be my only chance.

And that's when he reaches behind him, pulling out a revolver, and my plans are suddenly on hold.

"Sit down."

I freeze in front of the cot.

He cocks the gun. "I said, sit down."

"Cross, please," whispers Genevieve.

I drop down on my cot beside her.

Mickey grins. "Better. Now, just in case you get any idea of trying to do anything funny, remember that I won't hesitate to use this." He gestures with the butt of the gun behind him. "That door's on a timer. In ten minutes, it'll open again, and I'm walking out of here by myself. You can be alive at the end of the ten minutes, or you can be bleeding out on the floor. Your choice, da Silva."

Keeping my voice as calm as possible, I ask, "And what takes ten minutes?"

The creepy bastard licks his lip. "All depends on how good she is. So why don't you tell me?"

Next to me, Genevieve grabs my thigh.

I dare him to make another innuendo. I don't give a shit that he has a gun. If he's saying what I *think* he's saying...

Mickey sighs. "See? This is why I told the boss man that you should have your own cells. I wouldn't need to keep the gun out if you were tucked away, but it is what it is. I came here to get what I'm owed..." He pauses for a moment, laughing as if he said something funny. "Maybe not one of the Owed. If I was, it would've been a lot easier to get that Haven bitch to play nice without breaking her." His beady eyes land on Genevieve. "You gonna be a good girl, sweetheart, or you gonna need to be broken in, too?"

She blinks, stunned. "What?"

Mickey keeps the gun on me while addressing Genevieve. "See, now, the other bitch got booted when she went mute. I didn't need her to speak to suck my cock, but without her here... this is one of the perks of dungeon duty. If I want to get off, I'm getting off. It's been days. The boss said I needed to wait until you were settled in. Fuck it. I've waited long enough." His eyes slant over to me. "Don't try to be a hero, boy. Don't try to stop me. You can get your piece of ass when I'm done, but no one said you can't share her mouth."

He'll shoot me. This guy is just looking for an excuse to do it, and no one is going to stop him. No one is going to stop him from shoving his cock past Genevieve's lips, making her gag on his length if that's what he wants.

No one, but *me*.

I don't even glance at Genevieve. If I see the horror that has to be written on her face, I won't be able to control myself. A dead man can't protect her, so I need to be smart.

Too bad my brain seems to go haywire as Mickey keeps the gun trained on me while he uses his other hand to open his pants, pulling out his hard cock.

"No," whimpers Genevieve. "I... *no*."

Ignoring her, Mickey strokes his dick, making sure that neither me nor Genevieve can miss what he's doing. "Listen. Yeah? I'll make this is as clear as I can: I'm not leaving until my dick gets wet, one way or another. And that means I won't be going up to check in with the boss, or bringing down any more food for you. If I won't, neither will Noah and Brady. Hey. Two days made you hungry. Maybe a week will have you realizing that sucking me off isn't so bad when you get a meal out of it."

Genevieve trembles next to me—and that seals it. I need to be smart. I need to have a plan.

This is the only one I've got.

"Fuck it," I say, my voice a casual drawl that conceals the rage burning through my veins. "I'll do it."

Her fingers dig into my thigh, clutching me.

I pretend not to notice as I wait to see how this black-mailing asshole will react to my offer.

His face turns thoughtful, though his hand never leaves his dick. "Didn't take you for a fag, da Silva."

I expected as much. The slur, and the thoughtful caress as though he's not opposed to the idea.

"I'm not. But you said it yourself. You want your dick wet. One mouth's as good as another. The girl doesn't want to do it so I guess I have to."

The bastard's eyes light up. Not in amusement or excitement, though. That's sadistic pleasure, pure and simple. "You seem so eager. How can I refuse?"

Dumb fuck. He *should*.

I shrug. "Ten minutes, tops. Right? I blow you for ten minutes and you leave us the fuck alone."

"For tonight," Mickey greedily agrees.

No. *Forever*.

"Can I get up or are you going to shoot me?"

"Try something smart and I will."

I don't doubt it.

The second my ass starts to leave the cot, Genevieve reluctantly releases her death grip on me.

"Cross," she breathes out.

I peek over my shoulder at last, giving her a quick look that promises that I got this, before turning to face Mickey again.

His smirk tells me all I need to know. This is a power play for him. Just like my stepfather. He's a tough guy. A big shot. Someone obviously put him and the others in charge of the captives, and if he can be believed, he already abused another woman enough that she lost the ability to speak. I won't let him touch Genevieve if I can help it, and if I have to potentially trigger the memories of my own abuse to protect her, I *will*.

Mickey's getting off on my acquiescence already. I got it right when I said that one mouth's as good as another because he's gripping his erection by the base, angling the stubby cock so that I can wrap my lips around the head without any hesitation. He doesn't seem to give a shit that I'm a man. He wants his dick sucked, and the fact that he's got a Sinner willingly going to his knees might almost excite him more than forcing Genevieve to do it.

She sucks in a breath that might be a sob, but I don't turn around this time. To make my legs obey, to bend my knees, to drop to one, then the other in front of a naked cock... I need all my grit and determination to do this.

For her. It's for her, and I don't think I can handle seeing a flash of horror twisting her features right now—or after.

mariposa

NINE
ENOUGH

CROSS

I know what Genevieve thinks. That I'm a nice guy. *Sensitive.* Good. Even though she's aware that I'm high-up in the Sinners Syndicate, part of her is convinced I only got in because of my lifelong relationship with Rolls, plus my skill with my tattoo gun.

That's on me. When I saw all that innocence in her pretty blue eyes, I had this irresistible urge to keep it there as long as possible. If that meant hiding the darkness that's taken root inside of me long before the fire... I did it. For as long as she believed I was worthy of being near her—knowing we could never last—I needed her to see that *good* in me.

But I don't have the luxury of doing that anymore. I gave her my word that I'd protect her for as long as we're trapped behind that glass door. My butterfly is beautiful.

That's not my attraction to her talking, either. Anyone with eyes can see how gorgeous she is. Our jailers haven't hidden how they gawked at Genevieve, and I'm absolutely positive the cameras are aimed on her, especially when she's discreetly trying to use the open toilet.

So, yeah, I guess I was expecting something like this. One of these pricks thinking they can take advantage of her? Sorry, sick men will always prey on those they consider weaker than them; I know that one all too well. It was inevitable that someone would try, even with me here.

And I'm ready for it.

Because I'm *not* a good guy. Not anymore. For her, I *want* to be, but I've been a Sinner under the Devil of Springfield for close to a decade now, and that was after all the trauma I kept tucked behind an impassive mask. I know exactly what I'm going to do.

I might not have a gun, but that doesn't mean I'm defenseless. I'll only have one shot at this, too, and I swear I'll make it count as I drop down in front of Mickey.

After the fire, I blamed myself. If I'd just dealt with Chad myself, if I'd waited until I was grown and strong enough to fight back without threatening to tell my mom the truth... maybe she'd still be here. Ana Lucia, too, and Rafe. Every time that he slipped into my room and told me I had no choice... I fantasized about my revenge.

I never got the chance to get any back when I was twelve and overpowered by my stepfather.

Now?

As I thumb the corner of my mouth, then part my lips as though ready to suck down a beer instead of Mickey's cock, the dark side of me admits that I can't fucking *wait*.

The familiar tang of salt and unwashed skin nearly makes me hurl since he doesn't even give me a chance to prepare for it. As though trying to prove how much I'm at his mercy, he shoves the head of his cock past my lips and into my mouth.

I'd planned on waiting until he'd fit as much of himself inside as he could before I reacted. Maximizing the damage was the plan since I don't expect to survive what happens next, but I underestimated how much I *would* trigger my past when the tip touches my tongue and my teeth clamp down.

As a kid, I did the research once. With the right amount of force, a human could section and sever an erection with their teeth by clamping down with their jaw. I'd thought about doing it a dozen times, but was too afraid of the repercussions if I did.

Carlos was afraid.

Cross isn't afraid of anything.

I bite as hard as I can, and when my mouth fills with blood and something the same texture and size as a bite of a fucking hot dog, it's obvious that I took off the tip of his cock.

Not as much as I wanted, but by the howl that tears out of Mickey's throat, it's more than enough.

He jumps back, the bloody stump of his cock pulling

free from my teeth. I spit out the tip from my mouth just in time for him to kick me dead in the face.

My head explodes, and over the roar of pain that echoes around my shattered skull, I hear Genevieve scream.

My cheek is probably fractured. It's better than being shot, though that's probably because Mickey's initial reaction to having part of his cock bit off was to kick me away from him instead of using the gun in his hand.

But he'll remember that he has one eventually, and when he does, I'm dead.

That's okay. I think part of me knew I was the second I bit down.

He's still howling. "Get on your knees. Get on your fucking knees!"

A boot to my side has me flopping to my belly as my arms give out. I don't even have a second to respond to his demands before Mickey lunges at me, gripping me by my hair. He yanks it so hard, I have no choice to follow his pull unless I want to be scalped. I rear back, my ass against my boots. Another tug and I'm back on my knees again, forced to look up at him.

There's murder in his eyes, and a promise of retribution in every line of his face. Shock, too, and agony as he shoves the gun in mine.

Good.

The mouth of the gun bites into my forehead. "You're dead. You hear me? *Dead.*"

Yeah. I figured.

But it was *worth* it.

I grin, letting the blood dribble free from the corners of my lips. It trickles down my chin, sticky and warm and wet, and I dare him to shoot me all while thinking: *try raping her mouth now, asshole.*

It wouldn't have stopped there. I know men like him. If he forced Genevieve to give him oral tonight—especially with me in the same cell—what would have happened the next time he wanted to get off? Would he have decided she needed to spread her legs for him instead? At least he won't be able to do *that* with the top of his cock on the floor.

As I prepare for the bullet between my eyes, I feel at peace with my violence. Knowing that I've stopped one asshole from hurting Genevieve is enough, even if it costs me my life.

I have faith in Damien Libellula's reputation. He'll find her. He'll save her.

At least one of us will.

Mickey bares his teeth at me. His finger moves a fraction—

"That's enough."

—but he never pulls the trigger.

The second that rich, almost taunting male voice booms into our cell, Mickey bellows out a wounded cry, then removes his finger from the trigger, the cool mouth of the unfired gun from my skin.

He doesn't shoot me, but he flips the gun quickly, pistol-whipping me in the same cheek that's already busted. Maybe it's not fractured, though with the renewed explosion of agony nearly blinding me, it's hard to tell.

But fuck if I don't stay on my knees this time. If only to work my jaw, then spit out some fresh blood at Mickey, taunting the bastard the way he deserves... I stay on my knees as he pants, chest heaving, bloody cock a beautiful mess of red.

"You, *asshole*—"

"I said, that's enough, Kelly." The voice is firmer this time, his words cutting off Mickey's fury. "You listen to me. I gave you permission to fuck Haven's mouth so long as you didn't touch her cunt. Same thing with li'l miss Dragonfly here. But you don't kill unless it's on my orders. Do you understand?"

"My cock—" he gasps, wide, staring, tear-filled eyes focusing on the camera in the right corner.

"Yes. I saw what the Sinner did. You put him on his knees, you fool. With his history, did you really think he wouldn't retaliate?"

Ice slithers down my spine. *His history...*

Fuck. They don't just know my name. They don't just know my affiliation.

My history. The big shot talking over the loudspeaker knows about my stepfather.

How? No one does. Anyone who gave a shit that Chad Rogers was a pedophilic, murdering piece of shit is long dead. The courts didn't care, giving him the minimum sentence they could for the arson. The fact that three people I fucking loved *died* paled in comparison to the amount of damage to the neighboring houses. Justice is a joke in Springfield. Is it any wonder I became a criminal after all? I saw what playing by the rules got me.

My stepfather's hands all over me.

A dead family when I finally fought back.

Enough baggage to stock a department store.

But that's my cross to bear. For fuck's sake, it's the reason I shucked the name 'Carlos' in the first place, mockingly rechristening myself as 'Cross' instead. It wasn't a religion thing. My mother and bio father were both born Catholics, just like Devil, but after my 'dad' took off, she stopped believing in God and so did I.

Then she met and married Chad, and not even God could save me then.

No one knows. I made sure of it. I mean, when I went into foster care, changing schools three times in two years before I ended up at Springfield West, there were rumors that followed behind me. Rumors that maybe I set the fire, or that I was the one my stepfather was really trying to feed to the flames. It didn't take long for some punk kids to think I was fucking him, and while that was the one thing Chad *didn't* do—at least, he didn't fuck my ass, preferring to see me on my knees in front of him just like Mickey did—it didn't matter. Kids suck, and I spent my early teen years dealing with that shit, too.

As an adult? I've put it behind me as best I could. It's been almost twenty years. No one should know about my history with that pedo—but this guy does.

How?

I don't know who that is. No way he's going to tell me, and I guess I should be grateful enough that Mickey's boss seems to have some hard lines he won't cross. The hired goon can fuck Genevieve's mouth, but not her pussy, and even after I mutilated him with my teeth, he's not allowed to kill me. Kick me, slap me with the gun, sure, but shoot me? Not yet, at least.

I have no illusions that that means he's a good guy. A decent man. He's *caged* us, and allowed his hired help to SA a girl enough that she went *mute*. That's what Mickey said. She stopped talking, and now she's gone, and all that's left are my butterfly and me.

He won't let his men rape her *now*. I'm not dead *yet*.

That could very easily change.

I won't forget that, just like I won't forget that my initial suspicions have been proven correct. Those cameras work, and that means there's no way of knowing when the faceless boss is watching us—or what he's learned so far.

I need to do the same. He's still talking, and I force myself to listen to him.

"Besides," he drawls, "now you know better. There's a reason why you're the one to interact without our guests, Kelly. Back an animal against the wall. Lock him in a cage. Give him a bitch to protect... you're bound to see him go feral and use his teeth."

"But my *cock*—"

Through the loudspeaker, you can hear the impatience in the man's sigh. "Do shut up about it. I've already sent Baker down with a cup of ice. Grab whatever piece of it's missing off the floor, and stick it in the ice. There's a car idling out back. My personal surgeon will fix you up." He pauses a moment. "Can't guarantee that you'll get all the feeling in the tip back, but at least it's something. Now put that stump away. You don't want it flapping about when you move through the facility, do you?"

Mickey shakes his head, cheeks hollowing as he clenches his teeth, biting back his pain.

My face is on fire, but I'm just as stubborn. I won't let him see that I'm hurt, either. I'll survive it. I'd kill for some of that ice the other man mentioned, but I can make do without it.

Mickey? Good luck with that reattachment surgery, motherfucker.

He's obviously thinking along the same lines as me. Still holding his bloody cock, trying to tuck it beneath his ruined boxers, Mickey starts searching the floor for the piece of dick I spat out.

I see it. It looks as much like a piece of hot dog as I thought it felt like in my mouth, and I have half a mind to fling it beneath our cot to make it even more trouble to find. Pity that he scoops it up before I can, giving me one last murderous look as the ten minutes finally go off, the door sliding open behind him right as Noah comes clomping down the stairs, wearing a befuddled expression and holding a red Solo cup full of what has to be ice.

"Mick?"

"No one word, Noah," he grits out, limping out of the cage before dropping the tip of his cock into the cup. "Not one fucking word."

Noah clamps his mouth shut. And once the two men are gone, disappearing down the hall, I realize he's not the only who's gone quiet.

The man in charge of our imprisonment is silent—and so is Genevieve.

mariposa

TEN
SNOWFLAKE

GENEVIEVE

I ... I didn't know that was possible.

I think about sticking a finger between my teeth and biting down. It'll hurt, and I'll probably leave teeth marks in the skin and white marks on my nail, but I don't think I'm strong enough to, like, bite off the tip.

Is it because that creep was already hard when he came down here, expecting me to suck his cock? It all happened so fast. The fear that he might actually do it, the terror that Cross might have to watch me, and just how quickly he coolly offered to take my place...

I tried to tell him that he didn't have to. To be honest, I didn't think Mickey would actually *want* Cross to do it instead of me, but both men surprised me as Cross dropped to his knees and that horrible guard held his dick out to Cross.

For a split second, all I could think was how fucking stupid I am. I've been best friends with Christopher since we were *eight*. I was there when he liked girls, I was there when he liked boys, and I was there when he decided he liked both. When Cross told me that he didn't do relationships, that we could be friends, it never even dawned on me that he was probably so uncomfortable by my obvious attraction to him, he came up with an excuse so I'd stop coming onto him.

I don't know why he didn't just tell me he was gay!

I mean, I would've been disappointed, sure, but only because I never had a chance with him if he batted for the other team. I still liked him. I'm still in awe of his talent. I already decided that, if friends were all we could be, I could use another one. It brings my grand total to, like, *three* if I count my sister-in-law, but that works, right?

And then, just as Cross took Mickey's cock into his mouth, his jaw moved and, holy shit, I had no idea you could bite off the tip of someone's dick like that.

Mickey almost killed him. If it wasn't for that booming voice making him stop, he would have. I have no doubt in my mind that he would've, or that Cross was expecting that.

Only he didn't, and now it's just the two of us again, and by the time I break out of my admittedly stunned stupor, he's rubbing his battered cheek with one hand, using the other to cup water from the faucet and sip it.

I approach him carefully. "Cross? You okay?"

Mickey kicked him in the face, then pistol-whipped

him with his gun. If his cheek isn't fractured, he's lucky as hell, but it'll be purple sooner or later. His mouth is bloody, too, but I don't think it's *his* blood. Even so, before he answers me, he swishes around the water he sipped, then spits it out into the basin of the sink.

It's slightly pink from the blood.

He looks at it, shaking his head. "Just washing my mouth out," he says needlessly. And then he adds, "Gotta get rid of the taste."

I nod in sympathy. "The blood."

Cross starts filling up his hand again. "No. Not the blood."

Oh. He's talking about Mickey's dick, isn't he? "I hate that you had to do that."

He washes his mouth out again, and shrugs. "It is what it is." A pause, and then, "You ever suck cock?"

Cross knows I'm a virgin. I cringe to think about how desperate I was, but when we were hanging out, I wasn't shy about being eager to lose my V-card. Now I'm pretty sure that never would've been with Cross, but when it comes to other sexual experiences… "No. I haven't."

"It feels great when someone you're into is sucking yours. But having to be the giver… I can't stand the taste of cock."

And there's the confirmation. "It's good to know," I say.

Cross has been avoiding my gaze. Not now. He looks at me, almost like expecting me to be appalled by what he did—or what he said. "You alright, Genevieve?"

I have no right to think my mortification tops what happened to him. He got beat, his brains nearly blown away, for *me*. Realizing that I'm not his type is nothing compared to that.

"Yeah. I mean, given the situation, I'm as okay as I can be."

His laugh is hollow, fingertips probing his cheek. "Ditto," he says, "though I wish you'd be honest with me. Something's bothering you. No, don't deny it. Come out with it. I know what you've gotta be thinking about what just happened. Don't keep it in. Remember, we're in this together."

Right. Only one of us had a cock in their mouth and a gun to their head, though. "It's nothing—"

"Genevieve."

Okay. He asked for it. "It's just.. I didn't know you were gay, okay?" I hold up my hands, cutting him off before he can say anything. "Not that there's anything wrong with that. You wanted to be friends. I'm the idiot who deluded myself into thinking all those times we went out to eat were dates. It's okay."

"Genevieve—"

"Christopher," I blurt out. "If we make it out of here alive, I'll introduce you to Christopher. That thing with Jessie fizzled out. Maybe he'd be into a sexy artist like you."

I'm babbling. Part of that's because I feel embarrassed. The other part's because I'm trying not to think about how, if I'd just gone to my knees instead, Cross's mouth wouldn't still be this bloody.

His eyes flash as I mention Christopher, but then he says, "Genevieve. I'm not gay."

"Okay. Christopher is bi, too, so I get it—"

"I'm not bi, either."

I open my mouth.

He grimaces, and I'm not sure if it's because his face has got to be killing him, or because he wants me to drop it. "Genevieve. I promise you. I'm into women."

I don't understand. "Then why were you willing to, you know, do *that*?"

"It's not my favorite thing to do, if that's what you're getting at," he says in that flat tone that warns me against continuing.

I don't listen to it. I can't. "But you're straight—"

I'm used to Cross's sad eyes. I've never seen them this *angry*.

Not at me, though. I have no idea how I can tell that the anger is for someone else, but even before he says another word, I know he's hurting and he's upset, too, but his anger? He's not directing it at me, even as his voice turns hard.

"You had your older brother to protect you as you were growing up. It was my job to protect my younger brother and sister from my stepfather."

Oh.

Oh.

He's not saying... but he is, isn't he? To protect his younger siblings, his stepfather made him do *that*?

I know I should drop it. His tone is all but begging me to. Even the little voice in my head is chanting: Shut up, Gen. Shut up, shutup—

"Are they okay now?" I ask.

"They're dead."

I should've listened to the little voice.

What the fuck is wrong with me?

"Cross, I'm so sorry—"

"I was twelve. There was a fire." His hands ghost up his throat. "My stepfather set it after I threatened to tell to get him to leave me the fuck alone, but he didn't have the decency to die in the blaze himself. Just my family."

Lowering his hands, he twists his arm, showing me the names inked on his skin. "Ana Lucia was nine. Rafe was eleven. My mother didn't even make it to thirty." Cross huffs out a breath. "She had three kids and I fucking outlived her."

I lift my fingers to my lips. Look at that. I finally figured out how to shut up.

Cross slams the faucet handle down, cutting off the stream of water. He spins around, bracing the sink with his hands, his eyes never leaving mine.

"I know what bad men want, butterfly. Men like Chad. Men like Mickey. I would *never* let them get to you. I couldn't save my family, but I promise you this: I will save you. But you have to finally understand something. I know what bad men want because I *am* one."

No.

He's *not*.

I step closer to him, expecting him to shove off of the sink and storm away toward the glass door. When he doesn't, I move until he's within arm reach before I tell him, "You protected me. I don't care about anything else. That makes you a good man."

He shudders out a breath. "I protect those I care about," he rasps. "You? You are my *muse*. My inspiration. You couldn't be anything other than that because I couldn't risk bringing you into the darkness that is my life."

His chest is heaving. I lay my hand between his pecs. "You sound like Damien," I say, purposely putting a hint of a tease in my voice. "But you're not. You're Cross. And I care about you, too."

He bows his head over mine, pressing our foreheads together. "You're special, Genevieve. You deserve someone good."

"I found him," I murmur back. Slowly, carefully, giving him every chance to stop me... I slide my hand up his chest, moving it until I'm gently touching the side of his swollen face. "Cross?"

"Butterfly," he breathes out.

He thinks that I could never be with a man like him. That I could never love him. Learning the truth of his past... my heart breaks for him. Adding that to what I just saw him do? I'm so fucking impressed by the strength of my artist.

Cross trembles under my touch, yet I can't shake the feeling that he expects me to push him away.

Oh, babe. Don't you know that I never do what anyone expects me to?

I part my lips. "You said you were trying to get that taste out of your mouth before," I murmur.

His Adam's apple bobs as he swallows roughly. "Yeah."

"Then let me."

I've only had a couple of kisses before. I'm not completely inexperienced when it comes to that, though it's a little more intense when I'm trying to get him to open up without aggravating his fresh injury. I'm not worried about the blood that might still be in his mouth even if I probably should be. It's more that I don't want his cheek to hurt.

So I try to be careful.

Cross?

The moment my tongue touches his, he's like a wildfire ready to consume me. His heat sears me down to my core, and I'm not sure if I'm kissing him or he's kissing me, just that I never want to stop kissing this man ever.

And who knows what would have happened next if it wasn't for a soft rap-tap-tap at our glass door...

Cross groans into my mouth, but he immediately releases me. Dropping his hands to my waist, he eases me out of the way, then moves so he's standing right in front of me as I turn to see who is out there.

I doubted it would be Mickey. I thought it might be

Noah, returning after he brought Mickey to the car waiting to bring him to get stitched up if possible.

It's neither.

In fact, I have no clue who he is at all.

Once he has our attention, he opens the glass door and steps into our cell. Not too far, though, barely a step inside, and he's so confident that he can handle a five-three ballerina and a half-beaten artist, he doesn't close the door behind him.

He's also obviously not a moron because, like Mickey, he has his gun out.

This man has a pleasant face. His hair is a rich, inky black, styled similarly to how my brother wears his. His suit is the same shade of black. His eyes are dark, though his skin is very, very pale.

I feel like I know him, though, and that gives me enough nerve to demand, "Who are you?"

He shows off his hand. I think it's a mocking wave—until I notice something staring back at me.

There's a snowflake inked on his palm.

After seeing Cross's work, I know a shitty tat when I see one. That one is not shitty. I can't imagine how much time he spent getting the details of such an elaborate snowflake on such a sensitive, lined piece of skin, but unless it's crappy up close, that tells me has time, money, and patience.

Oh, and a pretty fucking high pain tolerance, too.

That's what his tattoo tells me. It's gotta tell Cross the same thing, but he must see something else I don't because he goes stiff in front of me, his voice low as he spits out, "I know who he is. *Winter.*"

Winter? No... that's impossible. Damien had a file about his would-be killer in his office. Christopher snapped a pic of it for me, so I know what Jimmy Winter looks like. And, yeah, now that Cross mentions it, his face does remind me of Jimmy Winter, but the rest of him?

"That's not Jimmy Winter. He had white hair."

"Dye exists," Cross mutters.

"Okay, fine. But he's *dead.* Sav— I mean. Someone killed him."

The dark-haired man gives me an indulgent grin. "Don't be shy, Ms. Libellula. I know very well what happened to my brother. How he didn't listen to me when I told him we needed more time to infiltrate Springfield. How we're used to wiping out single gangs, not one as large as the conglomerate created when Mr. Libellula and Mr. Crewes joined forces. How one needn't use death as a motivator unless it's a last resort." His lips twitch. "You kill a man, he's gone. You destroy him and, well, he has to live with what he lost."

Cross gulps.

Me? I'm stuck on one thing in particular this guy said. "*Brother?*"

"Twin," he agrees. "Very astute, Mr. da Silva. Dye exists. So does bleach, and Jimmy was a very big fan of it. Not me. So now that he's gone and we don't have to pretend to be the same man anymore, I've tidied up a few details about what it means to be a Winter. Starting with the hair."

You've gotta be fucking kidding me.

Cross doesn't seem as shocked as me to discover there are *two* Winters. "You know, I was beginning to doubt our guy's skill. If Winter had a twin, he would've figured it out. But two of you pretending to be one guy... wasn't there a movie like that? With magicians?"

"Perhaps. But, I assure you, that this is real life. My life, and now yours. *Johnny* Winter, at your service." His dark eyes gleam. "I hope you're enjoying your accommodations."

Okay. Whether he's screwing with us or not, I don't care. "What do you want with us?"

He seems pleased I asked.

"It's very simple. I want what my brother's always wanted. What the two of us sacrificed for, worked for all these years."

"Yeah? And what's that."

"Power," he says simply. "Territory. *Money*. But he didn't listen to me. All these years, I let him take the lead, pretending I was him so that no one knew there was Johnny *and* Jimmy. All I asked was that he listen to me. God knows I'm the brains of the operation, and he was the face of it even though we have the same face. But, alas, your sister-in-law just had to run him down." He sighs, and I get the feeling that he could care less that Savannah killed his brother. "And now *I'm* in charge."

"That didn't answer Genevieve's question, though,"

Cross says. "The Snowflakes deal drugs. They run guns. I've heard they're in the skin game, too. You can get power, territory, and money with all that. You went to a lot of trouble to kidnap us. To throw us in a cage."

"Yes, but that's because you've already forgot what I said. Some rivals... I want to destroy them. What better way to do that by taking what they love and bringing them to their knees?" His gaze dips to Cross's. "You know all about that, don't you, Mr. da Silva?"

Cross takes a step forward. I grab the back of his t-shirt.

Winter doesn't even react, keeping his gun at his side.

"I'm not like my twin," he says after a moment. "Death is so final. I really do prefer it to be a last resort. Like you said, I went to a lot of trouble to get to you." He ticks off fingers on his free hand. "There was that Sinner. Dave... Sanders? Yes. I think that was his name. I paid him close to a thousand dollars to keep an eye on you two, letting me know your routine, where I might be able to catch you. Oh, and there was that Dragonfly that my twin tortured. Oliver... sorry. I didn't get his last name before Jimmy gutted him. But he's the one who said, to get to Damien Libellula, we needed to go through either his sister or his wife. Only his wife had a tracker in her arm, and sweet Genevieve... she did not."

"How do you *know* that?"

He *tsks*. "Weren't you listening? Oliver told me. Keep up, Ms. Libellula, please. I don't often make personal appearances, and I don't like to waste my time. I have plans for you two. So, if you would, be a good little girl and behave yourself until I'm ready for the next part of it, and I'll what I can to make your time here more... acceptable."

I don't like the way he said that.

Neither does Cross. "Plans? Like what?"

Winter ignores him. "Anyway, I just wanted to assure you that none of my men have my permission to touch you. In fact, this stage of my plan hinges on it. That's why I had to make the trip down here myself so you could meet me in person and see how serious I am about that. If they try, I'll have them killed. I hope you understand."

Yeah. I'm not sure I do. "Hang on—"

Winter lifts his gun, just making sure we see it. "And if you assault one of my guards again, I'll have you killed. Is that clear?"

He smiles.

Goddamn it, I flinch.

Now, I just watched the man I love get brutalized. I watched him mutilate another man with his teeth. Neither one of them turned my stomach the way Johnny Winter's smile does after he just so pleasantly threatened to kill Cross.

I gulp, answering before he gets the chance to do that. "Crystal."

mariposa

ELEVEN
DAVE

CROSS

I keep waiting for the other shoe to drop.

Ever since Winter came down to 'introduce' himself a few days ago, I expected retaliation for the way I went after Mickey. Winter wanted me to believe that he's running the show, that until he changes his mind about keeping Genevieve and me in his compound, we don't have anything to worry about so long as I don't go after another one of his men.

I already bit off part of a man's cock. If someone did that to me, there's no one who could hold my leash tight enough to keep me from getting revenge. And if I couldn't? I'd hope that Rolls or Killian would avenge me.

Does anyone give enough of a shit about Mickey Kelly to come at me?

It doesn't seem so. Either his comrades thought he

deserved it, or Winter really does have complete control over his hired help, because the only thing that changes following Mickey's mutilation is that Noah and the bald guy, Baker, are the only two who bring us our meals.

We don't see Winter again. Mickey might still be recovering for all I know, but after Winter walked down the hall, he hasn't come back. We haven't heard him on the speaker in our cell, either, though I have no doubt in my mind that—wherever he is—he's got his eyes on the video feed from our cameras.

It's been a week. After what happened, I didn't sleep for at least the next eighteen hours, if not more. That was to be expected. Between having to relive the act, plus confessing as many details about my past as I felt comfortable burdening my butterfly with, I was fucking *triggered*. It wasn't even the old familiar fear that Chad might wake me up that kept me from falling asleep; the man's dead, but trauma does funny shit to a guy, even two decades later. Instead, I was terrified that one of the other hired goons might decide to take Genevieve for themselves.

For the first time since we've been stuck here, not even holding her close was enough to help me sleep. The opposite, actually. I needed to hold her while I was wide awake to make sure that no one could touch her without me knowing.

No one but me.

The days of pretending like my heart doesn't beat for Genevieve Libellula are over. I'm not going to weigh her down with my feelings. That would be cruel, especially when there is no way for her to escape me or them. But the moment she kissed me... she's mine now, and as soon as we've figured out a way to beat Winter at his game and get the hell out of here, I'll make sure the whole damn world knows it.

Genevieve shows off her spark when she notices the black circles under my eyes and figures out that I stayed up the entire time she was sleeping, then didn't take a few hours for myself after she was rested. She smacked me in the chest, telling me that if I'm going to suffer from insomnia, she's going to suffer right along with me.

I fold. The first time she yawned, then stubbornly slapped herself in the face to wake up again, I lie down with her and swear that I'll do my best to sleep. She turned into me, caressing the massive bruise that covers my cheek, before brushing her lips over mine.

I fell asleep that night with Genevieve's taste on my tongue, dreaming of a life where we could be together without all of the various mafia politics at play.

Since then, I've seen less and less of her fire. At first, I convinced myself that my baggage was too much for her. She wanted a gentle artist with a commitment phobia. What she got instead was a CSA survivor who inked the name of his lost family on his arm so that he was forced to see it every day, plus a visual representation of the flames that stole them from him tattooed all over his throat where the needle hurt the most. She was too innocent to push me away at first, but it seemed like, the more time that passed, the harder it was for her to accept that I might never be the sort of man she'd want as hers.

She still lets me cuddle with her every night. If I try to give her as much space as possible in this small cell, she clings to me. I know what's happening. I saved her from Mickey's assault, no matter how I did it. I admitted I'm attracted to her. She believed me when I told her I would protect her back when she believed I only thought of her as my friend. Now that I want *more*... there isn't anything I won't do for her, and she knows it.

She also knows just how far I'm willing to go.

I only wish I could tell if that's a dealbreaker for her or not.

If she was firmly in the life, or had experience with the type of trauma I've been through, none of what I did would've been surprising. If she was a civilian, I wouldn't even be asking that question. Normal people would've taken one look at me, washing Mickey's blood off of my chin, and run as far away as possible. But Genevieve... she pressed her cool fingertips to my blazing face, then kissed me.

Genevieve's brother has tried his best to keep her shielded from the realities of life in a criminal organization, but between her insatiably curious nature and her friendship with Christopher, she knows more than her brother probably expects.

As for me, I might not often be involved in seedier aspects of what the Sinners Syndicate do, but I'm a high-ranking, respected member of the Sinners due to my friendship with Rolls, the amount of time I've been loyal, and my gig as the official artist.

I had to be trustworthy to get the chance to ink the Devil of Springfield, even before he got the reputation he has now. When he called me to his penthouse apartment last summer, giving me the order to tattoo his delicate bride's ring finger with his birth name—*Lincoln*—I knew that I was as highly regarded by our mafia leader as I am by his trusted second-in-command.

Genevieve's seen the darkness inside of me. There's no tucking it back out of sight, but that just means I need her light more than ever.

I need my butterfly.

I'm not surprised she's slowly withdrawing from me. During the days, she's losing hope that we'll ever be found. Regardless of how he put it, Winter confirmed that this is payback for his brother's death. He wants Damien to pay, and he did that by stealing Genevieve from her family. I got nabbed because it was too good of an opportunity for him to miss. I'm a Sinner, and Winter's crew still wants to get the snowflake-embossed guns and drugs into Springfield. By taking me prisoner, he's showing Devil that no one in the Sinners Syndicate is untouchable.

And all because Dave Sanders sold me out.

Davey boy. What the fuck, Davey boy?

For less than a stack, one of my fellow Sinners told an enemy that I was high up enough to be a good score for Winter. I was right when I said that Genevieve was the main target. I was the poor Sinner who was with her, but the perfectly timed van strike was Winter's way of killing two birds with one stone.

He stole Genevieve to get back at Damien. I was just collateral damage.

I don't care. I would've willingly come along and marched myself into this damn cage with her rather than let her be taken from me. And if any of his hired guys think they can separate me from her now?

I'll make what I did to Mickey seem like foreplay.

Genevieve finally confesses that her quiet mood is because she feels guilty. She's upset that I'm stuck with her, no matter how I try to convince her otherwise, and there's only one thing I can think of to ask her in order to help get her mind off of our precarious situation.

Sitting next to her, my heart—and my cock—swelling when she instinctively leans into me, resting her head against my shoulder, I rub her forearm and ask, "Will you dance for me?"

She hasn't so much as twirled since the motorcycle crash. At first, she was favoring her good leg, waiting for the road rash to heal enough for her to move without pain. And while she spent hours at a time stretching, sitting in the splits, pointing her toes, and wiggling all parts of her body to stay loose, she hasn't danced at all.

A tiny hint of a spark appears in the depths of her pretty blue eyes. "There's no music, Cross."

I shift my weight slightly, turning so that I can tap my chest. "There's music in our heart, ain't there?"

For a moment, she just stares up at me. But then she laughs. "Oh my fucking God. That was so *cheesy*."

I know it was. Dipping my head, stealing a quick kiss, I tell her, "But I got you to laugh."

She cradles the edge of my jaw. "You did. And you know what, babe? You're *right*."

Babe.

Holy shit, Genevieve called me her 'babe'.

I'm thirty years old. I haven't been young in a long time. But to be her 'babe'…

I thread my fingers through her hair, tugging her close to me. "God, you're amazing, butterfly."

"I am," she agrees, her voice finding a little of its usual sass. "But just wait until *this*."

For a split second, I think she's going to lean back on the cot, pulling me down with her. I mean, *fuck*. That's what I want to do. Only the constant reminder that we're under surveillance has kept me from doing more than stealing kisses from this woman. I'll be damned if any of Genevieve's first sexual experiences take place in a cage, with a madman watching our every move, but if she initiated… I'd like to think I'd be a strong enough man to put a stop to it, but I can't honestly say that I'm positive I would.

But that's not what she does. One more quick kiss and she shimmies out from under my arm. Flashing me a grin, she moves gracefully off of the cot, standing in the center of the floor.

And then she dances. Humming under her breath,

her eyes closed, listening to music only she can hear, Genevieve dances—and I imagine her as a butterfly, flying free, far, far away from here.

———

LATER THAT NIGHT, GENEVIEVE'S HEAD IS IN MY LAP, ALL that pretty blonde hair spilled over my jeans.

Since she laid down with me again, I've been careful to angle my hips back as far as I can so that my aching cock isn't jabbing her in the skull. Now she's using my thigh as her pillow, staring up at the ceiling, a thoughtful expression on her face.

I twirl a strand of hair around my finger, admitting if only to myself how damn sick it is that I... I'm feeling pretty fucking peaceful. We've been trapped by a madman for a little more than two weeks now—fifteen days at last count—but despite the cameras, and the light, and the knowing that this illusion of safety can be shattered at any moment on Winter's whim... holding Genevieve close, as if I have any right to this innocent creature, I'm more at peace than I have been for most of my life.

It won't last. God willing, her brother will still rescue her. Sinners are loyal, too. Tanner is a bonafide genius. If we can be found through technology, he'll figure it out. The world is huge. At this point, I'm sure we can't be in Springfield or they would've found us by now. That doesn't mean they won't.

Right?

I'm staring down at her.

Her lips part.

My heart swells.

Her nose wrinkles. "Do I stink?"

I blink. "What?"

Genevieve angles her head so she's looking up at me. "I mean it, Cross. Do I stink? I think I do—and," she adds before I can say a word, "if you tell me I smell like roses or some shit, I'll know you're full of it. It's been ages without a shower, and that sink only does so much when we only have a sliver of bar soap to use."

Part of me is amused by the way Genevieve's mind works. The other part is actually relieved that, after her dance, she's regained enough of her spirits that she can actually stop to wonder about her hygiene.

"Well, you did work up a sweat when you were dancing," I tease.

She pokes me. "You wanted me to."

"I did. I only wish Winter felt sorry enough for me to let me have some paper and a pencil. Maybe if I gave my word I wouldn't stab one of his goons with it." I raise my voice. If Winter was watching the dance meant for me earlier, the least he can do is listen to me bitch at him now. "Hear that? I want a pencil, Winter!"

"Cross!" Genevieve turns, burying her face in my crotch. "I can't believe you—*oh*."

I suck in a breath. Yeah. There's no way in hell she can miss my erection now. "Butterfly?"

Her voice is a little muffled. "Don't mind me. I'm, uh, just getting acquainted with your friend here."

Watching her dance has done something incredible: for the first time in weeks, I feel light. I feel *hope*.

I also feel like maybe... just maybe... we might have a chance. Only that would entice me to stroke her scalp as I murmur, "I'm sure he'd be very happy if you wanted to give him a little kiss."

When Genevieve doesn't smack me for my tease, I realize I might've pushed her too far. "Hey. You okay? I was only kidding."

"No, no. I'm fine. I'm just reminding myself why it would be a very, very bad idea to give my first blow job while I'm trapped in a glass box with a pair of cameras on me."

"It would be," I admit.

Doesn't mean I'm not thinking about it now. About sharing that experience with Genevieve, about how amazing the heat of her mouth would be on my skin, and how erotic it would be to know that no one else had ever experienced that pleasure from her before.

"Cross..."

Someone bangs on the glass door of our cell. "Break it up, you two. This ain't no lovers' hotel. You want to eat, move it. I'm coming in."

Are you kidding? What happened? Winter saw the two of us actually content for once and sent his goons right on down to break up the peaceful moment?

Even worse, how did I miss the footsteps? True,

Mickey was the one who always seemed to stomp when he walked, and Baker is big enough that he can't help it. The man on the other side of the glass, holding the plate of... meatloaf and chips? I think it's meatloaf and potato chips... that's Noah. He's a beanpole, so that explains how he was able to sneak up on us.

And then I see that guy that came with him, and my heart almost stops before beating triple-time.

You wouldn't think he would be involved in something like this. A couple of inches shorter than the lanky Noah, with closely cut black hair, deep green eyes, and a pleasant if slightly unmemorable face, he's the type of guy that you nod at, then forget once he's out of your line of sight. He's wearing a long-sleeved dark blue shirt—on purpose, I'm sure, since I know exactly what he's hiding under there—and a pair of jeans a shade lighter, only highlighting the vibe that he's a new recruit on a first-day-of-work tour.

Noah turns to him. "You remember that combination I told you upstairs? For the keypad?"

The other man nods. "I do."

"Good. Take out your piece. You heard what he did to Mickey, yeah?"

His brow furrows. "This is the guy who—"

Noah mimes a chomp. "Yup. Saw the aftermath of it myself. He got off a good inch."

"Jesus Christ."

"Yeah. That's why you're going to be in charge of these two. We got a new guest incoming if your intel pans out.

If it doesn't, forget everything I said. Winter won't have you feeding them. He'll make you one of them."

The other man scoffs. "I have a rep in Hamilton. Winter looked into it before he accepted me into his crew. I already proved myself to him. When you get Falco's girl, you'll see. And I won't just be a waiter. I've got bigger plans."

Yeah, I think. He does, and I'm hoping like hell I know what they are.

Falco... I've heard of him. He's this new gun runner who's stationed on the East Coast. He's been partnering with Devil in the business lately, but if he has something Winter wants, it looks like Winter's plotting to take something Falco wants.

And this guy is supposed to be the one to provide it to Winter.

His dark green eyes glance off of me, running over Genevieve. There's none of the lecherous desire that filled Mickey's gaze, and for that I'm grateful.

I'd hate to have to pluck out a fellow Sinner's eyes, even if he's playing a part.

That's got to be what's going on here. How many times have I shared an energy drink with Devil's driver, nudging him about what he was running from, and knowing that it would take a lot to get his ass back to Hamilton?

Too many. But if that's where we are...

I keep my face neutral. If I even hint at recognizing him, we're all fucked.

Though I can't stay quiet when Noah plops the plate down without any preamble, leering at Genevieve like usual before turning to go.

I wait until the glass door has closed behind them to take a step toward it.

"I wouldn't be in here if it wasn't for Dave," I spit out.

Noah rolls his eyes, but just like I hoped, I catch the other man's attention.

"Dave?" The new guy... my old friend... is suddenly confused. "Name's not Dave. It's Luca."

I know—just like I know from the way his expression *looks* confused, but his eyes go hard, that he received my message, and he understood it.

Good. Even if it takes him a minute to break us out of here, that's fine. But hopefully he can pass the message on.

The Devil of Springfield needs to know he has a snake working for him.

I only hope that Luca St. James isn't one of them.

mariposa

TWELVE

NEGOTIATION

CROSS

I let down my guard too soon.

Ever since Winter said that he had plans for Genevieve and me, I couldn't get the thought out of my head. He was very clear: none of his guys was allowed to touch her. I was so relieved that I didn't have to worry about the remaining guards attempting to sexually assault her again, I allowed myself to relax a fraction.

Then Luca appeared yesterday. I know him. For the second chance that the Devil of Springfield gave him, he would *never* betray the Sinners Syndicate. So long as there is a Sinners tat on my arm, we're basically family. If he's here, Devil found us and sent him in.

I don't believe in coincidences. I believe in Devil's ability to control his man, Rolls's skills as a fixer, and the genius that is Tanner Maguire. Between the three of them, they would've found us eventually. Throw in Genevieve's overprotective older brother, and I figured we just had to survive long enough to be broken out of this place.

Now that Luca's here, he must know that it's another Winter who's running the show. Whether he goes by Johnny or Jimmy, it doesn't matter. He's a fucking Snowflake, and he's the enemy. He's also a very formidable enemy, and the fact that my fellow Sinners haven't come down here, guns blazing, just yet tells me that they understand how dangerous Winter is.

Getting a man on the inside is super smart. He can relay the layout and the amount of both weapons and enemies that Winter keeps wherever we are. Because it's Luca, I feel like it has to be Hamilton, but that's at least three hours away from Springfield; though that would explain why it took them as long as it did to find us.

Luca's not at the facility today. He's playing his part, and whether he's really going out and grabbing another prison for Winter, he's not with Noah when he comes down to bring our breakfast. He's not with Noah when he serves us some cold pizza for dinner, either. Both times it's Baker, and I hope that means the next time someone comes down, it's Luca, followed by members of the Sinners Syndicate.

So, yeah. I let down my guard because, after the second visit to our cell, I didn't expect another one until the morning—but right around the time that Genevieve usually starts to curl up in the bed, and I get the opportunity to hold her as we both sleep, we both hear footsteps.

Her pretty blue eyes go impossibly wide. I know exactly what she's thinking. The last two times we had unexpected visitors, Mickey wanted her to blow him, then Johnny Winter made it clear he plans to keep us down until he decides to blow us away.

Whoever's coming down, that can't be good.

Unless... unless it *is* Luca.

It's not Luca.

It's Noah and Baker, and while both men are armed, neither is carrying a plate. Any hope that Winter decided to add dessert tonight especially as one of his 'accommodations' dies a quick death when, unlike usual, both men step into the cage as soon as the door opens.

"Oh good," sneers Noah. "We made it on time. It's not past the princess's bedtime yet."

Genevieve climbed out of the cot as soon as we realized the footsteps were getting closer. Wearing the same sundress she's had on for weeks, it seems so much thinner, so much *looser* than it did when we first arrived.

With Noah leering at her, and Baker standing there as silent as the grave as always, she crosses her arms over her chest, a flash of temper crossing her face at the derisive nickname.

She hates being called 'princess'. I hate the way these two men are looking at her right now.

Winter said not to assault any of his men. He didn't say not to mouth off to them.

"What do you want? You brought dinner. Your fucking pets already ate the food. Happy? It's my bedtime, too. So why don't you go and leave us the hell alone?"

Baker snorts. Noah grins.

And I know I made a mistake.

"What do we want? Hear that, Baker? Pretty boy here wants to know what we want." Slowly, making it obvious that it's what he's doing, Noah looks Genevieve up and down, lingering on her crotch and her chest. She gulps, and he gives me another crooked grin. "We want to watch you fuck."

Genevieve sucks in a breath.

My body comes alive in the worst way.

What the fuck? No. *No.* I move between Genevieve and the men so that I'm blocking her from view. "You heard me before. Leave us the hell alone."

"What's the matter, da Silva? We've seen the two of you together. There's a reason the boss put you in the same cell together. Even if you weren't hot to trot when we ran that bike of yours off the road, she's a pretty piece of ass, isn't she? You'd have to be a fag not to want a taste of that." His eyes light up, and he laughs as though what he said is hysterical. "Then again, I saw what you did to Mick. Could've taken him out without sucking him off first, you know."

Baker grunts. "Unless he wanted dick in his mouth."

"I think you're right. He wanted dick in his mouth. Well, you two are taking too long. I want to see dick in pussy. And I want to see it now."

I shouldn't look back at her. I shouldn't—

Fuck.

She's not just crossing her arms over her chest anymore. She's hugging herself instead, shaking her head back and forth slowly.

Of course not. Of course she doesn't want me to fuck her. Why would she? Maybe before we were taken captive and she got to see this side of me, if I'd given in and claimed her like I wanted to, it would be different. I knew she wanted to fuck me then, but I was the noble idiot who kept her at arms-length. Now? These two think they can tell her we're having sex and she's going to gleefully fall back on the cot and spread her legs to me.

With an audience? With them watching? No fucking way.

But Noah won't drop it. "Come on already. We got new meat coming in, but tonight you two are the stars of the show. Isn't that where you belong, princess? Center stage?" He points at the cot. "There's your stage. Now get on it."

Genevieve is still shaking her head.

Turning just enough that I can keep the two men in my line of vision while also addressing Genevieve, I tell her, "Don't listen to them. They can't make you do it—"

"They can't," booms the voice over the loudspeaker. "But I can."

Genevieve lets out a soft moan. Do you know what I would've given to hear her make a sound like that at the thought of fucking me? Only not one that makes her sound terrified, but well-pleasured instead? Her moan should go straight to my cock, but that one went straight to my heart.

"Winter," I snarl.

"Yes," agrees the voice coming over the loudspeaker. Of course it's Johnny Winter. Who else would it be? "Listen to me. We can sit here and posture all night. Noah can be crude and homophobic, and you can pretend that you're not dying to get Ms. Libellula under you. But Mr. da Silva... *Carlos*—"

That name is a dagger to my chest, though the pain lightens a tiny sliver when Genevieve is suddenly indignant on my behalf. "His name is Cross."

She knows my history. I spelled out as much of it to her as I could because, damn it, I *wanted* her to know. In a sick way, I was trying to push her away because all I wanted to do was hold her close. If she learned the truth about me, she could walk away and I'd know that as much as I *need* this woman, I was never meant to have her.

And now Winter is trying to offer her up to me on a silver platter, and as visibly scared as she is, she's defending me. My butterfly is smart. She has to realize that I shed the name 'Carlos' like a cocoon after my family died.

I *am* Cross, and I get the feeling that she'll correct anyone who tries to say otherwise.

"So it is," Winter agrees, sounding so smarmy, I visualize beating his face in with my fists even though he isn't here. "It's also beside the point. I have your file here. Every adult"—and the bastard emphasizes 'adult' which makes me believe he's not completely full of shit, and that Dave wasn't the only one who sold me out—"relationship he's ever had has been with a woman. Not as many as you'd think, considering his appearance and his profession, but I don't think we'll have a problem getting what I want from him. After all, we could've nabbed the girl at any time. You hear that, Ms. Libellula? You should be grateful that I at least chose this Sinner to put in the cell with you. It could've been a number of others, and then they would've been the one to deflower you."

His plans... all along, his plan was to manipulate the situation so that *I* slept with Genevieve? When he told me that he wouldn't allow any of his men to touch her, it wasn't out of the kindness of his heart. Oh, no. He just wanted to make sure that, when Genevieve got fucked in here, it was by someone he could use.

A Sinner.

Me.

What's the plan? Her brother is the head Dragonfly. He's spent her whole life keeping her protected. When Jimmy Winter targeted Damien, his plan revolved around making it seem like Devil beat Damien to death and left him in an abandoned store on the West Side. Of course the Dragonflies would have to retaliate.

Boom, there goes Devil.

There goes the Dragonflies.

There goes the Sinners Syndicate.

And here comes the goddamn Snowflakes.

That didn't work. Obviously. But what if some questionable Sinner started seeing Damien's sweet, beloved younger sister behind his back? Not only that, but when Genevieve was at her most vulnerable, that same Sinner proved to be a villain who took advantage of her during their captivity?

If Winter doesn't kill me, Damien definitely will. There are cameras here. Center stage, right? No doubt it'll get back to her brother. I'm dead, and the Sinners will have to retaliate.

Same outcome, huh? At the very least, the truce between the Sinners and the Dragonflies will go up in smoke. Only Devil and Damien will still be alive, too busy fighting each other to notice that Winter is moving in.

And just like he wants, his enemies are destroyed without him having to assassinate them and make martyrs of them to their men.

It's brilliant. Sadistic, and brilliant.

And never going to happen.

"I won't do it," I grit out. "I won't rape her."

Genevieve's voice is soft as she whispers my name.

I fist my hands. "So forget it, Winter. Okay?"

Winter's sigh comes over the loudspeaker. "Why must everyone always do things the hard way? You think I haven't been watching you on the camera? Haven't seen how you look at her while she's sleeping? The kisses? I'm giving you what you want. Take it."

"The only one who can give me that is Genevieve," I spit back.

"Very well. It seems as if I need to be a little more persuasive."

"Nothing will make me—"

"Baker. You have impressive aim. Shoot him in the hand. The right one preferably since his file indicates he's a righty."

Genevieve raises her voice. "What? You're going to shoot Cross's hand? He's an artist!"

"Yes. See. That's also in the files," Winter says, a touch bored. "And maybe when he'll never work again, he'll realize he should've done what he was told."

"He's saying no because of me. Because you're a sick fuck, and you want to make me have sex for the first time on camera!"

"Well, yes. But, to be fair, if he hadn't been such a gentleman these last two weeks and already fucked you when I gave him ample time to do so, it wouldn't have come to this. Now, Baker. If you would."

I move away from Genevieve so that she doesn't get hit if his aim isn't as impressive as Winter thinks.

She dashes in front of me. "Fine. I'll do it. Okay? I'll do it. Just don't shoot!"

I grab her hand, tucking her behind me again. "Genevieve, no..."

She juts out her chin, though she's shaking where she stands. "I mean it. You... you know how I feel about you. I never thought it would be like this, but if it saves your hands..." Her eyes dart over to Noah and Baker. She bites her bottom lip, then nods. "I'll do it, Cross. I want to."

Consent under duress. Fucking great.

"I can't," I tell her. "Let them blow off my hands. I don't care. I'd rather have no hands than ever touch a woman who doesn't want me to."

Especially not *this* woman.

"Again with the making everything so difficult. Noah," calls out Winter. "Shoot the girl in her knees instead. Maybe when she won't be able to dance again, he'll realize just what his insolence has really cost him."

What?

"No," I bellow. "You can't—"

"Then start to undress, Mr. da Silva. The girl's agreed. You said she was the only one who could give you permission, and she did. Now time's ticking. If you're not stripped by the time I count to five, Noah will shoot her in the knees. I don't bluff. One—"

I yank off my shirt, trying to figure out a way to save Genevieve's career and her innocence.

"That's more like it. I want the tattoos caught on camera, just so you can't deny later on that it's you. Two."

"Call off your goons," I tell him.

"Do you really think that you're in the position to negotiate? Three."

Hoping like hell that Winter lied, that he *is* bluffing, I concede a little by unbuttoning my jeans, but before I tug on the zipper, I say, "Aren't you hoping to use this to prove a dirty Sinner plowed the Dragonfly princess?" I hate calling Genevieve that when I know she despises it, but if that's what Winter thinks... "Won't really have as much of an impact if it's obvious we're only doing it at gunpoint."

"You might be right. And I'd prefer her to look like she's enjoying it, not that she's afraid for her life." He pauses for a moment. "Fine. Finish undressing, then I'll send Noah and Baker away. If I'm satisfied by what's on the camera, they won't come back until your next meal in the morning."

"Genevieve stays in her clothes until they're gone," I growl.

Winter chuckles. "And you wanted me to believe you don't already consider Ms. Libellula yours? Take off the jeans, Mr. da Silva."

Before he can say 'four', I pointedly stare in the camera and remove my pants. I save time and take my boxer briefs off with them. Kicking them away from me while giving Winter my most defiant expression, I tell him, "Done."

"Quite impressive," drawls Winter. "Seems like we won't have to waste too much time with foreplay since you're obviously ready."

I won't apologize for being aroused. Sorry. It's my default state when Genevieve is around, and though I've been able to control myself since sneaking off to the exposed toilet and rubbing one out while Genevieve was *right fucking there* just seemed disrespectful and wrong, my body is so ready for release, I can't help it.

My mind knows better than to be excited that I'm

supposed to fuck Genevieve on command. Normally, my body would, too. But it's been nearly three weeks since I've come. I'm primed to explode.

At least I won't be able to torture her for too long. How much do you want to bet that, almost as soon as I work my way into Genevieve's virgin pussy, I go off right away?

Here's hoping, though I'm sure Winter won't be too happy with a two-minute show.

Not like I give a shit. This is about making this as easy as possible for Genevieve. And if stripping down to nothing, having my cock and balls and ass on display for a psycho and his two goons, fine.

"There. I did what you said."

"And you even made it by the count of five. Fair enough. Okay. Pack it in, boys. Go upstairs and wait for my next orders. Tonight? It's for our young lovers here."

And Johnny fucking Winter.

mariposa

THIRTEEN
HIS

GENEVIEVE

I've seen Cross naked before; at least, from the waist down I have. It wasn't on purpose. As attracted to him as I've been since the beginning, I'm not a perv. I'm not about to gawk at him unless he knows that he's completely naked and that my eyes are on him—like right now.

But it happens, you know? I'm sure he's gotten a glimpse of me before. It's kind of avoidable when the toilet is out in the open. It's only ever been a flash, though. Just an idea of what his limp cock looks like as he's finishing up a piss before he rinses off his hands at the sink.

Now? There's no avoiding seeing the majesty that is an aroused Cross da Silva.

I tell myself that his erection doesn't mean anything.

He's been cooped up in here with me for weeks. A stiff breeze could probably get him going at this point. I don't take it as a personal accomplishment that the thought of him having to fuck me has him already hard, though I can't help but appreciate the sight.

I've seen cocks before, but there's something about eyeing the one that wants to find its way inside of you that makes them seem so much... bigger. And Cross's is definitely impressive. I would've still been drawn to him if he pulled out, like two inches, but the six or so he has looks like it'll be a lot of fun to play with.

I just... how the hell is that supposed to fit inside of me?

It's supposed to, I tell myself. Don't worry about that. At least one of us knows what we're doing, and if that sudden surge of heat that flashes through me when I'm irrationally jealous of all of Cross's previous lovers has me eager to join them so that I'm his *latest* one... well, it's not like I didn't know he was more experienced already. I wanted to fuck him anyway, and if we go through with this, I will.

I hate that we have no choice. Like, I *really* hate it. I want him to choose me because he cares about me, and while he's already told me that he does, he hasn't even made a single move toward me other than the few stolen kisses we've shared.

And now we have to *fuck*?

"Tick tock," Winter says mockingly. "I upheld my end of the bargain. My men are gone. I'll be quiet. You can forget I'm here and simply enjoy yourselves. But I warn you: my patience with this is thin. Please. It's just sex. Do what I ask and let's move on with our lives, yes?"

Maybe for Winter it's just sex. But that creep knows very well that I've never done this before. I heard him. Asshole said 'deflower', and I almost want to fuck Cross just so I can finally be done with this purity bullshit for once and for all. The only reason I haven't had sex yet is because the opportunity never presented itself. I didn't *save* myself or anything like that. Hell, if Christopher had taken me up on my offer to fool around when we were sixteen and I was bored, I wouldn't be obsessing over it now.

But I didn't, and in a way I'm glad. Even considering the circumstances, I don't think there's anyone I want to experience this with besides Cross.

And to show him I'm not *that* nervous, and that I really *do* want to do this with him, I reach down and grab the hem of my sundress before I chicken out. It's gotten loose lately, whether because I haven't been eating as much or the material itself has been stretched out from being constantly on me, but either way it's super easy to pull it up and over my head.

So that Cross isn't the only one naked, I take a deep breath before pulling off my panties. I add them to the growing pile on the floor, then remove my bra.

It's slightly yellowed along the band from my sweat, and I feel like maybe I need to take a shower before we do this. I should be clean, right? I mean, I can't take a shower, but what about a quick splash at the sink?

"Tick, tock," echoes Winter, and it's like he knew exactly why I was hesitating—and isn't too happy about it. "Let's go."

Turning around, completely aware that both Winter and Cross have a full view of my ass, I swallow the lump in my throat and climb onto the cot. I feel a little better when Cross swiftly moves to cover me as I get into position, and when I look up at him and see the undeniable lust written in his eyes, I know that everything is going to be okay.

And, no, I'm not delusional at all, am I?

I figure, for the first time, lying down on my back would probably be the best. That way I can kind of just sprawl out and take it, and let Cross do what he knows how to do.

I shudder out a breath and wait for him to join me on the cot. He does, putting both knees on the mattress, and I can't help but notice that his expression has turned hungry as he stares down at my naked body.

"So," I laugh nervously, trying my best not to freak out that this is happening, that Cross obviously wouldn't have chosen to do this on his own, and Winter is somewhere probably unbuttoning his pants and pulling his own cock out like we're his personal porno, "how exactly do we do this? You, uh, just stick that thing in me?"

God, I hope it fucking fits...

Cross tears his eyes away from me, dropping his gaze

to his cock. He almost looks surprised to see how it's jutting out from the patch of hair covering his groin. Giving it a quick stroke, gathering the bead of moisture I see at the tip before inching closer, I wonder if he's going to do exactly that. Just climb on top of me so that his back is blocking most of me from the camera, then shove his dick in so that we can get this the hell over with.

Only Cross doesn't do that.

Instead, he shifts his weight, moving his body until he's maneuvered himself into the cradle of my legs. Going down on his belly, he shimmies backward until his knees are on the floor, and his mouth is hovering mere inches over my pussy.

I can't help myself. I blink, shivering slightly as the warmth of his breath hits my skin.

Winter sighs, the annoyance in his voice carrying through the loudspeaker—and making me close my legs as much as possible. Cross's shoulders get in the way of my thighs, but the response was as reflexive as my cheeks heating up as he drawls, "Really? Do you honestly think I have time to sit here and watch you do *foreplay*?"

"She's never done any of this before," Cross snarls, refusing to look anywhere but at me. "You have us where you want us. We're doing what you're making us do. But I won't hurt her. If I just start fucking her, she'll be hurt. That'll ruin your video, won't it? I have to get her ready for me."

There's a vow in the clipped yet heated way he snaps at our captor, a vow especially for me.

I relax a fraction. Instead of fisting the cheap sheets beneath me, I lay my palms flat on the mattress and try to keep my expression as calm as possible. If Cross knew my heart was racing so fast, I thought it might beat its way out of my chest, he'd put an end to this no matter what Winter threatens him with—

"Make it quick," Winter orders. "Otherwise I might change my mind and invite Noah to take your place."

"Never," Cross whispers harshly. The force of those hissed syllables blows even more *hotter* air out on the second one and, holy shit, does that feel incredible on my skin. "Genevieve is *mine*."

—okay, my hysterical mind amends, maybe that threat caught his attention.

But, wait... *mine*?

Am I—

Oh.

Whoa.

Did I think *that* felt incredible? How about when, completely ignoring Winter, his focus entirely on me, Cross uses two fingers to spread my pussy apart before burying his face in there.

Okay. I kind of figured that was what he was going to do the second his mouth was by my crotch. I mean, I guess I didn't think he would just *go* for it, and I'm a little bit glad that it didn't occur to me. I don't have much time to be insecure about my own pubic hair or how musty I've got to be after not showering, or whether he would've enjoyed what he's doing a lot more if I'd gotten the chance to freshen up before we started.

Then again, as he focuses on me and I do every fucking thing I can to forget about our audience, I honestly can't imagine he *could* enjoy it more. Between lapping at my entrance and using his nose to nuzzle my clit before he takes the little nub inside the heat of his mouth, he keeps panting softly, telling me how good I fucking taste.

"I knew it," he says, coming up for a second just to make sure he can meet my eyes again. His mouth is shiny with my juices, and I don't feel a little bit embarrassed by that until he dips his head again, humming against my pussy. "From the moment I saw you dance, my butterfly, I knew your pussy would give off the most delicious nectar."

Yeah. I highly doubt that. But if Cross wants to convince himself that I'm delicious, I'm all for it. Especially if he'll keep on licking me like that...

Jesus fucking Christ. How did I go so long without this? The sensations are incredible, and I know it's even better because it's *Cross* who's touching me with such reverence. It's like he considers me so holy, he's worshipping at the altar of my cunt, and if I hear him mumble, "Oh my fucking God," right before he takes part of my labia between his teeth, I'm more than happy to lead him to the church of Genevieve.

At one point, he starts dipping his finger inside of me. There's a little resistance, but the way he's taken to scraping his teeth over my clit is so powerful, I bite back the slight scream as he stretches my pussy out. One finger, in and out as he murmurs that I'm being such a good girl, and when I preen, shifting closer to his hand, he rewards me with a second one. I know what he's doing, too. He's mimicking what his cock is going to do, and if *that* feels as good as this does, I'm beginning to look forward to it.

His touch is possessive and sure, but he's gentle, too. Soft. He doesn't want to hurt me, and with every caress, I don't ever want him to stop.

Cross doesn't. We both know where this is going—how Winter will demand it ends—but he takes his time anyway. I'm hot and slick, and I'd be more embarrassed about how his fingers squelch as he fucks me with them, I'm that wet, if it wasn't for the fact that he's working my body, making it his. It does burn a little bit when he widens his fingers, scissoring them inside of me, stretching me so that I'm prepped for his dick, but I've got this.

Cross isn't so sure.

He glances up at me, concerns written all over his face. "You okay, Genevieve?" he murmurs.

"Uh-huh."

"I need to hear you say it. You with me? Because if you're not..."

I swallow. If I wasn't, I'd have to get on board and quick otherwise I wouldn't put it past Winter to punish us by tossing Noah at me like he threatened. I want to fuck

Cross. Maybe this isn't what I expected, and if I start to think about how he's being forced to do this against his will, I'll dry up like the goddamn Sahara desert, but if Noah comes in here...

I'd rather *die* than let him touch me.

"I am," I swear. "This... it feels fucking *amazing*."

Cross's eyes search my face. He must see the truth written in every line of mine because he lifts his hand, giving my side a quick squeeze.

"Think that feels good, butterfly? How about this?"

He dips his chin, sucking my clit into his mouth again. Swirling his tongue around the nub while finger-fucking me, I gasp. My body tightens, clenches, *convulses*. I keen, and Cross chuckles, the vibrations from his laugh enough to send me over.

I'm a virgin; at least, for the new few moments, I am. That doesn't mean I'm a puritanical prude. If my brother searched my room, he'd be surprised about the toys I have, even if I shied away from dildos and vibes because I wanted the real thing the first time I was penetrated. My rose is perfect after a long day of training, so I'm familiar with coming.

That? It hits me so hard, I *arrive*.

My legs shaking, my thighs squeezing his head so tightly, I flatten his ears against his skull, I realize that he could do anything to me and I'd forever let him.

Which is good because now that my body is as ready as it's ever going to be, it's time for the main event.

Cross is thoughtful enough to wait for me to come

down from my explosive orgasm before he gives my mound one final kiss.

"Beautiful," he whispers, and I just barely hear him over the roar of pleasure echoing in my head. "And *mine*." He drops his voice, low enough that Winter can't hear him—and I only hope I'm not hallucinating when he promises, "I've wanted to do this for a long time, butterfly. Take you and make you mine. Stop me if you don't want me to, but otherwise... I'll be good to you, I fucking promise."

I know he will. But 'mine'? Again?

Does he really mean it?

God, I want to be Cross's. More than anything, but is this part of the show? Or his way of trying to make sure I'm alright with what's about to happen? I can't tell, and I don't get the chance to ask before he's wiping the corners of his mouth with his thumb before slipping it between his lips, as though he can't bear the thought of missing out on any of my taste.

Cross savors it as he climbs on top of the cot, prowling forward on his knees as his cock leads the way. He rises up, chin angled down at me, though his striking dark eyes are on his fingers. He marvels at the stickiness keeping the two that fucked me slicked together. Flashing me a wicked smile as I lay flat on my back, boneless after how hard he made me come, Cross slips those two fingers into his mouth next.

He licks them clean. When he's done, he purrs. "*Delicious.*"

I haven't looked away from him, and I'm stunned by the change that's come over him. Shit. I can see the answer in his eyes. He might not have been so keen to hop into bed with me before, but after what we just experienced? I don't think anything could stop what's going to happen next short of me finding the energy to sit up, brace my hand against his chest, and tell him 'no'. I one hundred percent believe that. If I changed my mind, it wouldn't matter what Winter threatens us with. He'd stop and face the consequences after.

Because he won't force me. He'll never force me.

If Noah tried? I know firsthand how strong Cross's jaws are, and how talented his tongue is.

And as Cross eases his body over mine, lodging his cock at my entrance for the first time, I promise myself that I'll never forgive him if he decides to go all noble and stop this from happening for my sake at the last possible moment.

It would be his right to change his mind. I'd understand if he couldn't go through with it. But, God, I'd never forgive him.

Luckily, I don't have to worry about that because, thanks to the way Cross worked my body already, I'm as relaxed and as ready for him as I possibly could be with a blackmailing, malicious *kidnapper* making us be intimate. He gives his body a quick push, seating himself just inside of me, and then he holds himself up on his arms.

An apologetic expression flashes across his gorgeous features. My heart—that had finally slowed after my climax—skips a beat at how fucking beautiful he is. "There might be a pinch, butterfly. But I know you're going to be perfect." He hisses out a breath. "*Fuck*. You already are. This pussy... I'm already addicted and I've only just put the tip in."

"Give me more," I say, shocked at how husky and throaty my voice is. Probably because my actual throat is raw from all those stifled scream from before... "I want you, Cross." I've never wanted anything more. "I want all of you. Everything you have."

"I've gotta go slow. Take it easy." A muscle ticks in his jaw, his arms shaking at the effort he's expending to keep himself from pushing his dick all the way inside of me. "I don't want to hurt you."

"You can't," I promise.

He doesn't seem to believe me, or understand that my pain tolerance is high—and I'm so aroused, I hurt because I *need* him to fill me up. Nothing I can do will convince him otherwise, either. He takes his time, and, okay, I'm a little bit glad he did when the resistance goes from nothing to *everything* in a heartbeat. I suck in a breath, about to tell him that maybe I did change my mind—I'm so full, and I don't think I can take any more of him—when, suddenly, there's that pinch he warned me about, followed by enough pleasure to make the whole thing fucking *worth* it.

Cross swallows roughly. "Hey. You still okay?"

"Fucking great," I breathe out. My hands reach out, grabbing his back.

Hey. He's *inside* of me. I think I'm allowed to touch all that grey and black and beautiful ink like I've been dying to for so damn long.

Cross grins. "That's my girl."

He's right about that. With his cock stretching me out, I *am* his girl. For tonight, at least, and I'm going to savor that the entire time we have this connection.

Mine.

Hell, yeah I am.

The only downside is, with all the foreplay he did to work up to this moment, I kind of wish it lasted longer than it does. I'm sure Cross thinks the same. His thrusts start out slow, but almost as if he can't control himself, he picks up the pace until the cot is rocking, I'm sliding on the cheap sheets, and he's racing toward his own orgasm.

Like he needs to claim me. Like he's afraid that Winter will stop us before he does.

His fingers dig into my side, pinning me beneath him as he fucks me. I let him, our moans a symphony that drowns out the crackle of the loudspeaker I'm doing everything I can to ignore.

And then it's done. Knowing that he wouldn't last, he lets go of my side so he can reach between our sweat-slicked bodies. He tweaks my nipple, growling under his breath as I inadvertently squeeze his cock. The slight pain mingled with pleasure makes me close, and though I never expected to come just from dick alone, he starts using his thumb to rub my clit. Between that stimulation and his cock filling me up so completely, it's like I'm a part of *him* now, the pleasure becomes overwhelming.

I cry out his name and, in response, he bucks up into me, burying his face against my tits as he comes. And there it is. As quick as it began, over so fast that I'm still humming from when Cross made me come the *first* time, it's *done*—

"I must say, coming inside of her like that, Mr. da Silva? Not entirely expected, but it was a nice touch. Thank you."

—and I suddenly remember why exactly we did what we did.

Oh, fuck.

Winter's voice slaps me out of my pleasure-filled haze, making everything crystal clear as I realize that Cross totally just nutted inside of me.

No condom.

No birth control.

No protection.

Shit.

mariposa

FOURTEEN
OURS

GENEVIEVE

I wanted Cross, but not like this.

The second the slight hiss from the loudspeaker dies and doesn't start up again, Cross decides that we've done enough to 'satisfy' our creepy, voyeuristic captor. Without even meeting my eyes, he climbs off of the bed—off of *me*—and pads his way over to the sink, pausing only to snag his shirt.

He tears the sleeve right off, then inspects it for a moment as if it's the most fascinating bit of fabric he's ever seen. His face it still closed-off, his sweat-slicked hair sticking to his forehead, as he takes the sleeve over the sink and rinses it with water until it's mostly soaked.

Cross brings it over to me, muttering, "It's as clean as it can be."

"What do you need that for?"

"This? Oh. It's not for me, Genevieve."

Butterfly, I want to shout. Call me *butterfly*.

Cross squats near the edge of the cot. I glance down, unable to resist the urge to look at him. His body is so incredibly beautiful. With as many distinct, unique tattoos covering him, he's like a piece of art, and that's not counting his sculpted muscles and his trim waist.

I've always wondered just how much of Cross is tatted. Now I know for sure. His back is covered, his arms are covered, his neck and throat are covered, but once you hit his hips, all I see is delicious tanned skin.

Tonight was the first time I saw him without his shirt. Amazingly, he has this big space on the left side of his chest that's empty. Right over his pec, it's completely bare, making his copper-colored nipple stand out while the other hides amongst the ink on the other side. I want to ask him why, but then my gaze dips even lower, landing on his cock.

I know he came inside of me. I saw the look of surprise on his face as he did, and I know Cross didn't mean to do that. There's no taking it back now, and I can see a faint sheen of white cream covering most of his length from where his come mingled with mine.

That's not all, though. Because unless I'm imagining it, the white sheen has a hint of red to it.

Cross ignores his own mess, turning his attention to mine. As he swipes the soaked piece of sleeve over my thighs, I'm just in time to notice that there are red splotches there, too. For a moment, I wonder if I started my period—because that would just be perfect as a captive—before I realize exactly what that is.

I was a virgin when he fucked me before. I'm not a virgin now, and that little bit of blood is enough to prove it.

With a look of intense concentration on his face, Cross wipes it away from my inner thighs. Then, bracing me with the softest touch, he pins me down so that he can flip the sleeve over, then tidy up my pussy.

At first, I thought he was trying to erase any sign of what we did together, and I want to shove him away. However, before I can do that, he leans closer, dropping his mouth down so that he can press a kiss to my thigh before rising up, standing next to the cot.

The quick rub he gives his cock is nowhere near as sweet and tender as the way he cleaned me up. He grabs it, wiping the sleeve around it until the skin is clear. That done, he tosses the used sleeve to the floor before reaching for the rest of his shirt.

He's been quiet since he told me that the sleeve was as clean as it could be. I keep waiting for him to say something, but he doesn't. He goes through the motions, and I've heard enough about sex from Christopher to know that cleaning up after is essential—especially when we haven't been able to do more than give ourselves a sink bath in weeks—so I finally realize that that was what he was doing. I appreciate it, too.

But when he makes as though he's going to put on his shirt?

"Don't," I say.

He pauses, giving me a quizzical look.

I lick my bottom lip, then scoot over a bit so that there's room on the cot. "I like looking at your tattoos. Don't put your shirt back on."

He nods. "If you say so."

Cross drops the shirt, going for his jeans.

"No." I'm a little firmer this time. "No jeans." I swallow, rushing the words out while I still have the nerve. "I want you to lie with me like this. Just like this. To hold me."

And if something else happens...

His brows draw together. "Naked? You're asking me to climb back into bed and hold you *naked*?"

I nod.

He thinks he forced me into having sex with him. He told Winter that he wouldn't rape me, and from the way he's acting right now, that's exactly what he think he did. But maybe I did the same to him. I wanted Cross all along. He's the one who never showed any sign he was into me before we were taken, and despite the way he said 'mine', I'm pretty sure that was part of the act to make sure that we survive Winter's insanity.

But Winter is gone now. We don't have an audience, and though he's pointedly ignoring the fact that, without his pants on, I can see that his cock is already starting to harden under the weight of my stare, we already fucked once because Winter made us.

What if we wanted to take control of our own bodies now?

We're in a fucking cage. No denying that. Cross wants to believe that his fellow Sinner is our way out, but at least for tonight, we're not going anywhere.

So why not be together in a way that *we* choose?

He doesn't have to. I hope he understands that. But if he *wants* to…

I flutter my lashes at him. It's a wordless *please*.

Please don't hate me for what Winter made us do.

Please don't refuse me now.

Please don't let me go—

"Genevieve…" He exhales. "Butterfly," he says, and I know then that I haven't lost Cross yet. He might seem like he's a mile away from me despite being trapped in the same cell, but when he uses my nickname… I think I still have him here with me.

Now I just need to keep him.

"I need you," I whisper, putting as much honesty into my words as I can.

"I'm right here."

I pat the empty space on the cot next to me. "Come over here instead. Please."

Cross glances up at the camera, frowning for a moment. I think he's going to refuse, or remind me that we could be being watched as if I've forgotten, but I don't care. Winter got what he wanted.

Damn it, why can't we get what *we* want?

That's assuming that Cross feels the same. I won't

know unless I give him the chance to decide on his own. I already have. I'm not so sore and achy that I don't want to try this again—on our terms instead of Winter's.

His frown disappears. I swear, there's the tiniest bit of hope replacing it as he says, "You want me to hold you."

Here goes nothing, Gen.

"I want you to fuck me."

Cross wipes the back of his hand across his mouth. "What did you say?"

I refuse to even acknowledge the camera. Instead, I pat the cot again. "I love you," I say simply. This might possibly be the worst time for that sort of confession, but if those three little words are enough to chase away Cross's idea that he did something to me that I would've enthusiastically consented to under different circumstances, I'll be honest with him.

And, sure, there's being honest and then there's being *honest*, but no matter what happens after tonight, I'll be content to remember that, at the very least, my first time was with the man I loved—and now he knows it.

He doesn't respond the same. I try not to let that hurt. I'm not as manipulative as Winter, or even my brother for that matter. I'm just Gen, and when I tell someone I love them, I don't have ulterior motives. I love with my whole heart, and Cross had made his mark on it long before Johnny Winter ever came into the picture.

So he doesn't tell me he loves me, not with words at least, but he doesn't have to, does he? I know he cares. It was in the way he would've stood there and let them blow off his hand to protect me. In how he agreed to this because my ballet career was on the line.

There isn't anything Cross da Silva won't do to keep me from being hurt, and as soon as I realize that, it doesn't hurt me now that he can't say the words back to me. Even if it's not the same way that I love *him*, he cares, and I'm pretty sure that's what has him prowling his way toward the cot before easing his body weight down next to me.

He's on his side of the narrow bed, his right hand reaching out to caress my cheek.

I stare back at him. His bruise is starting to heal. What was purple the morning after Mickey kicked him in the face is a more mottled shade tonight, greens and yellows making up the edges of the injury. If you ask me, though, it makes such a pretty man even more impossibly beautiful. That mark is undeniable evidence of how far he'll go to protect me.

I inch closer until his hard cock is nestled near enough to my lower belly that I can't deny he's at least ready. And then, because I don't see any reason to dance around the subject, I ask simply: "Do you want to fuck me, Cross?"

His eyes search my face, but he doesn't answer. He also doesn't scoot away, and that's enough of an answer to have me making my first move.

I reach between us, giving him a quick stroke. He closes his eyes, his nostrils flaring as he clenches his jaw.

"Please, Cross," I say again, using both his chosen

name and the word 'please' since it seems to affect him more than any other. "I'm not forcing you just like you didn't force me. I'm just asking you a simple question. Say 'no' and we go to sleep, maybe forget tonight happened." Until Winter uses that video against us... "Say 'yes' and—"

"Yes," he breathes out, so warm on my face, I fight back a shiver. "I want to. Don't ever doubt that... but we shouldn't."

Not *can't*. Shouldn't.

I stroke him again. Instead of pulling away, he bucks against my palm.

Look at you, Gen. First time handling a dick and you're not doing too shabby.

I smile at him. "I think we should."

He groans. "Butterfly... you don't know what you're saying."

That's where he's wrong. I know exactly what I'm saying.

"When you were treating me like I was precious... when you were making sure I was okay... I could forget he was there. I knew he was, but until he spoke up again when you were done, it was just the two of us."

He nuzzles my neck, hiding his face. "I'm sorry—"

My stomach goes tight, and I wish it was from the renewed arousal I experienced when I saw my virgin blood on his cock. "Don't apologize. Please. That makes me feel like we did something wrong."

"I forced you to do it," he says, his voice a mumble.

"Cross, no. Listen to me. *He* forced *us* to do it. That was his choice. This?" I run my fingers up and down his cock again. "This is mine. Now it's our turn. If you don't want to do this with me, I understand. I'm certainly not going to force you to do anything. But if you want to… we can own the moment. Make it ours. Something special. Something that belongs to only us."

Cross curses under his breath, and I know that if I keep stroking, he's going to come all over my fingers. Not that I'm not interested in seeing that happen—I want to experience everything with this man—but I was serious when I said I want to make this time ours.

But he's distracted now as he glares up at the ceiling. "Those fucking cameras."

I don't like them, either—and I have a spark of brilliance.

Reaching over him, I grab the blanket from off the floor. "What if we put this over us? It might be hot, but no one could see what we were doing."

He scowls. "I should've thought of that before."

"Winter never would've let you. Remember? The whole point was a blackmail video."

Cross's scowl deepens.

I lay back down on the bed, grabbing his arm, tugging him so that he can start to climb on top of me again. "I'm not worried about that. Trust me. Right now, there's only one thing on my mind and it's *you*."

He doesn't have to let me tug him anywhere. If he doesn't want to fuck me, he could easily shake his head, get up, walk to the other side of the cell, and it would be over.

Instead, Cross rises up over me. Giddy with both relief and excitement and *need*, I think that he's about to give me what I want, what we both *need*, when suddenly he pauses.

His expression is back to being concerned. "Are you sure?"

Is he serious? "I'm very sure."

"But are you tender?" His fingers ghost over my pussy. When he draws them back, seemingly surprised to see how fucking soaked I am, his breathing kicks up a little. His voice is thick as he says, "I tried my best not to hurt you."

I laugh, hoping that'll be enough to wipe that slight worry from his eyes. "Please. I'm a *ballerina*. I've danced on a sprained ankle and broken toes. I dealt with road rash and a bike crash. My pain tolerance is pretty high." My hand goes up to his cheek again. "So is yours. Don't you think it's time we finally get to feel good?"

Cross claps his hand over mine, keeping the connection. Never letting go, he lowers his head, taking my mouth. At the same time, he throws his leg over my hip, angling his lower half so that he can grip his cock by the base and feed it right into my waiting pussy.

I gasp into his open mouth, the slight sting from before a distant memory as the overwhelming sensation of being stuffed by him overloads every other nerve ending.

Feel good?

That feels *amazing*.

Too bad it doesn't last—and I don't only mean how eager Cross is to fuck me that he ends up coming inside of me shortly after he plucks my clit, playing my body like a pro, making me forget again that when I scream his name, someone else might've heard me.

But that's tomorrow's problem.

Tonight?

I get to have Cross, and even before I fall asleep under him, I can already feel him drifting away from me again....

mariposa

FIFTEEN

SAVANNAH

GENEVIEVE

I'm glaring at the camera, holding my shoe in my hand.

Cross is watching me. He has his chin tucked into his chest, a closed-off expression on his face. His shirt is on again, which is unfortunate, and he's sitting on the floor once more, his back to the cinderblock, which is even worse.

All morning, he's basically said three words to me: "How ya feeling?"

If he cared how I felt, he wouldn't have waited until I passed out from a combination of endorphins and exhaustion to wiggle out of my arms, choosing to sit on the floor instead of the bed where he so carefully took my virginity.

And I know I wasn't being fair. He's as much of a

victim as I am. More, honestly, because I *did* want to sleep with Cross. In another world, in another time, I would've gladly had my first time with him... but it was me he didn't want.

Pretty words. Everything he said last night... that's all they were. Pretty words.

So I said, "Fine," and left it at that.

Besides, I knew what he was really asking me. Knowing full well that I was a virgin before Winter forced us to fuck for the camera, he's checking to see how my pussy is recovering from all the attention he gave it last night. He wanted to make sure I wasn't bleeding anymore, or that I wasn't super achy and tender down below.

My initial retort was to tell him to ram a cucumber up his ass a couple of times, then tell me how *he* feels, but that was the rejection trying to run my mouth. After how gentle and supportive he was last night, both when we knew Winter was watching, and later, when it was just us under the blanket, I thought that sex might've done something to bring us even closer.

But that's the Gen living in a fantasy world. The Gen who is naive enough to believe in things like 'love at first sight' and a hero who will do anything to save her. Twice now, Cross was pushed to do something he obviously didn't want to in the name of protecting *me*. To keep Mickey away from me, and to prevent Noah from firing his gun at my knees.

And what happened after that? With at least an audience of one, I finally got to see what it was like to sleep with Cross da Silva.

As much as I could, I enjoyed it, and I have only Cross to thank for that. He talked me through it, even going so far as to eat my pussy first so that I would be aroused enough to take him. He was gentle and kind; the perfect lover, just like I knew he would be. If it wasn't for the fact that he still seems to think that he *raped* me…

I know that's what's running through his mind. Last night, when he thought I was asleep thought I was just on the verge of it, he whispered as much. He apologized for forcing himself on me, as though he was the one who decided to fuck me on the cot instead of the both of us being threatened into the act. He sounded so mournful and upset, I couldn't bring myself to tell him that I heard him—and remind him again that he's got it wrong.

And that brings me to why I'm glaring at the camera while holding my shoe.

It's all I have. My shoes and the clothes on my back, so I might as well make do with what I've got.

I wing it at the camera. Damn it. My aim is so shot, I miss it by, like, three feet.

"What are you doing?" Cross asks as my shoe hits the tile of our cell.

I snatch it back. "I hate these stupid fucking cameras," I grumble. They've bothered me all along, but it's been three weeks. *Three weeks.* I almost forget about them for a time before Winter inevitably reminds me that they're there. And after last night…

"Are you trying to break it?"

"Why not? I know it's unlikely. I know there's two of them, so smashing the lenses on both... probably not going to happen. He's probably still listening to every damn word we say anyway, but..." I sigh, shoulders slumping. Feeling frustrated and rejected and *angry* at this whole awful situation, I drop the shoe, jamming my foot back into it. "Forget it. I needed something to do to distract me."

He doesn't say anything to that. Mainly because he's gotta be doing the same thing. If I know Cross—and, by now, I think I *might*—then he's obsessing over last night in a way that can't be healthy.

I can't even talk to him about it. Once we knew for sure that the cameras worked, we made a pact not to say anything that Winter could use against us unless we keep our backs to the cameras and our voices down. Even then, with my luck, he has microphones or other types of surveillance equipment in here.

Winter gets a kick out of reminding us that he's constantly watching. Any time Cross leans in, trying to whisper to me, his smarmy, obnoxious voice cuts through the cell. The only time we seem to have a little privacy is our designated 'night'; with the lights never turning off, we have to use other clues to figure out what time it might be.

It's firmly in the 'day' part of our routine. Baker came by earlier to slide a plate of somewhat stale blueberry muffins into the room. No Noah. No Luca. I remember how they mentioned that Luca was supposed to be bringing another woman down here, replacing the Haven woman who was 'relocated'—whatever the hell *that* means—and I wonder if that's where he is now.

Before Winter interrupted us the other night, Cross was able to press his lips to my ears and whisper that the new guard, Luca, isn't just another one of Winter's goons. He's Luca St. James, the Devil of Springfield's personal driver, who used to live in Hamilton, an urban center in the next state over from where we live. He's been a respected Sinner for the last three years, and if he's here? That means two things to Cross: that Devil sent him, and that wherever we are, it's somewhere near Hamilton if not the city itself.

I thought that meant he was our way out. He might still be, but if so, there's some real shitty timing going on. He wasn't there when Baker and Noah came in, telling us they wanted to watch us fuck, and if they found us earlier, maybe that would never have happened.

Maybe Cross wouldn't be sitting on the opposite side of the cage as though he can't get far enough away from me...

He straightens from his slight slouch. "Incoming," he mutters.

He's right. I hear footsteps, heavy ones, including the *rap-tap-tap* of a pair of heels stutter-stepping down the hallway.

My gut goes tight. Part of me wonders if, now that Winter got what he wanted on his camera, there isn't any more use for Cross and me. Especially if Winter arranged for a new prisoner, he might not want to deal with the Sinners Syndicate or the Dragonflies now. Plus, I feel bad for her. She has no idea what she's walking into—

—and then I see her profile as she's marched between Luca and Noah past the glass door of our cell and I think I might've jumped the gun on that one.

Because just like how Cross recognized Luca, I know that woman's face. Her hair is shorter than it was when I saw her weeks ago. She's dyed it again, making it more auburn than mahogany, and she has it in an updo that I've never seen her wear before.

Her clothes are different, too. Instead of the comfortable sweater and jeans she usually wears when she's lounging in the TV room with Damien, Vin, Orion, and me, she has on a tight maroon dress with long sleeves that flare out around her wrists. Her three-inch-high heels are the same color, and nearly as pointed as the stiletto I hope she's hiding under that dress.

Savannah.

That's *Savannah*.

Holy *shit*.

A bubble of relief mixed with hope rises up my throat. I force it back, refusing to give away the fact that I recognize her. Especially when Noah grabs her arm, shoving her faster past my cell, and she's careful not to glance my way.

It doesn't matter. Luca did it. He brought a new prisoner down to the cells.

But it's not another gun runner's girlfriend.

Nope.

It's my murderous sister-in-law.

CROSS CAN TELL RIGHT AWAY THAT SOMETHING'S different. He gives me a curious look, but I just shake my head.

I don't have enough details yet. Whether they changed their mind and snagged Savannah instead, or if she's here to... what? Infiltrate the place where I've been held captive these last three weeks? I could see that happening. If Luca confirmed that Cross and I were trapped in here before telling my brother where to find me, I could totally see Damien trusting Savannah to find some way to break us out of here.

If there's a flaw in my logic—that it should be impossible for her to free me when she's trapped herself—I pointedly ignore that, too.

I do finally tell him the identity of the newest prisoner later that night. And if I encouraged him to lay next to me on the cot so we could whisper beneath the blanket instead of stubbornly offering to sleep on the floor like I'm sure he wanted to, I don't give a shit. He's the one who told me that he can't sleep unless he's holding me.

I'm stubborn, too. I absolutely refuse to let one night change anything. If he wants to go back to being friends, if he never wants to fuck me again, *fine*. But after all we've been through, I think the one thing that will break me is losing Cross because of something Winter made us do.

So I cuddled up next to him and admitted that my sister-in-law, Damien's new wife who is also a Dragonfly enforcer, is the newest prisoner. Doesn't matter that she seems to have gone through a transformation before she came here. That's *her*.

He agrees with me that, between Luca and Savannah, our respective families have put the first stages of an escape plot into motion. Until they make their move, all we can do is wait.

It takes two days. If Winter suspects anything, he doesn't make it obvious that he knows. In fact, I wouldn't be surprised if he caught on to the sense of anticipation in the air and chalked it up to the obvious chasm that exists between me and Cross after the other night.

But two days after Savannah gets led to a cell, I'm curled up on the cot when the glass door slides open and both she and Luca rush in.

Cross was pacing again. He meets Luca in the middle of the room, clasping his hand, pulling him into a sideways hug. "Fucking finally," he says. "It's time, yeah?"

"Finally," Luca agrees. "Sorry, Cross. I would've tried to get you out of here my first night at this place but that wasn't the plan. Damien wanted one of his people on the inside to make sure that his sister was safe, and then as soon as we had the opportunity, the two of us would work to get you out. It's just the two of us here right now. She could drop the act of being Falco's girl and we could make our move."

"Savannah," I breathe out, rushing forward and giving my brother's wife my own much tighter hug. A giddy laugh escapes me as I squeeze. "Took you long enough to make your move. What happened? Finally missed my brother?" Relief has me a touch reckless as I pull back and add, "Or was it just his cock?"

Luca chokes on his breath in front of me while I catch Cross shaking his head out of the corner of my eye, a hint of the first smile in days tugging on his lips.

Savannah doesn't seem to mind. In fact, a hint of relief touches the corner of her mouth as she flashes me a quick grin. "Good to see that being kidnapped and held against your will hasn't changed you one bit, Gen."

Oh. It has. I'm sure I'm going to be traumatized for a fucking *while* after we get out of here. But when I have hope that we will? I'm giddy with relief.

I just wish I had the chance for it to last.

I've never forgotten the cameras for a moment. From the moment Luca let Savannah out of her cell before plugging in the digits on the keypad to ours, the clock's been ticking. Either Winter knows we're breaking out, or he will shortly. I'm listening for the speaker to crackle and for his voice to fill the room, so when it doesn't, I think we're golden.

And then Luca cocks his head. His dark green eyes seem even darker as concern fills his expression. "Did you hear that?"

No. No, no, no. I don't want to hear anything except my feet on the stairs as we make a break for it. I listen anyway, and I nearly wail when I know exactly what caught Luca's attention: footsteps over our head.

Cross's dark eyes seem to turn black. "What the hell, Luca? I thought you just said this place was empty except the four of us."

"It was supposed to be. Shit. That's why I went and got Savannah. No one else was coming in until later tonight, but Winter must've sent another guy over for backup." Luca scowls. "I knew he didn't completely trust me."

Well, yeah. To be fair, I'm kind of surprised he lasted this long. With Winter's ability to learn details about those he's screwing with, it wouldn't have taken a lot to figure out that Luca's a Sinner now.

Did he have his own reasons to let Luca in? A plot to get his paws on Savannah pretending to be Falco's girlfriend? I don't know, but she turns to Luca.

"Should I go back in my cell?"

Luca gives his head a rough shake. "No point. We knew we only had one shot at this."

Savannah curses under her breath. "The cameras. Fuck. I forgot."

I wish I could.

"Right. Winter isn't always watching them, but if he logs in and sees the four of us in here, he'll know something's up. Might as well stay here and protect these two while I go check to see what that was."

"Protecting Genevieve is my job," rumbles Cross.

Savannah's eyebrows wing up at the possessive note in his deep voice. "Right. That's fine. But unless you have a weapon that you've neglected to use since you've been in here—"

It's my turn to choke on my laugh. Since this isn't the time to explain just how powerful Cross's jaw can be in the right circumstance, I keep that little tidbit to myself even as he reluctantly admits that we have nothing more than the clothes on our back and the thin blanket covering our cot.

Savannah actually looks thoughtful when he mentions the blanket, but instead of entering into a dick-measuring contest with my lover, my sister-in-law recognizes that it's better to just accept that Cross feels protective of me.

Cross looks Savannah up and down. If there was any heat in his stare, I might've actually been jealous, but he's more scrutinizing than appreciative of her build. "What about you? Doesn't look like you have a weapon, either."

"Couldn't risk carrying it myself. I'm pretending to be Camille Hedges. She's arm candy for this hotshot, Falco, and would never be armed. But that doesn't mean I'm helpless. Damien's been teaching me self-defense lessons for months now."

"Fine," he concedes. "You can help me protect her."

Savannah can be a bit of a smart ass at times, too. I learned that once I got to know her. Like Cross, though, she carries the weight of her own traumatic experiences with her. I'm not so sure what they are—only that, if you ask me, being forced to marry my brother would've been traumatic to anyone—but her eyes are sometimes as sad as Cross's.

Now? She simply nods, and Cross motions for me to get up and stand by them. Savannah is in front because, well, there's nowhere she can really hide in this tiny room. Cross is standing at my back, prepared to move if necessary.

I don't know who I'm expecting when, a few tense minutes later, the footsteps come closer and instead of it being Luca coming back to tell us everything's okay, it's fucking *Noah*.

Damn it. God*damn* it.

The gangly guard with the ponytail gapes when he sees that Savannah is in the cell with us. He points at her, points at Cross and me, then races over to the keypad. He came down here with a gun in his hand—not food—and I wonder if that's because he expected to see Luca.

The door slides open. He marches in and, before he says a word, he raises his gun.

It must be a warning shot. Unless Winter gave the order to take us out after all, but considering his aim is wide and, rather than blow Cross away, his bullet ends up in one of the cinderblocks, I'm not so sure about that. It doesn't matter. The fact is that he shoots past me, closer to Cross, and his instincts have him pushing me out of the way right before he falls forward and ends up on his knees on the floor.

Now I know why Savannah was eyeing our blanket before. With the echo of the gunshot still ringing out, she grabs the blanket, tossing it in front of Noah's face. It's only a split second's distraction, the material blocking his sight just long enough for Savannah to kick out at his knee before he can get off another shot.

Noah stumbles sideways. Instinctively, he throws out his hands—and the gun in his grasp goes flying in front of him even as he twists his body just enough to latch onto Savannah's slender shoulder, shoving her to the ground. Not expecting his brutal hit, she actually ends up on the floor while the big man recovers his balance just in time for his discarded weapon to land by my feet.

I think he's about to make a break for it, lunging forward to grab his gun. Some part of my instincts—self-preservation perhaps, or the Libellula blood running through my veins—has me swooping down, grabbing the weapon by its butt.

I've never held a gun before. I've wondered what it would be like, but Damien was careful to keep any firearms out of the house once sixteen-year-old Gen professed an interest in them.

As part of my obsession and morbid curiosity of my brother's criminal empire, I entertained myself by learning all about the business when I wasn't playing my part, dancing away my fascination. This one is a semi-automatic pistol with a single round of bullets—but that should be enough, right?

I have every intention of passing it off to Savannah. I

mean, she's the killer here. The enforcer. I'm a ballerina. Cross is an artist. Savannah is a killer... but Savannah is staring in horror as the big brute reaches behind him.

And I realize that Noah must have another gun there.

If he shoots again, he'll go for Savannah. I can't go back and tell my brother that his wife got killed because of me. And what if he aims for Cross—

"Shoot him, Gen," orders Savannah. "Shoot the fucker!"

I know that death is a part of the life. Damien's killed before to protect the Family. Vin's an enforcer with a bicep full of leaves so I can't even pretend that he's a Libellula who doesn't murder. Same with Savannah. She might've married into the family name, but she has four leaves.

Four deaths.

Four murders.

I'm not a killer.

But as I close my eyes and squeeze the trigger, I think I've just become one.

mariposa

ESCAPE

CROSS

After three weeks in a fishbowl of a cell, it took a single gunshot to shatter my butterfly.

I saw it happen. I was helpless to prevent it. So determined to keep Genevieve out of the line of fire, I pushed her out of the way after Noah's gun went off. The bang was explosive, the shower of cinderblock dust for where he struck the wall raining down on my hair, but all I could think about was getting Genevieve down.

I overcompensated in my panic. She moved out of the way, but I lost my balance, falling to my knees. At the same time, Savannah got bowled over after she threw the blanket in Noah's face to distract him and he barreled into her. A fucking comedy of errors, with the outcome being that Noah's gun skittered its way in front of Genevieve and my butterfly picked it up.

Savannah shouted at her to shoot, and she did, and I watched her *break*.

I could blame Damien Libellula for keeping her so coddled and under wraps that she found the life fascinating without ever facing the realities of it. She got her first glimpse when we were ran off the road and taken captive. Another glimpse when they starved us for days before bringing food down in an obvious ploy to manipulate Genevieve into sucking off the guards.

Then I did, and seeing the brutality I was capable of didn't turn her against me. I thought it would, but Genevieve always understood that life in the gangs was rough. I protected her and that's all that mattered. Even after they made me rape her—because that's what it was, it was *rape* because prisoners can't consent and I should've fought harder to keep her from what happened —she excused my behavior.

But I know this woman. She's made of fire and light, music and joy, and though three weeks in this hell didn't quite steal that from her, seeing the aftermath of how brutal *she* could be...

As I push myself off of the floor as Noah drops down dead, I know that that just might've done it.

Genevieve is no trained marksman. She didn't even know I carried until I admitted that they stole my weapon while we're unconscious, and she admitted that she's never even held a gun before. For a first timer, she couldn't have made a better shot.

Proximity had a lot to do with it. That close, she

couldn't miss Noah, and the shot got him dead center. He was gone before he hit the floor, leaving a bloody mess and a visibly shaken Genevieve holding his gun.

Savannah slowly rises as I take the gun from Genevieve. She doesn't resist. Trembling, her pale blue eyes staring straight ahead as if she can't see a thing, I remove her fingers from the handle and switch the gun from her grasp to mine.

"Butterfly," I whisper, using my nickname for her to get her attention. I don't know what I would've done if it hadn't worked, but she blinks once, her sight coming back to her as she looks up at me in ill-concealed panic. I make a soothing noise and use my free hand to tuck a lock of hair behind her ear. "It'll be okay. I promise."

I just hope I'm not lying when, as soon as the final echoes of the gunshot die down, I hear more footsteps.

These ones are welcome.

Racing for the glass door, punching in the code since it slid shut again, Luca looks from the shell-shocked Genevieve to the dead man on the floor, glances up at the camera, and thins his lips in barely concealed fury.

"He got past me," he spits out. "I don't even know how he did. I heard footsteps, but when I got upstairs, I didn't see anyone. He must've slipped right on by when I checked one room, then hit the stairs before I noticed him."

"It doesn't matter," Savannah tells him. "One dead Snowflake, two dead Snowflakes... as soon as we figure out where Winter is, he'll be another leaf on my bicep.

But that's later. We have to get the fuck out of here before someone else shows up."

"I did a quick sweep."

"You take the back and hold on to that gun," Savannah says to me. Suddenly, she has a stiletto knife in her grip, and I'm too stunned by the sudden turn of events, I can't even imagine where the hell she got it from. Luca maybe? Who the hell knows? "Luca, grab Gen and keep your gun out, too. Sandwich her between us, keep her safe. I've got point."

"Cross," breathes out Genevieve. "I need Cross."

Savannah doesn't even hesitate. "Right. Cross, stand with Gen. If anyone else comes, we're getting her out of here. Luca, you're in the rear."

No argument from either of us, though as Savannah Libellula gives commands, I have a newfound respect for Genevieve's brother for not trying to cage a woman like this.

Now if only I could get him to understand that Genevieve deserves to be free, too...

As we finally leave that fucking cell—and Noah— behind, Luca quickly explains the layout upstairs so I know what to expect. Turns out, this is a two-floor compound about as wide as the Libellula manor. The downstairs is specifically designed to host prisoners that Winter decides to shut up down there. Upstairs, he has a lab that worries me, a kitchen, a bedroom that the guards traded off using when they stayed over, and an empty waiting area for anyone who stops by and thinks that

Winter Enterprises is a legit business and not just a front for a criminal organization run by a psychopath.

There's attached storage, too. Luca says that the actual drug part of their operation is in Nevada—because, yup, Winter and his gang are based in Nevada and have just slowly been moving across the United States until they finally hit the East Coast—and this facility was designed to host their gun supply before distribution, though that was shut down before Luca got hired on. As of now, the only reason to keep this compound running on a skeleton crew was due to the cells in the basement.

No wonder the first Winter set his sights on Springfield. If he took out both the Dragonflies and the Sinners, he'd have free rein to push his Breeze and his weapons, and the money and crew to do it since he's already conquered at least eight other states with various properties all over the country.

When Devil first saw the snowflake on the butt of an unfamiliar gun, and Rolls warned me to keep an eye out for anyone asking to be tatted with the same mark, both our leader and his second made it seem like the man behind the snowflake was an upstart, pushing his like targeting Springfield.

Then Damien met with Devil and said that Jimmy Winter was dead and the Snowflakes were history.

Well. At least one positive thing came out of being captured and used as a pawn in a sick game masterminded by Johnny Winter: we know that the Snowflakes might just be a bigger problem than we thought.

Luca agrees. "When we get back to Springfield, stay alert, Cross. I only talked to Winter a couple of times. When they pushed me in front of him as an interview and after, like, five questions, he smirked and told me I was hired. Then when I offered to get a prisoner for him to show him I was legit. He's not all there. There's no way of knowing how he'll retaliate."

I nod, trying not to say anything that might further agitate Genevieve. She hasn't spoken another word since she asked for me, and as I keep my free arm tucked around her, holding her close, I can't help but feel like a part of her... she's slipping away from me.

Winter won't not be a problem until he's dead. Too bad he's nowhere near the facility.

Luca confirms that Winter is rarely on-site. He didn't even come to this side of Hamilton—because that's exactly where we are—to meet with Luca. They did that in the back of a dive bar at least ten miles away. Now that Noah's been taken out, the facility is all clear, and we have no trouble as Savannah leads us up and out.

Luca is still muttering to me, pissed that the escape plan got as fucked-up as it did.

"This was the only shot we had. It was just supposed to be me at the compound until dinner. Winter said he had other shit for the guys to do, and I figured it might be a test, but we couldn't wait. I guess Noah was the test. Winter must've sent him to make sure I was on the up and up."

Because Noah wasn't supposed to be here, but he was, and my butterfly was forced to kill him to save us all.

Genevieve stiffened at the mention of Noah's name. I rub her upper arm, pointedly ignoring how cold she is, then shoot a look behind me at Luca.

He gets the hint and shuts the hell up.

Less than three minutes after we hit the stairs, we're exiting a side door that leads right to a parking lot.

There are four cars out here. Three of them look too pricy to belong to Noah; the last one is a beater at least fifteen years older than the others. I recognize the long black car as Devil's. When Luca hurries over, opening the rear door—back to his driver duties—and Lincoln Crewes steps out in all his glory, I'm not surprised.

There's a nondescript black car parked two spaces away. Through the windshield, I see a large man with closely cropped dark hair and a pair of Libellula blue eyes a few shades darker than Genevieve's.

He lets himself out, and when he marches around his car, going for the driver side of the red Maserati next to him, I know he's wasting his time. I'm right. Damien Libellula doesn't wait for his cousin to open the door for him like Luca did for Devil. He shoves the door open, stalks out, and murmurs something in another language under his breath before he swoops Genevieve up into a tight hug.

I didn't want to let her go. Knowing that this is her family, I had no choice. Right before he grabbed her, I took my arm back and stepped away.

That's her brother. Her *brother*, Cross. She disappeared and he spent at least two weeks having no idea if she was safe or not. You have no fucking reason to be jealous of her brother.

And maybe if I keep telling myself that, I won't want to rip Damien away from my butterfly…

It's not Damien who releases Genevieve first. After a few more seconds, she wiggles out of his grip, immediately turning to find me. She ducks under my side, clutching my dirty shirt, and I feel peace for the first time since she was forced to fire that gun.

Damien Libellula has a fierce reputation. Not as bad as the Devil of Springfield, but when his pale blue eyes land on me and I see nothing but ice, my stomach goes cold.

It's a split second of him scrutinizing me before his elegant features soften once he sets eyes on his wife. He holds open his arms, and Savannah walks right into them.

I squeeze Genevieve close as the married couple have their reunion.

"Ragna mia, you are a miracle." Damien presses a kiss to the top of her hair. "Now, please, help my sister into the car. Vin will drive you home. I'll be right behind you."

Savannah moves over to Genevieve. "Come on, Gen. I'm dying for a good meal and a shower. And Orion. You missed him, too, didn't you? Let's go home and see Orion."

She blinks, still clinging to me. "Cross? Are you coming with me?"

Her question is a plea.

Damien's voice lashes out like a whip. "I'd like to take to him first, sorellina."

"Dame, I—"

He gentles his hard tone. "Genevieve, please. I'll see you at the manor. Let me talk to your man here."

As though needing him to recognize that I have some claim to her, hearing him call me 'her man' has Genevieve reluctantly letting go of my chest. She pats it once, then walking as though in a daze, allows Savannah to guide her to the black car and help her into the back seat.

Me? I know better.

That cold lashing voice? It was a sign of a frigid temper, worse because it's not as heated and explosive as a man on the verge of losing control. This is a man in *complete* control, and even more dangerous because of it.

So I'm not surprised at all that, the moment Vincent Libellula speeds away with my butterfly, Damien turns that whip on me.

"You will stay away from my sister," he orders.

Excuse me? "All due respect," because, after all, he is the head of the Dragonflies *and* Genevieve's brother, "but I can't do that. I love her."

Damien's face ices over. "It's a trauma bond, nothing more. You don't love her—"

"I do—"

"You can't. If you loved my sister, you never would've put her in danger in the first place."

My mouth clicks shut. I have nothing to say to that.

And for him to accuse me so justly, Damien knows. He knows about my growing friendships with Genevieve that turned into something more, and how we were only able to be caught because I took her out that fateful afternoon.

I wouldn't put it past him to know *everything*.

Damien moves into me, so close our chests are almost touching. "I blame myself, too. If it wasn't for me, Gen never would've been targeted. I know that. I accept that. It's part of the life, and I'll make anyone who hurt her pay for it. But you... you don't want to hurt her, right?"

The word is torn from my chest: "*Never*."

"I thought as much. So, listen to me: you stay away from her. And I'm not being a dick." Yes, he is. "Okay," he allows, "maybe a little. But that's because she's precious. You'd agree."

I jerk my head once. A nod.

"Exactly. And you have to know she's special. Whatever happened in there... she didn't deserve any of it. Don't you realize what will happen if you try to cling to her now that you're out? You'll remind her of what happened."

"I'm the only one who understands—"

"Very true," Damien says, interrupting me. "And that doesn't change my point. Genevieve needs a clean break. No reminders. She needs to stay home where my Dragonflies can keep her from getting mixed up with Winter again."

I swallow roughly. "I can keep her safe."

He raises an eyebrow. "Do you honestly think so? Because, forgive me, but I think we just went through a lot of trouble to pull your ass out of there, too."

Again, I shut up because, damn it, he's not wrong.

Devil's looming shadow suddenly falls in front of me. The leader of the Sinners Syndicate had hung back before, but now he stalked away from his fancy car, stopping once he reached Genevieve's brother and me.

"Damien," he growls. "For the sake of this damn truce, I gave you the two minutes with my guy you bargained for. Time's up. Cross. We're taking you home."

I want to refuse. I want to tell Damien to kiss my ass, that Genevieve is *mine*, and take her home with me. I want to lock her up in my apartment where I can keep her safe and sound in case Winter comes after her again, and lie with her in my bed as I finally get to explore her without cameras on us—

Holy fucking shit.

Holy *shit*.

He's right. The lead Dragonfly is *right*. All I wanted to do was set my butterfly free, and within minutes of us breaking out of that cell, I'm already planning to put her in another glass jar. Is it okay because *I* want to keep her? Fuck, no. I stole her first time from her, and I think that I should have the right to touch her again?

What the hell is wrong with me?

He's right. Damien told me to stay away from Genevieve because it would be the best thing for her. Seeing me would be an obvious reminder of what she went through. My skin against hers... how could she ever let me touch her without remembering being forced to?

I will forever be a trigger for her own trauma. And Genevieve will always be flames to me.

There's no way we can be together, and that means we have to stay apart.

Besides, this is the Devil of Springfield. You don't refuse Lincoln 'Devil' Crewes, especially not when you wear the Sinners Syndicate's trademark devil horns and tail on your flesh. Then again, I saw how he was with his wife shortly after they were married. I was the one who tatted his full Christian name on her ring finger to make sure everyone knew who she belonged to, and I was gathered with the rest of the syndicate when Devil went down on her after proclaiming her his queen—then setting an example by blowing Twig away when he dared to question Devil on his methods.

I'd do the same for Genevieve, I realize. Even before I knew she felt for me a sliver of what I feel for her, I admitted I was obsessed. Now I know that I can't live without her... but I'm going to have to.

For my butterfly.

So I nod at her brother in solemn regret, and Damien says, "Good. Then I trust we have an understanding."

I guess we do.

That done, Devil waits for me to follow him into the

backseat of his car. Once we're both seated, he raps the glass separating him from Luca, and says, "Let's bring our boy back. And then take a couple of nights off, Luca. You deserve it."

"You got it, boss," he answers.

The car starts, and we're off, leaving the last of my battered heart behind me.

Devil waits until we've sped out of the compound's parking lot before he asks, "You doing okay?"

No. "I survived."

I survived the captivity. How the hell am I going to survive being apart from Genevieve?

Devil searches my face. I do everything I can to shut my expression down and give nothing away. It must work because, after a moment, he leans back in his seat. His legs spread open, hand landing on the Sig Sauer that is his constant companion.

With an expectant look in his dark eyes, he nods at me. "In that case, I want you to tell me everything you know about this second Winter…"

mariposa

SEVENTEEN

AFTER

GENEVIEVE

No one will tell me where Cross is, and I feel like I'm going to lose my damn mind because of it.

It's been four days since we were rescued. At first, I was in shock. I won't deny that, and when Damien came home and met me on the ground floor where I refused to leave until I saw Cross again, he told me that his priority was to make sure I was okay.

Dr. Liz is dead—and good riddance. But we have a new doc that Damien is vetting, and against my will, he brought Dr. Vargas with him to the manor. One check-up later, I was told that I was exhausted, dehydrated, I'd lost ten pounds I couldn't afford to lose in the first place, my road rash had healed into a series of scars that hopefully can be covered up by tights, and I was definitely in shock.

I was told to take a warm shower to chase away the cold from the shock, drink fluids before Damien threatened me with an IV, and get as much sleep as possible to help in my recovery. The doc suggested I actually be hospitalized, but Dame shut that down real fast.

So did I. I just wanted Cross.

Why didn't he come with Damien? The only thing I got out of my brother was that Cross told him it was better if we went our separate ways after spending the last three weeks cramped together in the same cell. I couldn't believe it, but what else could I do?

Sneaking out was my first plan, to be honest. I gave all the proper lip service to the doctor, promising I would take care of myself, but in my brain, I was halfway to Sinners & Saints to see Cross—and then I went to my bedroom and discovered that that won't be happening anytime soon.

Damien cut down my tree.

The tree that's been outside my window since he built this manor for his family? *Gone.* My escape? Nonexistent.

And when he looked at me without any remorse as he made me promise that I would never sneak out again, I think I hated my brother for the first time ever.

The shock did fade. Sleep did help, even though I find it much harder to sleep in a bed by myself. All I wanted was Cross, though, and I settled for convincing Damien to replace my phone for me if I'd at least come downstairs for breakfast that third morning.

I have a dumbwaiter that leads from the kitchen to

my bedroom on the third floor. I thought it was the coolest thing ever when Damien had it constructed just for me, and it comes in handy when I'm in the middle of a marathon training session. I could just nip out of my studio, grab a bite from our cook, and go back to dance some more.

I'd skipped every meal with the family since I returned until I got the phone. But when I dialed the number I memorized and couldn't get through to Cross, I realized I was blocked. Texts didn't go through. I even googled the number for Sinners & Saints and the Devil's Playground, searching for someone to get through to him, and failed miserably.

Damien's words still echo in my ears after I threw a fit and nearly smashed the new phone: *I'm so sorry, sorellina, but I didn't want to hurt you. He made it very clear, now that you're out of that place, he needs to move on without you. It's not your fault, but his. So don't cry...*

I didn't cry. But since I also didn't believe him, I threw my brother's ass out of my room and have refused to speak to him since.

Something's wrong. I want to know what he said to Cross when I was too out of it to fight to stay and listen. Oh, he denies it, and Savannah's careful to change the subject when I ask, and Vin... after nearly losing Damien, then me, my cousin is on a tear, joining one of Devil's men in their search to exterminate any Winter strongholds in Springfield. But no one will tell me anything about Cross, and I feel like I'm going insane.

I still won't talk to Damien, and I made it clear that until I get into contact with Cross, I'm not changing my mind.

My brother isn't the only one I'm avoiding, either. In fact, if it wasn't for Savannah being Orion's owner, I'm stubborn enough to lock myself in my room and not interact with a single soul while I work through my trauma and obsess over what the hell Cross is doing since he's not with me.

I've never been a pet person, but that was because Damien wasn't. I used to beg when I was a kid for a cat or a dog, but he rightly pointed out that his job keeps him busy, ballet keeps me busy, and it wouldn't be fair for any animal to be adopted, then neglected.

Orion came with Savannah when she moved to the manor. While she was plotting her way out again—which was as obvious as it was when Savannah fell for Damien and decided to stay—Orion roamed over the entire manor like he owned it. That included my studio and my bedroom, and the first time he scratched at my door after I closed it, I realized that while I could keep the humans out, it wasn't fair to do that to Orion.

And, with Orion in here, eventually Savannah finds her way to my room, too.

Today she comes in under the pretense of making sure that Orion's doing okay, and once she sees he's sprawled out on the end of my bed with me, she gives me a knowing look.

"So," she begins, rocking back on her heels, hands in

the back pockets of her jeans, "are you ready to sit down and talk to your brother yet?"

"Depends? Will Damien let me see Cross first?" I toss back.

I try not to pay too much attention to the little voice in the back of my head that says, if Cross wanted to see *me*, he'd find a way. He doesn't have an older brother keeping him basically trapped inside. He could be here...

Savannah sighs, settling on her heels. "I don't think that's a good idea."

I flash her a half-smile. "Agree to disagree then. But until I can hear Cross tell me that he wants to keep his distance himself, I have nothing to say to my brother."

Usually, Savannah won't push it. I'm sure Damien is using her as a go-between with Savannah reporting everything I say back to him so that he can give the illusion that he's respecting my wishes by not imposing on me in my personal space.

But something's different today. I noticed it when she walked in, a little more hesitant than before, like she has something on her mind.

And then she says softly, "We know what happened between the two of you right before you got rescued," and my heart just about stops.

Though I know the answer already, I can't stop myself from asking, "How?"

"He sent a video."

Those goddamn cameras. I knew Cross wouldn't have

told my brother about it, but Winter... that fucker *would*. Hell, he told me that video was made specifically to mess with my brother. I should've known, but excuse me if that was part of my trauma I needed desperately to block out.

Can't now.

Savannah's expression is so apologetic and reminiscent of Cross's, I want to scream, but instead I listen as she adds, "Devil's guy traced it when we got the file yesterday, but it came from the facility where you were kept."

So no help there since my brother's spies have eyes on the facility and it's been abandoned directly after our escape. At least, if he was gonna send revenge porn of me out to my older brother, he could've had the decency to let himself be tracked down by it—or do something about Noah's body.

I force another smile to my lips. "Tell Dame we're even."

Savannah frowns. "Even? For what?"

I shrug. "I saw more than I ever wanted of you two. Now you guys watched me lose my virginity."

"We didn't watch, Gen," she says softly. "As soon as your brother realized what the video was going to show, he turned it off. He threatened all kinds of unholy things if anyone ever saw it. Tanner traced it, then deleted every single megabyte of that file. It's like it never existed."

Damien tried something like that once. I fell during a performance, and as an admittedly dramatic teenager, I declared my life over when I saw the clip circulating online. He tried everything he could to get it erased, but since it's still up now if you know where to look, he wasn't successful.

"The internet is forever."

"Tanner Maguire says otherwise," is Savannah's firm retort. "But now I understand why you refused to let the doctor do a rape kit on you—"

I fist my hands at my side. "I wasn't raped, Savannah."

"I know," she says, and if she's just trying to calm me before I start throwing pillows around my room again, that's fine. Regardless, I'm not going to let anyone think Cross did anything to me that I didn't want him to. "But I have to ask... was there protection?"

If she'd watched the video, she would've known there wasn't. I shake my head.

She shudders out a breath. "I figured. Okay. So. This is gonna be awkward as fuck, but since it's better coming from me than your brother... you might want to take a couple of tests, Gen."

I'd thought the same thing, then shoved it out of my mind. Cross wasn't a virgin. I knew that. I also believed him when he told me he hasn't had any one-night stands in the last year for no other reason than he wasn't inter-ested in having one. I chose to think that meant he was clean, and prayed that he hadn't lied to me.

He said he would protect me. Keep me safe. Never let me go... and that was a huge whopper, wasn't it?

"I think I'm fine."

"But are you pregnant?"

My heart skips a beat. "What did you say?" Savannah gives me a bewildered look, and I quickly clarify my surprise by adding, "Okay. I just told you I was a virgin when I went into the cell. That doesn't make me an idiot. I know that unprotected sex can lead to a baby, Savannah, so if you could stop looking at me like that, I'd appreciate it."

She winces. "I didn't mean—"

"I know. And it's fine. I've thought about that. I don't know if it's too soon to tell"—God, it's only been a *week*—"but if it happened, we'll call Dr. Vargas back up and he'll help me get an abortion."

Savannah doesn't react to my blunt statement; at least, not right away. I know that she's open to the idea of having kids. Years ago, Damien decided to get snipped so that none of the desperate women who wanted to be Mrs. Libellula could baby-trap him. He has no idea that *I* know—thank you, Christopher—but not too long after he and Savannah got hitched, my brother went and got his vasectomy reversed.

So she might want kids with Dame one day. Me?

No, thanks.

"You really have thought about it," she says after a moment.

"Yes," I tell her. "And I won't change my mind, either."

I've always been pro-choice. A woman's body belongs

to her, and abortion is healthcare in my mind. I don't regret sleeping with Cross, no matter why I had to, but if he left some of himself behind? I'll take care of it, and though I don't want to without getting some closure from my artist first, I'll move on.

He sure as hell did.

mariposa

EIGHTEEN

CROOKED

CROSS

The new soldier looks down at his fresh ink and frowns.

In my rolling chair, my back goes stiff, my body still. I'd already finished the shading on his devil horns and the matching tail, and was grabbing the plastic wrap to bandage him when he sat up and started scrutinizing it. The frown is just enough to catch my attention out of the corner of my eye, and I wait.

Pax's frown deepens.

I drop the plastic wrap down on the tray, knocking over the leftover ink onto the paper towel beneath it. "Something wrong with your tat?"

The kid startles. I know why, too. Like most Sinners, I have a rep in the syndicate. I'm cool-headed with a steady hand, more quiet than anything, the stereotypical artist who uses his own body as a canvas. I'll joke around with those I know well, though not even my closest pals know the depths of my past beyond the fact that a fire stole my family, and that I moved from one neighborhood to another until I settled in with my final foster placement at fourteen. I was a loner in high school who found an unlikely friend in golden boy Royce McIntyre, and with Rolls being Devil's second-in-command now—and my being the syndicate tattooist—that's the reason behind my elevated status on the West Side.

If the new soldier knew I bit the tip off of Mickey's cock because he threatened to sexually assault my butterfly, he wouldn't have shot me a side-eyed look after frowning at my work—though he sure as shit nearly slips off the leather chair when I snap at him.

Pax wasn't expecting it. Too bad. So I kept to myself before, and am even more of a recluse since being rescued with Genevieve. That doesn't mean I'm going to sit here and let him act like my work's not good.

No one frowns after I get done with them. Confidence in my needle is all I have left, and I've done hundreds of Sinners brands, from Devil himself to even his sweet, little wife.

So when Pax shakes his head and says, "Nah, man," I can't let it go.

"You're still frowning, newbie."

Pax bristles at the nickname. Glancing down, he twists his forearm so he can get a better look at the design.

I wait some more.

He offers it to me. "I dunno. It look crooked to you?"

I grit my teeth at the implication. My eyes are bleary, my head pounding, and this twenty-two-year-old kid has the nerve to pick apart my ink? I came all the way to the back offices of the Playground to tat him because that's my job, and because I always do a Sinner's brand on-site instead of at my studio, but no matter how much my world feels like its spinning off its axis, there's one thing I will always pride myself on: professional tattoos every single fucking time.

"You approved the stencil when it went on," I remind him.

Depending on the client, I either draw freehand or use a stencil as a guide. The devil horns are muscle memory at this point, but since this was Pax's first tat, I let him choose the size and position of where he wanted Devil's brand on him.

He went big and bold, right on his forearm so that he could show it off all over Springfield. Because it was his arm, not mine, I made sure he okayed the stencil, then got to work.

Crooked? Hell, no. It's fucking straight.

He squints. "I mean, if I look at it like this—"

"It's straight."

There's something in the edge of my voice that warns Pax from saying another word. He swallows, nods, and I pick up the plastic wrap. Clean up the client first, I tell myself, then clean up my station.

Once that's done, I give him another rundown on the tattoo aftercare before I let him escape from my space. Pax mumbles a quick, "Thanks," and bolts through the open doorway, nearly colliding with the man strolling in at the same time.

Poor Pax. Even I can muster a little sympathy for him when he sees he nearly steamrolled our fixer—and Devil's right-hand man. The new soldier babbles out a quick apology, then disappears down the hall before Rolls can finish glancing down at the barely visible crease on his thousand-dollar suit jacket. Probably to the Playground for a drink to celebrate his near miss, I'd bet, before I stop thinking about him at all.

Though I do think that maybe I'll stop by, too. I know the odds of sitting in a far back booth and spying Genevieve dancing in the middle of the dance floor are ones even a degenerate gambler like Rolls would never take, but my exhausted mind and battered heart can't help except hope a little.

Then again, as Rolls moves into the room, holding an energy drink in one hand, jerking his thumb behind him with the other, I'm thinking that drowning my sorrows in a shot of whiskey isn't on the table right now…

He nods at me. "Everything good, Cross?"

"The tat was straight," is all I say as I snap off one of my plastic gloves.

"Of course it was," Rolls easily agrees. "If it's your work, no doubt." A tiny smirk tugs on his lips. "You offer the new kid that numbing cream you've got?"

I snort. "With the way he came in, swaggering like he owned the space? Get real, sunshine."

"Just making sure I wasn't the only one you wanted to watch squirm. I mean, my devil hurt like hell, but I should've let you numb me up when you gave me my seahorse."

I remove my second glove. "Your fault. I offered last time."

"Yeah, yeah. Just saying, I think that's the last ink for me for a while. I wear my loyalty to Devil and our crew on my side, and my love for Nic near my junk. I think I'm good now."

"Well, if you decide you want any more, I'm only a call away. And," I add, still stewing over what just happened, "it'll be fucking straight."

Rolls quirks his eyebrow at me.

I shake my head. "Forget it. What's up? You need me for something? Devil told me to give Pax his tat, then I could head back to my shop. But if something came up…"

Rolls isn't just the syndicate fixer. Among all of his other responsibilities, he long ago made himself the head of clean-up for Devil. Whether it's an informant who needs to be taken care of, or a body that needs to disappear, Rolls is in charge of it. True, he's got a crew of his own that do the dirty work, but if he needs an extra hand and came to see me, that might just be the distraction I so desperately need.

Shame he shakes his head as he says, "Nothing like that." He lifts his hand, flicking a strand of blond hair back into place until he's perfect again before he adds, "But since you mention it... you got clients to see tonight?"

Considering I haven't bothered opening up Sinners & Saints for walk-ins yet, and any clients on my books were canceled after everything that happened, I don't. I'm good enough that I'm worth the wait, and when I feel like focusing on something other than a Sinners brand, I'll open up again.

Just... just not yet.

Then I glance up at him, catching the slight tension in his too-handsome features. Fuck. I should've guessed already. He's not here in his role for our syndicate.

He's here out of concern for his old friend.

I've been expecting this. To be honest, I've been *avoiding* this. Once I accepted that what I had with Genevieve had to be left behind in Hamilton, it was a struggle to return to the life I had before. Rolls was part of that. Tattooing was the biggest part. Attending meets, checking in with the state of the syndicate, helping to unload the trucks when the latest shipment of guns came in... all things I used to do that I just... I can't do anymore.

I breathe. I eat. I don't sleep, but that's nothing new. And I only keep the last shreds of my sanity by telling myself over and over again that this is for her.

This is for my butterfly.

She'd hate me if she knew. The way I basically ghosted her after being there by her side all those weeks... she sure as fuck hates me now. It's better that way, but sorry if one thing I can't handle more than anything else is being around a happy fucking newlywed like Rolls McIntyre.

But he's here now, and I don't want to blow him off. Rolls doesn't deserve that. It's not his fault that right when I thought I might have a shot of happiness, like everything else in my life, my dreams of a future with Genevieve have gone up in smoke.

She's better off without me. I know that. God fucking knows that Damien Libellula would also agree, but even when we were in our early twenties and just coming into the life, Rolls always pushed me to find a sliver of something to look forward to.

Back then, I found it in my needle. When it was one in my arm or one in my hand, I went art instead of H, and I was... fine. Part of me was searching for that muse, hoping for that spark, but if it never happened, then whatever.

Now it has—and it's torture going back to the way it used to be.

The emptiness. The loneliness. The constant ache behind my eyes, and the endless thoughts running like a train through my head as I basically beg for the sweet release of sleep if only to forget for a few blissful hours that I held my butterfly in my hands only to set her free.

Free... I snort under my breath again. Whether it's a gilded cage of her own making, or one where her older brother holds the key, there's no denying that Genevieve is just as trapped now as she was when Winter kept us behind that glass wall.

And, like then, there's not a damn thing I can do about it.

So, locking down my emotions as I pretend not to see his concern for me, I simply say, "None scheduled, but that could always change."

And if it doesn't, that's fine, too. I have other shit to do, and if I can dodge Rolls getting to the point behind his unexpected visit, I will—and then I can get to it.

To be fair, I shouldn't be *that* surprised he stopped by. Besides the fact that his new wife works as a waitress for the Devil's Playground, when Rolls isn't doing his other syndicate duties, he's also in charge of the nightclub. He spends most nights here, running the casino in the back, making sure the girls upstairs are taken care of, and keeping the drinks flowing and the music pumping.

But that's the thing. He should be at the Playground, not the back offices where Devil meets with his inner circle, Tanner has most of his computer setup stores, and I keep my second studio sterilized and stocked. Regardless, Rolls knew where to find me tonight—checking here instead of tagging me on my phone or stopping by Sinners & Saints—and I'm sure neither one of us is leaving until he tells me why.

Royce 'Rolls' McIntyre is as much a Sinner as the rest of us. Still, he's a good guy at heart, and devoted to those he considers his. Whether that's Devil or me, his wife or those in his clean-up crew like Killian and Jose, he has a slight tendency to mother us—which, yup, is the reason why he's here now, and he proves it when he can't help but use his free hand to gesture at my face.

"Or you could head on over to your apartment and get some rest." Rolls clicks his tongue. "You look like shit, buddy. Like you haven't slept in days."

Right. Because I really haven't. Not for more than a couple of hours at a time anyway.

He holds out the energy drink he brought with him. "Here. Something told me you might need this."

I wave him off. "I'm good. Thanks."

Rolls's brow furrows further as he lowers his arm to his side. "You sure? You normally guzzle this shit by the gallon."

I used to. It's not even the memory of the nasty caffeine headache I spent three days dealing with before it subsided enough for me to feel human again that got me to quit the stuff. Turns out, only being able to sleep soundly with Genevieve in my arms wasn't a fluke. I haven't slept for shit since we broke free of Winter's prison, but the idea of chugging an energy drink to be coherent has lost its flavor.

I told her once that there were worse things I could be addicted to. I meant it, and I'd only begun my fascination with her then. Now? My Genevieve withdrawals are even more fucked-up than those caffeine ones.

I pat my chest. "Gotta start thinking about the ol' ticker. Wouldn't want it to up and explode on me. Especially not after all the trouble you guys went to to bring me home."

Rolls moves closer to me, giving my shoulder a squeeze. "Never doubted we would for a moment," he swears.

I didn't, either. Nope. It was whether I'd still be in one piece when they finally tracked us down that I wasn't so sure of it, but as long as Genevieve made it out, I didn't care. Now we both did, and it's as painful living without her as I imagined it would be.

I don't shake Rolls off. Part of me wants to, but I'd never disrespect my oldest friend like that. Instead, I change the subject to one guaranteed to get him away from the one I'm eager to avoid.

"Enough about me. How've you been? How's your wife doing?"

Rolls's whole face lights up as he shifts his position, leaning with his suit jacket up against the wall at his back. "Nic? She's doing great. Not too happy with me that I won't let her leave the Suites until I've introduced Winter to ol' Woody the woodchipper, but she's been helping Ava out with the baby while Devil's taking care of Sinners business."

I still can't believe I missed it. That Ava finally gave birth while Genevieve and I were trapped in that cell. I haven't had the chance to meet Devil's daughter yet, either, though that's probably to be expected.

When I've spent every minute I'm awake obsessing over my butterfly, I've barely had time to keep my studio going, let alone pretend like some part of me didn't die when I had to let Genevieve go.

But her brother was right. I would only remind her of the trauma she went through, and he said that before he knew that I was forced to fuck her on camera. For God's sake, she was a *virgin*. She'll never have sex again without thinking about how her first time was stolen from her.

I did that. And I can tell myself all I want that I had no choice, that they would have shot her in the knees if I didn't, but that only explains the first time I fucked her.

The second time? She might've been the one to come on to me, to tell me that she needed to own the act on the heels of being forced to take my cock, but I would've done anything to get back inside of her. I didn't need to be convinced, and a good man wouldn't have been.

A good man would've known that she'd just been sexually assaulted—that we both had by Johnny Winter and his goons—and told her that we could wait until we were safely out of the cell again.

A good man wouldn't have lost control twice, coming inside of her, trying desperately to mark her as his even when he knew that she never would be.

A good man...

I'm not a good man. But, for Genevieve, I'm trying to be. And if that means I have to keep my distance, staying away from her for her own good, I will.

I promised I would protect her. I failed when we were trapped together. I won't fail this time.

So I blocked her number so I couldn't be tempted.

Then, because I'm a fucking hypocrite, I take a ride over to the East End on my bike just to be as close to her as possible whenever I can.

Who needs sleep when I can torture myself by staring up at her window like some lovesick Romeo standing beneath his untouchable Juliet's balcony?

Don't think about Genevieve, I tell myself pointlessly. I'd be better off trying to convince myself to stop breathing. It's that hard to do, and I rub my chest, grasping for something else to distract Rolls and me both.

"Baby doing good, too?" I ask.

Rolls cracks open the energy drink. He holds it out to me, I refuse, and he takes a swallow. His handsome features twist as the taste hits him. "You like this shit?"

"It grows on you."

His look tells me that he's not so sure he agrees, but he takes a second sip anyway. "Baby Clare's doing just as great. That's something else that grows on you, too, I guess."

Oh? "What do you mean?"

Rolls's deep blue eyes gleam. "My Nic's having a little baby fever of her own. I told her let's get this trouble with the Snowflakes sorted and we can start giving it a serious try ourselves."

I know Rolls. Even when Nicolette was one of our waitresses and supposedly off-limits to Sinners, he was so obsessed with her, he wagered ten grand on a bet to win a night with her. I also heard a couple of guys talking about how he disappeared into a Playground supply closet with her before they even started dating officially. Add that to how possessive he was of her when he brought her to me so I could do her cover-up and... yeah.

In a way, I guess I'm just shocked she didn't get knocked-up as quickly as Devil's bride did. Still, I raise my eyebrows at him and ask, "What the hell have you two been doing already?"

He grins. "Lots and lots of practice."

mariposa

NINETEEN
IMPOSSIBLE

CROSS

My answering laugh sounds rusty and unused, and it nearly shocks us both as it bursts out of me.

To be fair, I don't think I've laughed since I was sitting in my studio all those weeks ago, with Genevieve swinging her entrancing dancer legs as she absently flipped through my book of designs. She was always saying the most amusing things when we were first getting to know each other—when I foolishly convinced myself I could be satisfied with being her *friend*—like her sunny personality and her sass could be the foil to the lingering darkness inside of me that I've never been able to shake.

Rolls visibly relaxes a little at the sound of my amusement. "Good to see you haven't forgotten how to do that," he teases.

My laugh dies down as I swap it for a sigh. "They caged me up, Royce," I say, using his real name. Unlike me, he doesn't even react. He's as much Royce as he is Rolls, while I've buried the last of Carlos a long, long time ago. "They treated us like dogs." The way they starved us, then threatened to make us eat off the floor. How Mickey wanted to force Genevieve to blow him, then greedily agreed when I offered in her place. How they would've shot us if I didn't *mount* her and *rut* her, no better than a mindless animal. "Worse than dogs," I spit out. "I'm surviving, sunshine. That's the most I can do right now. Everything else is a bonus."

His expression shadows over just as quickly as I lost my laugh. "I know. It's hard sometimes. Trust me. I *know*. But that's why I'm here. When shit gets rough, you need to know you're not alone."

My gut goes tight. Rolls is right. Of course he is. I'd expect no less from this man.

But the words... they're familiar, too, and that affects me more than the sentiment behind his statement.

I said something similar to him once, years and years ago, right after everything went down with Rolls's younger cousin and that Dragonfly girl he was obsessed with. Back when Rolls wrongfully convinced himself that the brewing war between the East End and the West Side was all his fault because he was there the night Heather Valiant was shot and killed, and when Devil made it clear that he was backing up his second even if it meant war between the Sinners Syndicate and the Libellula Family.

Tensions were high. Bodies started dropping, and none of us knew who to trust. I didn't care about any of that. I went and visited my old friend just like he searched me out tonight. I told him how much it hurt to lose the ones you tried to protect, and even if he barely knew Heather, she'd turned to Rolls when Jake McIntyre wouldn't take no for an answer. Just like I did for Genevieve, Rolls promised to protect her—and the poor girl died anyway.

No surprise that he blamed himself for it even if he wasn't the one who pulled the trigger, and I know him well enough now to see that he always will. Just like I'll never be able to think of Ana Lucia, Rafe, and my mother without wishing I'd been home the night they died.

Could I have saved them? I was twelve. The fire burned so quickly... so, no. I couldn't have saved them. But I wouldn't have had to live the next twenty years with survivor's guilt if I had died with them.

Genevieve... I *did* save her. But I lost her just the same, and even though Rolls is right here with me, I can't shake the loneliness that is my constant companion.

If I admit that to Rolls, he'll worry about me even more than he already is. I can't let that happen. It's bad enough that I was gone without a trace for two weeks before Tanner figured out where Winter was keeping us. We're out now. Life fucking goes on.

I know that better than most.

So, again, I change the subject. I ignore the ache in my head and the sensation of grit in my tired eyes to tease Rolls about what names he would choose for any future McIntyre baby. I promise I'll find the time to clean up a little and head over to the penthouse of the Paradise Suites to pay my respects to Devil, Ava, and baby Clare. I even half-heartedly accept a dinner invite at Rolls and Nicolette's place, and if I make an off-color comment about the time I did Nicolette's cover-up and had her bare tit staring me in the face the entire time I inked a seahorse over the shitty dragonfly her abusive ex etched into her skin, Rolls is good enough to let it pass without becoming as jealous now as he did then.

Once he seems sure that I'm short-tempered due to lack of sleep, but otherwise as okay as I can be, he tosses his empty energy drink in my trash can, then tells me he'll check in with me again about that dinner invite.

I make a noncommittal sound in reply, and let out a breath when he finally leaves.

Getting up from my seat, I fish the can out of the trash so that I can toss it in my recycling; with the amount I used to go through, I got into the habit of making sure I always recycled the aluminum. Grabbing the handle, I pull the door closed. A quick flick of the lock and I won't be disturbed by any other Sinners 'just walking by'.

I'd paused in cleaning up the rest of my station when Rolls walked in as Pax was leaving. I make quick work of it now, and as I'm about to put my tattoo gun away, I pause. Something Rolls said rattles around in my exhausted brain, and for the first time in weeks, I feel a jolt of clarity.

Only it's not a shot of caffeine from an energy drink that clears my brain a little. It's the sudden burst of inspiration that slams into me coupled with his words.

I wear my loyalty to Devil and our crew on my side, and my love for Nic near my junk...

I've lost track of how many tats I have exactly. I've done them all, except for the ones on my back. Those were gifts to me by the mentor who I first apprenticed with, but as soon as I knew that a life of ink and the buzz of a tattoo gun was my calling, I used my own body as my first canvas.

It was another addiction. The hit of dopamine I got from the pain as the needle dug into my skin, combined with the satisfaction of another piece of permanent art done flawlessly on my flesh was a rush that rivaled any drug for me.

I haven't been inspired in so long, but after talking to Rolls... I know exactly what I want to do.

I'm an old pro when it comes to swapping out my needles from used to fresh, pouring out the colors I'll need, and sticking the little ink cups to my tray with a dollop of vaseline. As soon as I'm prepped, I grab the large lighted mirror on its stand and move it nearer to my seat. Tugging off my shirt, I toss it over the headrest of my leather chair before glancing down at my chest.

I've never tatted my hands. No actual reason, really, other than that I know how much of a bitch it is for hand

and finger tattoos to heal properly. I need my fingers; another reason why I wasn't surprised Genevieve gave in and allowed me to have sex with her when it was my hands on the line. I've left my thighs alone and my cock ink-free for the same reason as my hands.

But the left side of my chest? My heart died the same day that my family did. I never thought I'd feel love again—and then I met Genevieve. We can't be together. I accept that. It's not even because our respective gangs were once rivals and enemies—like we're living a modern-day version of *West Side Story*—or that she's too good for a damaged man like me. She is, of course, but if we'd never had been taken captive together... if we'd gone from rivals to friends to eventual lovers... there might've been a chance.

There isn't one now. To pursue Genevieve would be selfish as fuck, and I can't do that to her. Not when I can finally admit what I've known from almost the first moment I saw her dance.

I love her. She owns my heart—and as I grab the disposable razor and start shaving the nearly invisible hairs that cover my left pec, I decide to prove it.

Even if my butterfly will never know how much I belong to her, at least I will every single time I look in the mirror.

It's better than seeing the monster that stole the last of her innocence.

WHEN WAS THE LAST TIME I SLEPT FOR MORE THAN A couple of hours at once?

That's the question that's running through my mind as I park my bike as near enough to the back of the large white manor as I can without getting caught on Libellula's cameras. Considering I've already been run off by three different Dragonflies—and the old butler who came marching out from inside the big house—over the past few weeks, I've gotten a pretty good idea of their limits by now. I still push them, though, because I *need* to.

I need to see the light on in her studio, too. I strain my ears, hoping that the music from the third floor might filter down to me. Wishful thinking, yeah, since the roar of cars driving down the consistently busy roads would drown it out, but no one said that I was being rational.

In my admittedly delirious state, I know I'm not.

When was the last time I slept for more than a couple of hours at once? When I was holding Genevieve in my arms while we were in Winter's damn cage, and since that's never going to happen again, this is the next best thing.

It's been a week since Rolls came to visit me after I did Pax's Sinners tattoo. For the sake of my old friend and his palpable concern for me, I tried to sleep after I finished inking my chest. I did everything I could in the nights that followed. Melatonin. Benadryl. Any over-the-counter sleep aid I could get from the corner store. They all managed to knock me out, but staying asleep only to wake up alone in my bed?

Impossible.

I brace my boots on the asphalt, snorting under my breath as I realize how much my life's changed. For years, my childhood trauma meant that waking up alone was a *good* thing. The nightmares of my bastard of a stepfather sneaking into my room to do whatever the fuck he wanted affected my insomnia for so damn long. Doesn't matter that he's dead and rotting in some unmarked grave, provided by the prison because—as his only kin— it was understandable that I'd refuse to do anything for his remains but spit on them.

I'm thirty. Almost two decades of that man owning my nightmares and making it so that I could never have a bedmate didn't quite disappear when I held Genevieve in my arms, but the demons were quieted. To protect her in a way I couldn't Ana Lucia and Rafe... I wasn't the victim. I was the savior.

Until I was the villian.

This last month, my nightmares all include Genevieve simply disappearing. Like, *poof*, she's gone, and I have to resist the urge to ball up my fist and plow it into the first hard surface I see whenever I think of her ceasing to exist.

So long as she survives, I could give a fuck what happens to me. I thought that in the cell we were trapped in, and it means even more to me now.

She's up there, and though I expect to be run off before I can really get comfortable, this might be the best opportunity I have to just sit on the seat of my bike and know this is as close to her as I can get.

Once a month, the head of the Sinners Syndicate and the Libellula Family meet up with the mayor of Springfield to make sure that the guns keep selling, the drugs keep flowing, and that the SPD know what side of their ridiculous—and clearly crooked—thin blue line they need to stay on. Genevieve's brother won't be home for a while. Devil will find a way to leave the meet early so he can return to his wife and newborn, but Rolls usually goes to those dinners, too. So does Genevieve's cousin, the big guy who acts as Damien's bodyguard. Vincent. He's the one who threatened to snap my neck for breaking his Genny's heart when he found me out here, and I almost let him because *fuck*. She doesn't understand that I'm hurting just as much. Even more, most likely.

But I deserve the pain. She doesn't. And I only hope that, the longer we're apart, the easier it is for her to forget me.

To forget those weeks in the cage.

To forget what I did to her...

Leaning forward on my handlebars, I get comfortable. My gaze is locked on the gauzy yellow light streaming from behind the curtains on her windows. I've never been inside, but she's told me how the entire third floor is hers. She's up there. That's all that matters to me. The lights are on, she's home, and I'm more at peace on my bike, watching her window from a distance, than I would be tossing and turning and by myself in my bed.

I lose track of how long I'm staring up there; when no one comes out straight away to tell me to get lost, I figure I found a good spot to keep watch over her. Eventually, Libellula will return and I'll have to head back to the West Side, but for now, I'm content to just spend the rest of the night out here where I am.

And that's when, suddenly, the back door pushes open and a feminine figure steps out onto the porch.

I jolt up, attention snared so quickly, you'd think I was a fish caught on the line.

Genevieve—

My heart skips a beat, then sinks just as quickly. No. That's not my butterfly. The woman heading down the porch stairs has dark hair, not golden blonde, and while she moves with a purposeful step, it's nothing like the innate gracefulness that first drew me toward Genevieve.

I can't make out her features, but it's clear enough that she's not my girl. Since the only other people who live in the manor are the cook and the housekeeper— both older women—and Damien's wife, Savannah, I'm assuming that must be her. It's too hard to see if I recognize her from this distance.

But she sees me. I know she does. I also know now that she's almost as dangerous as Damien Libellula himself. She's a Dragonfly enforcer, and if she decided to take me out, I have no doubt that she could—or that it would please her brutal husband.

Only she doesn't. Instead, turning slightly and tilting her head back as though she's searching for the same window that I was, Savannah notices the light on in Genevieve's room—and the missing tree outside her window that means my butterfly can no longer sneak out like she'd been doing before we were caught by Winter's men.

I noticed that my first night I rode by the manor. Even if Genevieve *wanted* to see me again, her previous way out was cut down. Add that to the countless new cameras put up on Libellula's personal territory and he wasn't taking any chances of his baby sister leaving the manor without him knowing again.

Would she, I wonder. If I hadn't made it impossible for her to reach me—if I'd told Libellula to shove it, and been selfish enough to claim my butterfly as my own even though I would only hurt her in the end—would she come to me? Or did I lose her before she was ever really mine?

I don't know, but after Savannah pointedly lowers her gaze, turns again, stares at me for a few seconds, then walks back inside of the manor, I spend the next couple of hours obsessing over *that* next...

mariposa

TWENTY
MATCHMAKER

GENEVIEVE

I try not to remember the first time I met Savannah because, well, that would involve reliving the moment I burst into Damien's bedroom without knocking, expecting to find him organizing the million suits he has in his closets but actually getting a front row seat to him getting his knob polished.

Like, I knew he had sex. As much as he tried to hide it from me in some 'noble' sense of protecting my innocence, my older brother is an objectively handsome man with a shit ton of money and power. I never bothered him with it, but all through high school, then later when I was part of Madame Durand's company, so many of the girls tried to get close to me because they had eyes on the prize: becoming Mrs. Libellula.

Is it any wonder that I stuck close to Christopher, who

while definitely attracted to men, never made a move on Damien? That alone made him a keeper, plus how loyal he was to me at the same time as he was there to temper some of my more irrepressible urges. I would've gotten into so much more trouble as a kid if it wasn't for Christopher, and even as adults, he always looked out for me.

Did I suspect Damien put him up to it? Duh. I'm not a moron. From the moment Christopher joined the Family as Damien's personal assistant, I knew that keeping tabs on me would be one of his duties.

But I also knew that, unless I was in danger, I could trust him. For years, Christopher allowed me to have at least some semblance of a normal life, and I'm so grateful for him. I'm even more grateful when Savannah told me that Christopher was the one who alerted both her and Damien to the fact that I was missing.

He knew I'd gone to see Cross the day we were taken. It was inevitable that he'd think that Cross had something to do with my disappearance, especially when he turned up gone, too. That's why it took a week before their focus shifted on blaming him to thinking that maybe we were taken together.

Once Cross came up gone, Devil got involved. If there's one semi-decent thing that came out of this whole disaster, it's that the truce between the Sinners Syndicate and the Libellula Family has never been more rock-solid. If Winter wanted to further his twin's cause of taking over Springfield, he royally screwed up there. Banding together to bring me and Cross home safe made the two mafias unbeatable.

Devil had his tech guru, Tanner, figuring out where we'd been hidden. I'm still hazy on the details *how* exactly, but when I asked Savannah, she told me that it's better not to ask about his skills and just be grateful he uses them *for* us instead of *against* us. Luca went in first because, as part of the criminal scene in Hamilton before he fled to Springfield, he had an in. I still think Winter knew he was letting in a spy, but since that fucker's gone ghost since we left his facility, there's no way to know about that, either.

With Luca in place to check out the layout of the compound where we were kept, Savannah was selected to play the part of Falco's girlfriend. I kinda feel bad for Dame when it came to that. He had to choose between his new wife and his beloved kid sister, and even Savannah knew that he would pick me.

She cops to it readily, then later slips something about the first night we met I didn't know: how, in the middle of her going down on Damien, and after I burst into the room before high-tailing it back out again, she made a comment about thinking that *I* was his wife. Besides that being super gross to even think about, Dame doesn't do bigamy. But remember: Savannah and Damien got married after Savannah *stabbed* him. Their marriage was a power play that actually ended up working out so far, but he told her that she'd be a victim of one of his enforcers if she so much as laid a finger on a hair of my head.

Instead, the two of us become fast buddies, bonding over her kitty, and now Savannah is both one of his enforcers *and* the woman who helped rescue me and Cross from Winter.

She's more than that, too. I can forgive her her taste in men—because if Cross had shown himself to be like Damien in the beginning, I would've never fallen for him —because of how she's basically replaced Christopher as my partner in crime these days.

I still haven't talked to him. I know he's on thin ice with the Family because, after confessing that I was suddenly missing, he had to tell Damien all about how I've been sneaking out for years. I'm pretty sure the only reason he still has his neck in one piece is because he kept me safe every time I did. That, plus I'd be really pissed off if Damien slit my best friend's throat.

I don't blame Christopher. It's more that I'm ashamed that my reckless actions got *him* in trouble. So when he reached out right after our rescue and told me he understands that I need space and he'll give it to me, I jumped at the chance to put some distance between us.

Damien? He can fuck off for all I care. I might've forgiven him if he hadn't chopped down my tree in a fit of brotherly entitlement. Like, I get it. He wants me to stay in the manor. I guess I should be grateful that I put my foot down and refused him to agree that he could chip me with a tracker and he *let* me, but with Cross acting like I don't exist, it's not like I wouldn't have agreed to not sneak out again until this whole thing with Winter is done.

No one can find him. No one knows what he's planning, or if he finally got it through his thick skull that Springfield will never be Snowflake turf. He's vanished, and when weeks pass, turning to more than a month that I'm a basic prisoner in my room, I start to get the old familiar itch to go out into the world again. I want freedom—

Ah, who am I kidding? I want *Cross*.

He couldn't have made it more clear that he doesn't want me. Rejection fucking sucks, but I'm a big girl. I should just be happy to have experienced so many firsts with him.

My first love.

My first fuck.

My first *kill*.

And my first heartbreak...

Savannah doesn't leave the manor, either. Not really. When she first came to stay—and I nearly had a fit when I thought Damien had a secret girlfriend he up and married without telling me about her—she was as much a prisoner as I am now. Once she proved her love and loyalty to my brother, she could leave as she pleases, but Savannah prefers to stay in at the manor unless she's going out as one of Dame's enforcers.

I've discovered that she's a homebody who enjoys binging movies and TV shows in our big home theater room, curled up next to Orion, while eating popcorn and talking to me about what we both think will happen next on the screen.

I haven't watched television since I came home. The theater room is on the second floor of the manor—Damien's turf—and I'm still avoiding him. He thinks I'll get over his heavy-handed treatment of me eventually.

Don't hold your breath, Dame. I know how to hold a grudge when it counts.

As though he can sense I need his company, Orion has been my shadow. If he's not with Savannah, he's with me, and though he's not quite the man I want to sleep next to, Orion has been my buddy in bed for weeks now.

He's there now, curled up at the end of my bed while I fluff my hair, checking it out in my mirror as Savannah nods in approval.

"It looks good, Gen. I really thought that pink would suit you."

"It's really nice," I agree.

When Savannah went to the drug store to grab another box of dye, going from that auburn color back to her deeper brunette shade, I impulsively asked her to get me some, too. I wanted color, I wanted pizazz, and though I drew the line at coloring my whole head, she helped me paint in a few streaks in the front before dipping the ends of my blonde hair in the pink dye.

It was equal parts to give me something to do, to shake up the sameness of every fucking day, as well as knowing that Damien would purse his lips in disapproval if he saw what we'd done.

Oh, well.

That's not all she bought for me at the drug store, either. When I couldn't ignore the reality any longer, I finally acquiesced and allowed her to pick up a pregnancy test. I'd hoped that sleeping with Cross twice without any protection wouldn't leave a bun in my oven to take care of, and the test boasted a ninety-nine perfect accuracy.

I really, really hope they mean it because I'd never been so relieved to have a test with a negative result.

I don't want kids. Not anytime soon. Maybe not ever. I'm only twenty-five, and I planned on dancing professionally 'til I was at least thirty. If I kept myself in shape, there was no reason I couldn't. I might not ever dance on a big stage again, but there are more than enough local companies where I could dance for a few more years.

I haven't watched television. I haven't danced, either.

Which is why I can't help the pang in my chest as Savannah says, "And it's the wash-out stuff, too. Give it a couple of weeks and it'll be gone. The next time you're preparing for a performance, you won't have to worry about having pink hair."

Only one problem: I'm not sure there'll be another performance.

What happened in Hamilton... it broke me. Cross walking away with no reason, no remorse, and no closure?

I don't know if I'll ever heal.

But God bless Savannah, I guess, who is definitely Damien's mouthpiece these days. My brother is the one who put me through dance lessons, ramping them up when I told him I was serious about it at ten. He's gone to every performance, helped bandage every injury, and if there's anyone who knows how much dance means to me, it's my brother.

My studio stays dark. I don't put music on.

He's gotta be shitting himself in worry.

Closure, I think again. One way or another, I need closure...

"Did you see that Riverside plans on doing *The Nutcracker* for November?" Savannah asks as I turn away from the mirror, moving to sit on the edge of my bed.

I give Orion a stroke. The big orange-and-white cat quirks open one big green eye, starts to rumble like a motorcycle engine, and goes right back to sleep. "They do every year."

I should know. When I was nineteen, I got the part of Clara. They usually get a younger girl to play her since the character is around twelve or so, but I was small enough that it worked. They wanted our Clara on pointe so the casting team looked for dancers with impressive skills, and it was one of my first big credits after I left Madame Durand's studio.

But I've always wanted to dance as the Sugar Plum Fairy. It never fell into place for me, and depending on how my July audition went, I was hoping that this would be my year for *The Nutcracker*.

Not anymore. I haven't done so much as a grand jete since I came home again. I just... I can't do it. I thought my love of dance was strong enough to get me through anything, but as it turns out, loving another person—and having them reject you like you're nothing—is enough to steal my former passion and joy.

So when Savannah starts mentioning the upcoming schedule for auditions at the end of the month, I cut her off. "Any update on Winter?"

Savannah pauses for a moment. She runs her gaze over me, and I see the moment she realizes that I'm not ready to talk about ballet just yet. Of course I'm still fixated on Winter and my captivity. She has to know that I can't stop thinking about Cross, either, but it's much safer to talk about the bastard who put all of this into motion.

Damien would find a way to change the subject. That's why I like Savannah because she takes a look at me, gauges what she thinks I can handle, and says, "No update yet. Once he realized I wasn't Camille, he withdrew his people from Falco's territory since he didn't have anything to use against him. He's gotta know it would be a death wish to come after Springfield. But Tanner thinks he might be targeting the crew in Harmony Heights."

"What's Harmony Heights?" I ask.

I can't help myself. Not only do I want to be involved when it comes to taking out Winter, but I've always been fascinated by the various local mafias and criminal organizations. You think that would've changed after everything I've been through, but not quite.

Only I've never heard of Harmony Heights before.

"It's this small hamlet in the southern part of the state," Savannah explains.

"Weird name," I note.

"Weird town," agrees Savannah. "You think Springfield's bad? This place is run by criminals, but that's better than that one."

"I don't get what you mean."

"They've got this not-so-secret society who runs the show there. Everything from the businesses in town to who gets to marry who, this order is in charge. They've got money, too, and a lot of pull. I guess, from what Damien told me, Winter thought he could take over that order by taking one of the member's daughters. Haven something. I forget. It didn't end well for that part of his operation."

Haven. "I don't know if it ended well for her, either," I mutter.

Savannah cocks her head, curious.

"Remember? How there was another girl being held in that place with us? Her name was Haven. One of the guards made fun of the fact that he sexually assaulted her so bad, she went mute."

My pretty sister-in-law's face turns murderous, and in that moment, I remember just how formidable of an enforcer she's become. "What a monster! Is that the one who lost part of his cock? 'Cause to do that... I really hope they couldn't reattach that fucker."

"Me, too. I never even knew it was possible to do that, but when Cross did—"

I stop short.

Savannah goes still.

Cross.

He's on my mind constantly. I haven't been able to forget him one bit. But his name... since the moment Damien told me that Cross said it would better this way before blocking me everywhere... I haven't actually said his name.

Until now.

She hesitates, then says, "Give him time, Gen. You both went through something really traumatic. You're healing. Maybe he is, too. And when he realizes that he needs you as much as you need him—"

I know she's only trying to help. But that? That's not helping.

"He doesn't want anything to do with me ever again," I blurt out. Blurt out... no. I *explode.* The words I've kept bottled up inside of me come out with such heat, I scare the shit out of poor Orion. He yelps, jumping off the bed as I throw open my arms. "Friends, Savannah. He promised me we could be friends. And then when I needed a friend the most, he *disappeared.*"

"Gen—"

I'm not done. "I thought he cared about me. I thought there was something there. Going through that together...

shouldn't that have made us stronger? But he threw me away like trash! All that time we spent together... before... after... and he walked away without a fucking backward glance!"

Her expression goes soft. I know she's going to calm me, but maybe I don't want to be calmed.

Maybe this was the release I've been waiting for—

Savannah turns her head, glancing at my window. "Are you so sure about that?"

The quiet yet firm way she says that takes all the wind out of my sails.

Why is she staring out my window?

"Savannah?"

She moves next to it, gesturing for me to join her. Not sure why, but suddenly very curious, I do—and she points.

"You can't see him from here, can you?"

"What are you talking about?"

Savannah gestures out of the window with a little more oomph, toward a blind spot behind the back of the house. "There. You can't tell from this spot, so if he's been parking his bike right over there, you'd never know."

I still don't get it. "Why would he be out there?"

"That's something you'd have to ask him. But I promise you, I saw him. I'm not the first one, either. Vin ran him off a couple of times recently. Frankie came out, shaking one of his wife's wooden spoons. He always leaves, but he always comes back."

He always comes back...

"But *why*?"

"I don't know, Genny. But don't you think it's time you stop hiding out in your room and find out?"

She's not wrong. That's *exactly* what I've been doing. I could blame Damien for keeping me his prisoner, but if I wanted to go… could my brother really stop me?

No. But as I stayed in my room, licking the wounds from Cross's rejection, I could stay away from Cross, too… but what if I didn't any longer?

"He blocked me. I can't get through to him," I argue.

"Over the phone, yeah," she agrees. "But what about in person?"

She isn't suggesting what I *think* she's suggesting… is she?

I was too proud to go to his studio to beg, though the thought did cross my mind once or twice. But that's not the only place where I can find Cross, is it?

I smile, and Savannah lays her hand on my shoulder. "Don't worry about a thing. I'll take care of your brother."

And I'll take care of Cross.

"Thank you, Savannah."

She shrugs. "Hey. You and Cross saved my cat. Least I can do is help play matchmaker."

I've been avoiding Christopher for weeks. He wanted to give me space. And yet, when I pick up my phone and send him the first text since we went radio silent, it isn't ten seconds before he replies:

> Hey. It's been a while, but you busy tonight?

> Not at all. Your brother's had me doing paperwork for ages. I'd love an excuse to forget it for a couple of hours.

> Why? You need to get some fresh air?

That's how I used to phrase it. When my bedroom got too stifling, and I thought that I'd scream if I spent another minute in my studio, staring at a hundred Genevieves looking back at me, I would tell him I needed air, and he'd be waiting for me at the corner of our street in no time—just like Cross used to do.

Just like Cross *still* does.

I haven't given up on him yet. And, sure, I can call it closure all I want, but we have something. Something solid. I don't care that he walked away after Damien talked to him. I wouldn't put it past my overprotective brother to try and convince Cross that I'd be better off without him.

But Cross? He should've known better.

I'm basing what I do next on nearly twenty years of friendship. Hoping that I can still rely on Christopher to put me first when it matters, I send him another message.

> Savannah thinks I should.

I hope he understands that, at least tonight, I have my sister-in-law backing me on this. Considering Damien might not get too pissy if he realizes that the two most important people in his life outvoted him, that should make Christopher feel a little better about bringing me back to the Devil's Playground where this all started.

I can be there in ten. Should I park in the usual spot?

I think about it for a second.

And then I smile.

Cross should've known better, but so should Damien. I've never been the perfect mafia princess, easy to control, no matter how much I pretended—or what Damien deluded himself into believing.

I stayed in the manor like a good girl for too long. It's time for this butterfly to break free.

Nope. I'll meet you at the front gate.

I toss my phone onto the bed. Christopher will be here in no time.

As for me? I have to get ready to bait Cross da Silva.

Because one way or another? I'll know exactly where we stand after tonight.

mariposa

TWENTY-ONE
MINE

CROSS

I might've avoided Rolls McIntyre—and the Playground itself—since his impromptu visit to my setup in the back offices, but my oldest friend will still look out for me no matter what.

You know how I know? Because Genevieve wasn't in the Devil's Playground more than ten minutes before one of the Sinners out on a night off recognized her as Damien's sister and immediately tagged Rolls. Knowing that her connection to me is infinitely more important, Rolls called me right away to let me know.

He told me what she was wearing: a black-and-white mesh top over her bra, a pair of black booty shorts, and black boots. When he added that she had dyed part of her hair pink, I thought he was screwing with me. That sounded so unlike my butterfly, I wondered if she had a secret twin, just like Jimmy Winter did.

And then he sent me a fuzzy camera phone pic. The neons and flashing lights in the Playground made it hard to make out details, but that was undeniably Genevieve.

Fifteen minutes after I got the text, I've parked my bike and stalked into the nightclub, searching for her. It doesn't take long. Very few people inside have the inherent grace that Genevieve does, and I spot her in the middle of the dance floor almost immediately.

She's not alone.

I'd heard she came through the door with fucking *Christopher*, but he's not the one she's dancing with now. Some toothy blond frat boy is parked behind her, too close for my liking. He's grinding his cock against her ass, all while Genevieve smiles and dances next to him.

Hell, *no*.

I don't stop until I'm inches away from them. This close, I can hear Genevieve's sweet voice over the bass as she leans in and says matter-of-factly to the wallet: "Did you know that it's possible to bite a guy's cock right off?"

I'm stunned. Part of me can't believe she's mentioning what she witnessed in Winter's facility so casually, while another part is stunned to think that she might be *bragging* about knowing that fact.

Shaking it off, I tap her on her shoulder.

She spins around and I see that she didn't just paint the tips of her hair with the pink color. She has highlights in the front, framing her face.

My heart nearly stops. She's that gorgeous—and the way her face goes from flirtatious to furious in an instant has me almost taking a step back to escape her barely concealed anger.

Then I remember what she was doing when I found her, and I move *closer*. "Your hair."

She fluffs it out. "You like it?"

Yes. The pink color toward the ends of her golden hair isn't only just incredibly attractive, especially to a guy like me who loves to decorate his body. It helps her lose a little of the innocence that used to cling to her when she would wear her ballerina hair up in a bun. Loose and wild and *pink*... I love it.

I shake my head. "Say goodbye to your friend, Genevieve."

"Why would I do that?"

"Because you're coming with me."

Her eyes widen a bit before her lips quirk upward in a secretive little smile that replaces her earlier anger. She doesn't even turn to look at the man she was both tantalizing and terrorizing, waggling her fingers instead as she moves toward me. "And where exactly do you think you're taking me?"

Home.

I don't answer her. Snatching her fingers, clutching them in the heat of my hand, I start to tug her behind me. Not roughly, never roughly, but if I don't walk away from the man who was attempting to grind up against her, he might lose a couple of his.

And that's just for starters.

Clutching Genevieve to me, I wind my way through the crowd. She probably expected me to lead her out through the front door. I don't. As a Sinner who spends far more time in the Playground than I should, I know all the ins and outs of this place. Within minutes, I've brought her to the back alley outside the south side of the Playground.

I see her notice my bike, though if she recognizes that I replaced her white helmet with the pink butterfly on it after the last crash, she doesn't say anything.

That's okay. *I* do.

"What were you doing, talking to one of the wallets about cocks?"

That catches her attention.

Spinning around so she can face me, Genevieve smirks. "That's nothing. I told one guy that I killed a man. He didn't stick around to dance long after that. Another one groped my ass. I wasn't above watching him turn green when I told him the same thing I just told my *friend,* then snapped my teeth at him. You didn't give me a chance with this one before you hauled me out here." She pouts. "I didn't need your help, you know. I can take care of myself."

The gun goes off.

Noah drops.

Genevieve pales...

"I know that," I admit. "But you're on Sinner territory, butterfly. I'm the one who protects you here."

That was probably the worst thing I could've said.

Her pretty blue eyes turn hard. "Is that how it goes? I'm Dame's problem on the East End, but if I *dare* to step off of Dragonfly turf, you'll get off your high horse enough to act like you give a shit?"

So she's angry again. *Fiery.*

God, I *missed* her.

I can't let her see that, though. All those weeks when I stayed away... they would be for nothing if she knew how I really feel. How I've been the walking dead without her, and how I dream of that last smile she gave me after we were rescued before waking up to the nightmare of a life without her.

And that's if I *do* sleep.

So, instead of coming clean, I do what I do best: I lock my emotions up tight, keeping my expression impassive as I ask her, "What are you doing here?"

Okay. That might've been more of a demand, and I gave away too much with it, but I can't help it.

And then she *answers,* and any hope of simply sending her on her way and heading back to my empty apartment dies a very quick death.

"Isn't it obvious? I was a virgin for twenty-five years. Now that I'm not anymore, I found out I like sex. I want to have more of it. And, sure, I know how you feel about my first time, but I didn't lie to you, Cross. You made it worth it. Fuck the cameras. Fuck the people who think they can use it against us—"

That catches my attention. The second she admitted

that she was trolling for some ass had my head roaring and my mouth clamped shut before I said something I couldn't take back, but then she said *that*, and I take an actual step away from her.

"What did you say?"

"You didn't know?" When I shake my head, she tells me, "Winter did what he said he would do. He sent that video of us to my brother."

No wonder Damien warned me away from his sister. I should be lucky he didn't gut me the second Genevieve was out of sight.

"When?" I rasp out, to see if it was a close shave—or if I need to be even more wary of Damien now.

"I don't know exactly. Doesn't matter anyway. He didn't watch it, and one of your guys said it's as good as erased."

For Genevieve's sake, I'm glad to hear that. For mine... my gut twists, and I mutter, "I bet you wish you could forget just as easily."

"God, you're such a sorry fucking *ass*. You know? I thought you were sweet. Sensitive. A real artist-type. I saw your sad eyes and I wanted to make them happy again. But you... you just like being miserable, don't you?"

"I don't like it, butterfly. I'm just used to it."

The fire of her temper ebbs some. The flames don't die out completely, they're still there, but when she speaks again, she gentles her voice. "What happened to your family... what that man did... I won't ever dare tell you that you need to move on. I never knew my mother.

My father was a piece of work. If I lost Damien back in May, I don't think I'd be here now. But you survived. Cross, you exist. Don't you deserve to be happy?"

"What are you doing here tonight, Genevieve? I mean, besides lecturing me."

I went too far. I know it the second the words leave my mouth. This back and forth had been as flirtatious as it was explosive before her pity triggered me, but the way Genevieve recoils now right after I lose control, I have to admit: I fucked up, and there might not be any way of making it right with her.

And then she fists her hands on her hips and snaps, "I told you already. I've got an itch to scratch, and if you don't want to be the one to take care of it, I'll find someone who will."

A vein pulses in my neck. I *feel* it, and it's probably due to the way I'm resisting the urge to launch myself at this tempestuous woman and take care of both of our repressed needs.

But I can't do that, so I just raise my eyebrows and play it fucking cool. "At the Playground?"

"Why not?" she shrugs, drawing my hungry gaze right to the cleavage revealed through her mesh top. "That's where I found you, isn't it?"

"Well, tonight *I* found *you*."

"Okay." Her lips twitch, and I can tell she's feigning amusement this time. "What about hate sex? Let's see. I've had pity sex with you once already. Well, you had pity sex with *me*. At least hate sex would tick off another one of the boxes I'm dying to try."

I snort. "Oh, butterfly, you need to actually hate someone to have hate sex. And I know you don't hate me."

Not the way I hate myself at any rate.

"I guess we'll see, won't we?" And then, before I can put an end to this, before I can regain my self control and march Genevieve back inside, she does something so reckless... so undeniably fucking *hot* and *reckless*... that I admit that this was inevitable from the moment I heard her say the word 'cock' in her sweet voice to another man.

I don't care that she was threatening him in a round-about way or that it was a throwback to our captivity. I know what she meant—

—but Genevieve doesn't know what she's asking of me as she bumps her chest against mine, laying her fingers against my achy cock, tilting her head back as she demands, "Fuck me tonight or I'll find someone else who will."

Butterfly...

She says she wants tonight.

I'll demand *forever*.

"Listen to me," I say, swallowing my groan. Having her so close... my body goes tight and it takes everything I have not to thrust against her palm. "I fuck you, this is it, Genevieve. You understand that? I'm not staying away anymore. I tried. God fucking knows, I *tried*. For you. Because you deserve better than me—"

"I *love* you."

"You just think you do," I grit out. "Because I was the only one you had to hold onto when we were being held by Winter. I promised to protect you. I did a shit job of it, but I made you believe in me. Of course you think you love me—"

She slaps me. Not in the face, but in the chest, right between my pecs. "Stop."

It takes me a second to realize she released me, and another to really understand she hit me. I frown. "Genevieve?"

"I said fucking *stop*, okay? I didn't want to think you were like my brother. *Fuck.* You know why I fell for you in the first place? Because you *weren't*. You were careful with me, sure, but not because I was Genevieve Libellula. That was because I was your butterfly. But you never acted like you knew better than me. We were friends." She scoffs. "*Friends*. And I was okay with that because you at least treated me like an equal. You didn't hide me away like Damien does."

"No. And that's how you ended up getting taken by Winter."

"That wasn't your fault!"

I shake my head.

"Now you listen to *me*. Cross? It couldn't have been your fault. I mean, unless you were in on it. Unless you planned with Winter and those assholes to lock me up—"

"I would *never* do that."

"Of course not! But it sounds crazy that I'd suggest that, right? Well, guess what, genius? It sounds crazy to me when you try to blame yourself for something you didn't do. You were a victim, too—"

I turn away from her. And there it is. I've always been a victim.

Genevieve marches around me, gripping my chin in her delicate fingers, using more strength than I'd given her credit for to yank my head, jerking it down so that I'm forced to look at her.

"Shitty choice of words on my part. You're no victim, babe. You're a survivor. We both are."

"Babe," I echo. "I wanted to be your 'babe'."

"Yeah, well? You were supposed to be."

A lump lodges in my throat as I see the fire in Genevieve's eyes. I swallow it roughly. "Supposed to be?"

Fuck. She's turned me into a mimic, repeating everything she says. But I can't help it. 'Supposed to be'... does that mean she's given up on me? On us?

I should want that. That's exactly what I should want to hear. I'm no good for her, and if she wants to pick any man from the Playground's dance floor and let them into her body—into her *heart*—then I need to back the hell up and let that happen.

Yeah. *No.*

"You're mine," I grate out. "You want to be fucked? You come to *me*. No one else. I popped your cherry. You bled on *my* cock. That pussy belongs to me."

mariposa

TWENTY-TWO
HEAL

CROSS

Once again, I'm reminded that Genevieve Libellula is a mafia princess. A civilian woman would hear how possessive I suddenly became and beat feet down the street.

My butterfly?

Without breaking our stare, she grips the waistband of her tight shorts and wiggles them down to the asphalt. She steps out of them, then does the same thing with her panties. Before I know it, she's naked from the waist down except for her shoes, and before I can marvel over how amazing she looks with her trimmed pussy on display, she turns around.

I growl under my breath, my hand going right for my erection. I keep it tucked behind my jeans, but I can't stop myself from stroking the hard flesh through the rough material.

And then she braces her elbows on the seat of my bike and bends over, sticking her ass out and says, "Am I? Prove it."

"Mariposa..." I breathe out.

She glances over her shoulder at me. "What was that?"

"Mi mariposa," I tell her again. "My butterfly in Spanish." Dropping low, I untie the laces of both of my boots before rising up again and kicking them off. "I haven't used a word of Spanish in years. I used to be fluent, but Chad beat that out of me years ago."

Genevieve starts to get up. "Cross—"

I lay one hand on the small of her back, keeping her bent over for me. With the other, I unbutton my jeans. "No. Don't feel sorry for me. Be flattered. When I saw your ass and pussy just now, I forgot English for a second. It's a good thing that I could rely on Spanish. Maybe I'll use it more now." I rub her soft skin before releasing her, saying a silent prayer when she stays down. "You're right. I survived him. I survived Winter." With two free hands now, I yank my shirt up and over my head, then shove my jeans down past my ass. I don't stop until they're off, too, and I'm butt-fucking-naked outside of the Playground. "I just don't know if I'm going to survive *you*."

Glancing over her shoulder at me, her eyes sparkle in invitation. She goes up on her tiptoes, letting me see how her folds glisten for me. "Only one way to find out."

"Remember," I growl, grabbing my cock. I'm already so hard, it won't take much to have me going off like a rocket. Since I want to be inside of Genevieve when I do, I brace my legs behind her, then use her juices to cover the length of my cock before I position it right at her entrance. "You're the one who wanted to fuck."

I feed the first two inches inside of her, gritting my teeth when her warmth envelopes me.

She goes still. I pause, making sure she's with me all the way, only for her to snort. "With that lead pipe of yours ready and raring to go, babe, I'm not the only horny one here. You want to fuck me, too. Don't deny it."

"I'm not denying anything."

Genevieve swallows and goes up on her toes again, taking more of me. "I've never regretted doing anything with you. Not the first time. Not now. But if you're going to—"

I bottom out inside of her, stealing the last of her words as she trades speech for a soft, "Oh."

"You okay?"

She nods. "Yeah. I guess I just forget how stuffed you make me feel."

"Then let me remind you, butterfly," I murmur, withdrawing just enough that she'll feel it when I push back inside of her.

She squeals.

It's music to my ears.

"Just like that," she groans. "Do it again."

"Don't be so demanding, Genevieve," I tease.

She sniffs royally even as she takes my cock. "I'm a Libellula. I was born to be obeyed."

"Is that so?"

"Yup. But, like I said... if you don't want to fuck me, I'm sure I can find some else who will."

In answer to that, I quicken my thrusts. Genevieve moans and, instead of bracing herself on her elbows, she lays her belly flat on my motorcycle seat. I grip her hips, holding her there, and *fuck* her.

"No way," I grunt as she pants my name under her breath. "You're mine."

She pushes her ass back against me, and the moment suddenly becomes charged. "You stayed away."

"For *you*."

Genevieve goes still. Instead of meeting my thrust, she freezes before turning to look over her shoulder and snap, "So fucking help me, Cross, if you try to tell me that you tortured us both by abandoning me for *my* sake, you can pull out and leave me the hell alone."

She's not bluffing. As worked up as we both are, she'll pull her shorts back on and walk away as if this meant nothing.

As if *we* mean nothing...

I grip her hips, clutching her to me as I bury my cock so deeply inside of her, she'd have to crawl over my bike to escape me.

If she told me to get off, I would. If she told me to stop, I'd listen. If she told me she regretted bending over my bike, I'd hate it, but I would have no one else to blame but myself for letting my butterfly flutter out of my grasp.

But I need her. Fuck it, I've been nothing without her.

And it's time I give up on this ridiculous attempt at being selfless. I tried. I fucking *failed*. I love this woman, and if she's willing to give me another chance, I'm going to take it as much as I'm taking her.

"Try," I tell her, knowing better than to dare Genevieve but unable to stop myself. "I gave it a shot, Genevieve. I tried to stay away. I never wanted you to look at me and relive the nightmares of that place—"

"How could I, Cross?" she demands, still meeting my gaze. "You're the only good thing I remember about that hellhole. When you were gone, that was all that kept me going." She inches away from me, but trapped beneath my weight, there isn't anywhere for her to go as she whispers, "I even stopped dancing."

My stomach drops. I even start to deflate a little, losing my erection. "You never stop dancing."

"You were gone. So was the music in my heart. But tonight, when I saw you coming for me from across the dance floor, that's the first time I wanted to use my body for anything other than existing from one moment to the next."

I start to withdraw from the warmth of her body. What she said... it's so eerily similar to how I felt. Both as a kid when my family perished, and then when I purposely walked away from Genevieve. "I'm so sorry—"

"No," she snaps, and the ferocity has me freezing in

place. Well, that and the way she reaches behind her, jabbing her fingernails in my ass cheeks. "You stop fucking me, then you'll be sorry. I was bluffing. I don't care anymore about why you were gone. I just got you back. At least stay with me for now."

As if trying to keep me closer, she squeezes my cock, trapping me in a vice so tight I couldn't pull out if I wanted to. My erection comes roaring back to life, but hearing her beg me to stay?

I bow my body over her, pinning her in place as I quicken my pace, giving her every inch I have. "Forever," I gasp as she scratches her nails up my spine. "You and me, butterfly. We're forever."

She makes a soft sound in the back of her throat. I can't tell if it's because she's struck speechless at my fervent vow, or because she starts spasming around me, coming as soon as I started pounding into her, but instead of trying to get away from me, she arches her back, taking all of me.

And as I drop my head to her neck, suckling on her skin as I thrust, waiting until I sense my body ready to explode, I make sure to give her every last drop I have.

I give myself permission to come once she does. It was a messy fuck, frantic and emotional, but with my post-nut clarity, I realize that she can't be comfortable with my bike seat digging into her belly. I thrust a few more times, if only to remind her that I'm here, that I'm not leaving just because we both got off, then I slowly pull out.

A sense of masculine pride fills me as I watch my come dribble out of her well-used pussy. Bending behind her, I press a kiss to her ass, then use my finger to gather up as much of the moisture as I can before dipping it back up inside of her. Once I'm satisfied that I did, I run my palm over her ass cheek and murmur, "You feeling okay, butterfly?"

"Mm."

I laugh. Good enough.

Rising up, feeling a hundred pounds lighter than I did earlier tonight even though I only lost a couple of ounces, I ease my arms under Genevieve's. I murmur to her to hold on before lifting her up off of my bike.

She's boneless, but in a good way. Her expression is one of pure satisfaction as she reaches up, twining her fingers in my hair, holding me to her.

My heart is racing. I'm out of breath, but as I look down at Genevieve, I finally find the words that I should have said a long, long time ago: "I love you."

She blinks, as though not sure she heard me right. "What?"

"That's the short version. I love you."

"I..." Her brows draw together. "Okay. Wait. That's the short version. What's the long version?"

I press my thumbs to her cheeks, still staring into her pretty blue eyes. "I've watched my world burn, nothing left but ash. But you, mi mariposa, my butterfly, mi amor... you are the undying flame that's transfixed me, and the reason I can love again. I love you, Genevieve

Libellula. And I meant it. This isn't for tonight. This isn't for now. This is *forever*."

And that does it.

The sated look from two seconds ago slides right off of her face. I see a flash of pain, then she shoves me away from her. Swooping down, searching the pile of discarded clothing, she tosses my shirt to the side, reaching for her shorts.

I stop her by squatting down, grabbing her wrist. "Talk to me. Genevieve... I spilled my guts out to you. I opened up my goddamn heart. What did I do wrong?"

She hollows her cheeks, but she doesn't break free of my loose hold. "See. I knew you didn't get it."

"Get what?"

"When I called it hate sex before. You thought I was talking about me hating you." She laughs, though the sound has no humor in it. "Yeah, right. I tried to hate you, you know. For throwing me away so easily..."

"I didn't," I cut in. "I was there. You didn't see me, but as much as I tried... I couldn't stay away."

"Oh. I know." At my look of surprise, she gives me the smallest smile. "Savannah saw you the other day. She told me tonight before she helped me sneak out of the house."

Well, that makes a little more sense. Something told me that Damien Libellula had no idea that Genevieve was here, but if she didn't care, I wasn't going to, either. I doubted he relaxed at all when it came to locking her up to ensure her safety, but if Savannah let her free so she could come to me... maybe I have a better chance of making this work than I thought.

And then Genevieve adds, "I wanted to hate you. I couldn't. I loved you too much. But you... You don't love me, Cross. You *can't*."

No. I *shouldn't*.

But I do. I have from the start. My mistake was in doing exactly what she accused me of before: treating her like her brother instead of her partner. Instead of her lover. I thought I knew better, that she'd be safer without me, but I was *wrong*.

I gather her up in my arms.

I'm standing in the middle of a Springfield alley, my ass out, my cock semi-hard as if it has hopes of getting back inside of Genevieve where it belongs. I don't want to think about what my bare feet have been stepping in. Anyone could walk out and see us. The bus boys taking out a load of garbage. One of the waitresses coming out for a smoke. *Anyone*... but I don't give a shit.

Right now? This moment is for my butterfly and me.

And as she melts against me before dissolving into tears—tears that could mean so many different things—I accept that Genevieve was spot-on when she called us both survivors.

We're just survivors who we still have a shit ton of healing to do, but we're going to do it.

Together.

mariposa

TWENTY-THREE
FOREVER

GENEVIEVE

I've finally made it upstairs to Cross's apartment.

Victory!

Heading to his place was my idea, and for a couple of different reasons beyond just wanting to be intimate with him in his space. As much as I wanted to stick my middle finger up at my brother by inviting Cross back to my room—making him pay for meddling in my relationship like that—I knew better. Savannah was risking her own marriage by doing the same, helping me sneak out earlier tonight. I have no doubt in my mind that Damien will forgive her, but if he found Cross in my bed?

Yeah. That might be a little too much too quickly.

Besides, the Devil's Playground is so much closer to Cross's apartment than my home on the East End. So, once I assured him that I was okay, *honest*, he helped me pull my shorts on again, keeping my panties as a trophy that he proudly shoved in one of the pockets of his jeans. Cross took his spot on his new bike once we were both dressed, making it clear that he's considered the back seat mine since the moment we first met.

The fact that he had my personalized helmet—also a replacement to boot because we lost the first one *and* his bike in the crash—strapped to his saddlebag is proof of that.

Turns out, his old friend Rolls was the one who tipped him off that I was here. Whatever outcome Cross expected after following me to the Playground, there must've been a part of him that knew I would be leaving with him one way or another. Whether it was because he was treating me like a little girl and dropping me off at home for my brother to take care of, or he actually saw me as a woman who knew what *she* wanted, I have no clue, but seeing that helmet... realizing he went out of his way to replace it while we were apart... I knew that Cross da Silva was still mine.

He sure as hell fucked me like I was *his*.

I'll be feeling this one tomorrow. Going up on my tiptoes, letting him bang me from behind while I clung to his motorcycle... yeah. My lower belly is red, my legs wobbly and weak—which is exactly why he needed to help me get my clothes back on—but I don't give a shit.

He loves me. To hear this man tell me that he does, to *believe* it... I would've done a lot worse than egg on his jealousy before tempting—*daring*—him to fuck me.

The sex was great. I'm still so new to it, but after the weeks he stayed away from me, I'm more than willing to make up for lost time. Especially since he agreed to bring me to his place after he finished letting me cry all over his naked chest.

I was ready to take him again. He refused to shuck his clothes once he let me upstairs, pointed out his kitchen, his bathroom, and, finally, his bedroom. I could tell he was just as aroused as I was, but he offered me something to drink instead.

Cross poured me a glass of orange juice. It was either that, water, or lemonade since, to my surprise, there isn't a single caffeine product in his fridge. When I pointed it out, he said he never got hooked on the energy drinks again, and considering the deep purple circles under his eyes, I don't think it's because he's learned better sleeping habits.

I took a few sips while he dropped a gentle kiss to the top of my head as he rubbed my back.

Okay. I know I freaked him out. Anyone who knows me knows that I'm a whirlwind of emotions. I don't hide them. I don't keep them back. I'm an open fucking book, and I can go from one extreme to the other, swinging like I'm a goddamn pendulum. But tears? I can't tell you the last time I cried.

Cross has never seen my tears. Then again, the last time I was with him, he didn't have that massive butterfly on his chest.

Outside of the Playground... the entire time he was

fucking me, he took me from behind. Sure, I looked up and over at him, but I was watching his face. I noticed it last time. When Cross is fucking me, *he* is open book. He doesn't put up that guarded expression, and his eyes... his eyes seem to come alive. Not even the circles hid the love and affection and *need* that was in his eyes.

Did I look at his chest? Fleetingly. I appreciated what a gorgeous piece of man he is, but I was too distracted by the sensation of him hitting every single nerve inside of me while strumming my heart at the same time. The lights at his back silhouetted him. He has so much ink on him, I didn't notice that he added more.

And then he finished. His possessive yet soft touch as he stuck his finger back up inside of me sent another shudder of pleasure through me, but it was when he got up and turned me into him that I saw the butterfly on his chest.

It's the exact same design that he drew for me the night we met.

He told me once that tattoos are permanent, regardless of things like laser removal. He would never put something on his skin that wasn't a permanent fixture in his life, and yet... that's *my* butterfly.

To see that, then to hear him call me his and *mean* it? I broke down. It happened. I wouldn't have done it if I wasn't cruising on a shit ton of endorphins from my orgasm, but I cried and Cross held me the whole time I did before wiping away my tears.

If he'd suggested I go home, my emotions would've

swung all over the place again. He didn't. He asked me where I wanted to go, I said his place, and that's where he brought me.

That's where I am now.

After I told him I was done with the orange juice, he took me by the hand and led me to his bed. Cross shook his head when I asked if we we're getting undressed.

"I just want to hold you," he murmured. "I can only sleep when I hold you."

And that's how I found out his insomnia has been even worse since we were separated. I couldn't even gloat. All this time, I thought he was living his life, happy to be rid of me, but he suffered as much as I did. Worse. Savannah knew he was skulking around the manor, but according to Cross, so did Vin and Frankie and a couple of other Dragonflies.

He didn't sleep. Oh, no. He came to watch my window instead, confirming that I was at least safe, even if he couldn't be with me.

And why couldn't he be with me?

Damien.

Just like I suspected, my stupid fucking older brother was the one who put the idea in Cross's head that I would be better off without him. There were no threats. Damien's too smart for that. Why threaten Cross, knowing that if it got back to me, that would only push me away when he could use Cross's own insecurities to keep us separated on the guise of being the doting older brother?

Doting?

Try *controlling*.

If it wasn't for Cross grabbing my hand after I jumped up off the bed, prepared to storm all the way back to the East End to confront Damien, I might have. This time, it was his turn to beg as he pleaded with me to stay.

Cross da Silva wanted *me* to stay.

How could I refuse?

Especially when, after I crossed my arms and plopped back down with a huff, he distracted me by pulling his shirt off again. Not the pants, which is a downright shame, but he yanked off his shirt, letting me look my fill at the butterfly on his chest.

When I finally got my tears under control, I admitted almost sheepishly that the surprise of seeing his tat was what turned me into a weeping fountain in the first place. He changed the subject then, reminding me that we were both naked and anyone could stumble on us at any moment, but as I turn into him, tracing the wings on his chest, I won't let him change the subject now.

Beneath his decorated skin, his heart beats. As he breathes softly, already halfway to sleep now that he has one leg thrown over mine, his hand nestled possessively on my hip, I swear I can see the butterfly's wings flapping.

I press a kiss there.

It's not a fresh tat. After hanging out with Cross at his studio for those six weeks straight in the beginning of our 'friend'ship, I can tell the difference between a fresh one and one that's healed some. This one is at least a couple of weeks old.

He confirms it. "I couldn't have you with me. Stupid, I know that now, but I honestly believed it. So I did the only thing I could. I gave you the place of honor on my chest."

I remember thinking how odd it was the first time I saw Cross without a shirt that every inch of his torso and back had various different types of tattoos on them except for the space over his left pec. I never asked because, well, it didn't seem appropriate then, but now?

"I always wondered why you kept this part of your chest bare."

"The spot over my heart has always been empty," he says, lifting his hand to stroke my cheek with the pad of his calloused thumb. "That's because it was meant for you, butterfly. For the person I gave my heart to."

Now, really? How can you expect him to say that in his deep, sexy voice, his fingers roaming over my cheek, his head resting on his arm as he watches me with heavy-lidded eyes?

I scoot closer, cupping his face in my hand. His lips part, and I kiss him at the same time as I move so that I'm nearly on top of him.

For all his blustering before that we needed sleep, that we could fuck later, he's not resisting me at all as he flops onto his back, letting me spread out on top of him. I bend my head, tonguing his nipple before rubbing my cheek against his butterfly tat.

Then, because I still haven't had the chance to see what it was like to suck a cock for myself, I start to shimmy down the length of his body.

I'm just about to fit myself in the cradle of his legs when he goes still. The anticipatory look on his face as soon as he realized where I was heading is replaced by one of confusion, then, just as quickly, one of frustration.

"Don't worry, babe," I tease. "I might not know what I'm doing, but I didn't know what I was doing when it came to fucking, either. Good thing for you I'm a quick learner."

I nip his happy trail before reaching for the button on his jeans.

"Genevieve..."

"It's okay," I promise. "I mean, if *you* want me to do this. If you're tired—"

"I'm always tired. That doesn't mean I would reject what you're offering me, but no. It's just... didn't you hear that?"

My fingers hovers over his button. "Hear what?"

He listens for a second, then shakes his head. "Never mind. I thought—"

Using my thumb and forefinger, I flick the button open before grabbing the zipper pull lightly between them. "It's just you and me, Cross. And if you want to stay up a little longer... you don't know how much I've fanta-sized about this."

Cross's jaw goes tight as he folds his arms behind his head, pillowing it at the same time as providing a little lift. His core tightens, the tattoos on his lower torso rippling as he crunches just enough to be in a position to watch me as I slowly, seductively work the zipper down.

His voice develops a hint of gravel as he admits, "You? Fuck me, butterfly, but I've dreamed about you taking my cock between your lips since the first time you smiled at me."

Hearing that, a mischievous grin tugs on those lips. "What about now?"

"Don't tease me," he pleads, and my grin widens.

That was totally begging. Do you know how fucking powerful it feels to have a man like Cross da Silva begging for your touch?

I'm hoping that I wasn't boasting before when I said I could make this good for him for my first try. I mean, I always thought of it like licking a lollipop or eating an ice pop. Lick, suck, nibble... and because this is *Cross*, I'll use teeth, but never the way he was forced to.

He's heavy in my hand as I reach inside of his underwear, releasing the hard flesh. I'm not surprised that, as soon as I pull him out, he's already sprung. If there's one thing I learned about Cross while we were trapped, it's how often he was aroused around me—and how careful he was to hide that fact.

The time for that is over. It's such a boost to my own self-esteem that he found me attractive at my worst, and after everything we've been through, is eager to touch me now.

Only it's my turn to experience *him*.

I dart my tongue out, taking an experimental lick over the head. That's supposed to be the most sensitive part, and from the way he sucks in a breath, I'm thinking that's right.

I swirl my tongue around it, working myself up to taking the whole head inside of the heat of my mouth.

As greedy as I am, I know better than to try to swallow his whole length at once. I'm already finding it hard to breathe with as much of him as I have in my mouth, but I'm determined to do this.

It becomes easier once I remember I have a nose to breathe out of. Mimicking the act of fucking, I start to bob my head a little, doing everything I can think of to make this good for Cross. I keep one hand at the base, squeezing him, while I dare fleeting glances up at him to see if he's enjoying himself.

His eyes are still heavy-lidded while his chest is barely moving, coiled and tensed as he holds himself back from either going off in my mouth straight away or, following my lead, thrusting into it.

Cross sees me peeking, and a slow, sensual grin makes him even more undeniably sexy.

"Do you know how fucking hot you look, your lips stretched around my cock, all that pretty hair falling into your face? The pink, butterfly... when I think of you now, I think of sunshine and pink."

I let him slip out of my mouth so I can have a breather. Holding him with one hand, I push my loose hair out of my face so that I can look up at Cross. "And sex?" I tease.

"Yes," he agrees throatily. "But also fucking *forever*. You make me believe in happy endings, Genevieve."

My heart jumps. Yeah. Good answer.

I stroke him, circling my thumb and forefinger tightly around his slick flesh as I squeeze. "The pink's not forever," I admit, because no matter what, *we* will be. "It's a wash out. Next time I audition, I'll be back to boring blonde."

"Nothing about you is boring," Cross says, and the deceptively lazy look on his face sharpens into one of complete honesty. "You keep me guessing. You make me *feel*. You make me *want*."

"Oh?" I tug on him, swiping the head of his cock over my bottom lip. "And what is it you want?"

"*You*." His chest shudders, his cock seeming to jerk in my hold. Releasing one of his hands from its position behind his head, Cross pats his chest. "Now up," he orders. "You started this, butterfly, and I know where I want to finish it. Bring that pussy over here. I'm dying for—"

I'd barely let go of him when Cross starts to sit up. That same curious expression from before flashes over his features as he says. "Wait. That time... I know I heard something."

"What was it?"

He doesn't even get the chance to answer me because we *both* hear it.

"Gen! Genevieve Libellula! I know you're in there."

I gasp, and Cross closes his eyes. "Fucking hell. I thought he'd at least wait until tomorrow to start shit. I mean, I saw Savannah. Wouldn't he rather be fucking his wife instead of stopping me from fucking mine?"

My girlish little heart goes pitter-pat when Cross mumbles that. Now, I know he's not actually proposing to me. For a man in the life, it's not as easy as that anyway. When a Sinner or a Dragonfly finds a woman that they don't plan on letting go, things like marriage licenses and weddings are more... suggestions than anything else.

This man has a butterfly tattooed on his chest. With a thick black outline and the same detail work as his initial drawing, but dark pink wings that almost match the color I put in my hair the other day.

He removed his pants and fucked me on his motorcycle within minutes of seeing me grinding with another guy.

He told me he loves me...

Yeah. I'm his wife.

And it's time my brother realizes that I stopped being the little girl he raised a long, long time ago.

mariposa

TWENTY-FOUR

DAMIEN

GENEVIEVE

One bonus to being five years younger than Cross plus a professional ballerina, even if I'm a little rusty? I'm quick and I'm fast and I dance out of his reach before he can try to convince me that going downstairs and confronting Damien is probably not the smartest thing to do right now.

Of course it is. Wait? Me? Oh, no. Besides, with Damien bellowing like a wounded rhino out there, I should go see him before someone puts him out of his misery.

Third Avenue isn't really open after dark. I'm not too worried about Cross's neighbors hearing my brother, but as annoyed as I am with him, I still care for him greatly. He's not just my brother. He's the head of the Dragonflies. He might have a truce with the Sinners, but what if some other enterprising gangster takes advantage of Damien being on Sinners turf, searching for me?

I know he's not an idiot. If he's here, odds are he either has Savannah or Vin with him.

Both, it turns out. Savannah is sitting in the front seat of Dame's flashy red Maserati, with Vin's legs up almost by his ears as the big guy is crammed into the back.

Damien is waiting outside of the studio, tapping his foot on the sidewalk as I struggle to get the door unlocked. By the time I do, Cross has caught up with me, but he knows better than to get involved as I march outside of his studio to confront Damien.

Nope. Like Savannah and Vin, Cross is *my* backup.

"Damien Libellula." I perch my hands on my hips, glaring up at my older brother. Like always, his hair is perfectly styled, highlighting that silver streak of his. He's wearing another of his expensively tailored suits, like this is just another business meet for the head Dragonfly, instead of a worried brother coming after his sister. But that's the thing... *how* did he find me? "You swore that you wouldn't put one of those stupid trackers in me."

Unless Savannah snitched. I glance over at her, knowing that my voice carried enough that, through the open window, she could hear me. She gives me an answering shrug and rolls her eyes at Damien's back.

I stifle a chuckle. Hey. She's the one who chose to marry him.

Clearing his throat, Damien pulls my attention back to him. He gives me a pointed look. "You swore that I wouldn't have to worry about my sister sneaking out anymore."

I jut my chin at him. "I didn't sneak anywhere. If you were checking your precious cameras, Dame, you would've seen me strolling on out to meet Christopher at the gate."

Damien raises one eyebrow. "Would that be the same Christopher who hung onto his job by the skin of his teeth after he came to me and admitted that you went missing the first time? Or the Christopher who called me up when he discovered you slipped out of the Devil's Playground tonight?"

Oh. That's how he found me.

I can't even get pissed at Christopher. It's bad enough he had to take the fall for years of my risky behavior, but after Damien gave him a second chance, I should've known that he'd go running to my brother the second he couldn't find me.

Whoops. I guess I was too busy getting banged by Cross to remember that Christopher was my ride tonight. When I disappeared right after I waved him off after Cross found me dancing with another man, it wouldn't take a genius to realize I left with him.

Where else would we go? Since Cross owns the tattoo parlor and lives above it, it was a pretty safe bet we'd have gone here.

Does that mean Damien had to head across the city to confront us?

He takes in my mussed hair, askew and definitely racy

shirt, and crooked shorts. His gaze travels over Cross's unbuttoned jeans and shirtless chest.

My brother is *forty*. I remember telling him after I accidentally walked in on him and Savannah that first time, I never expected him to be a virgin at his big age. Thanks to Winter being a voyeuristic freak with a mean streak, Damien knows I'm not a virgin anymore, either. Even if he tried to pretend that that first time didn't count —since, look at him, the thought of his baby sister getting laid is turning his tanned complexion a little bit green— the scent of sex clinging to us, coupled with our obvious states of undress and... yeah.

We were fucking like bunnies earlier tonight, and Damien knows it.

Hell. If he hadn't interrupted us, we might've been well on our way to round two. As it is, I'm talking to him with the taste of Cross's cock in my mouth. His wife worships his cock. Why can't I worship *my* lover's?

And the fact that impulsively reckless Genevieve was seconds away from snapping that at Damien when we're both emotionally charged and our significant others are standing right there is a bad, bad idea...

Then again, since I want to head back upstairs with Cross, that's all the more reason to send Damien on his merry way—no matter how I can.

I try the easy way first.

"Well, you found me. I'm perfectly safe. Look." I gesture at myself. "Managed not to get kidnapped by one of your enemies and tossed in a cell this time, left to rot unless I fucked my cellmate." Okay. Maybe I'm still really pissed that Damien turned Cross against my 'for my own good'. "Aren't you proud?"

Damien winces. He doesn't even pull the old 'pinch the bridge of his nose' move and sigh like usual. The distinguished mafia leader *winces*, and I just don't care.

I dare him to answer. Again, he clears his throat, and then his icy blue gaze lands on Cross.

"Butterfly," Damien says thoughtfully. He nods at Cross's chest. "Looks fresh compared to the others."

"Fresh enough," Cross agrees. "But it was a long time coming."

"Mm." He turns to me again. "Sorellina."

Little sister.

Yeah. I know. That's what I've always been to Damien.

"Fratello," I retort.

Brother. It's about all the Italian I know, and mainly because of how often Damien called me 'sorellina' when I was younger. But that's the key word there: younger. I will always be fifteen years his junior. That doesn't mean I didn't grow up.

I did—and whether he likes it or not, it's time he realizes that.

Damien can see something shift in my expression. He gives his head a royal shake, then gestures toward the car. "Come. We're going home."

The hell we are.

At my side, Cross stiffens. His expression is closed-off, but I look at his eyes and I see resignation. I challenged him to reject me again on his terms, whether he realized I did or not, by showing up at the Devil's Playground. Did I know that he'd be there? Actually, I doubted he would be. But after everything that happened with Johnny Winter, I figured that there'd be more than a few Sinners lurking around the nightclub who would recognize me and jump to be the one to tell Cross that I was there.

It worked, too.

Part of me guessed that Damien was the reason behind Cross's sudden silence. Cross admitted as much. But then he promised me forever, and backed it up with the reveal of the butterfly on his chest.

The least I can do is accept it.

I step back lightly on my feet, grabbing his bicep. "No. I'm staying here. With Cross."

Damien firms his jaw. "Genevieve."

"I said no, Damien." I squeeze Cross's arm. "I'm not a child anymore. I'm twenty-five-years-old. If I want to spend the night at my boyfriend's house, I'm going to do that. Unless you'd rather I take my boyfriend home with me?"

"Boyfriend," murmurs Cross.

"Okay. Boyfriend does sound kind of juvenile," I admit. "But I thought, if I said 'lover', Damien might blow a gasket. Besides, you're the first boyfriend I've ever had."

"The only boyfriend you'll *ever* have," he interjects.

I laugh. Now how did I know that would be his reaction? "Right. Still, I've never got to use the term before. Let me have it for now."

Cross sighs in almost mock resignation. "I guess it'll do until you call me 'husband'."

I kiss his butterfly, and for a second, I completely forget that Damien is still standing right there. It's usually so hard to ignore his presence, but over the years, I've had some practice at it. Besides, as far as I'm concerned, I made my stance very clear. I'm not going anywhere with Damien.

Not now.

Not until I forget how stinking pissed I am at him.

Knowing my moods, that won't take long, but for fuck's sake? Can't he at least let me have tonight?

Seems like that answer is actually *yes*.

We look at each other, my brother and me. Something passes between us, and Damien bows his head just enough to have my heart fluttering in my chest.

"Well," he says, "it seems as if I might've interrupted something that I would've much preferred not to interrupt. In that case, I'll leave you two to it. But Genevieve? I expect you home tomorrow for dinner."

I try not to let my smile widen too much. "I need studio time. Don't forget, I have that new company to audition for. Remember, Savannah? Riverside? So I'll be home early and I'll stick around—but only if Cross can eat with us."

Damien exhales. "If he must. But just dinner. If you want to spend the night with your... boyfriend, then you can do so here."

"It's called fucking, honey," calls out Savannah.

"Thank you, cara mia," responds Damien. "And just to prove that your husband hasn't forgotten the word at all, I'll make sure to lead you right to the bedroom once we're home again."

Vin groans. "Can you drop me off at Il Sogno first? I could use a glass of wine before I pretend like I'm not the only Libellula not getting laid tonight."

"I think that can be arranged, Vin. Especially since it seems as though I was a little hasty to think Genny needed another rescue." Damien smiles indulgently at me as he reaches the driver's side, then nods at Cross. "In fact, I'd be more concerned about her young man here."

Cross's arm lowers, draping around my waist as he tugs me close to him. "I think I can handle her."

Savannah's husky laugh carries over to us on the still night air. "That's what he thought, too."

As Damien lets himself into the car, head shaking even as he immediately grabs for Savannah's hand, I can't help but grin.

If my relationship with Cross ends up half as strong as the one Damien found in his would-be murderess, I might just get my happily-ever-after after all...

mariposa

TWENTY-FIVE
FIRE

A WEEK LATER

I smell smoke.

The instant the tell-tale aroma hits my nostrils, I'm already wide awake. I never thought I'd be grateful for a lifetime of insomnia and shitty sleeping habits, but though I only went down about an hour ago, sleeping fitfully at best, I smell smoke and I'm *up*.

Where is it? I breathe in, trying to make sure that I'm not imagining it. I cough, and I'm sure I'm not. That this isn't just the remnants of a lifetime of remorse over surviving a fire by constantly dreaming that I'm in one.

Then my fire alarm starts to blare, the high-pitch nearly deafening me, and it's clear that this isn't my worst nightmares come true. This is happening, and I need to get out *now*.

I fell asleep in my t-shirt and jeans. With Genevieve staying at her brother's house last night because she's going to meet with a new company in the morning, there was no reason to strip down, especially when I doubted I'd get any sleep at all. I need to be holding onto my butterfly for any peace, but as the alarm seems to quiet in my frantic mind, I'm so fucking grateful that I slept alone.

When I look at Genevieve, I still see flames, but I never, ever want her to experience fire.

I don't have any shoes. There's no time to grab them. I don't even think about necessities like keys or my phone or ID or any of that shit. It's only about getting out before the fire finds *me*.

My apartment is on the second floor. I never minded the cramped space because I knew for sure that there was a window off my bedroom that led right to a fire escape, and to me, that was more important than more square footage. If my family had a way out, they might have survived, and in any place I lived after that, I always needed an escape.

Now I race for it, grabbing the edge of the window.

Shit. Whether it's my fear spiking or my sudden anxiety making my hands worthless, I can't get a grip on the window. It's like someone glued it down or something, and no matter how much effort I put into it, I can't get it up.

Okay. *Okay*. The fire alarm is still blaring, the smoke

is getting thicker, and since the upstairs consists of my sleeping area, my bathroom, and the kitchen, I can sweep my gaze over the entire space and see that there's no fire up here.

That means the fire is downstairs—and so is my only other means of escape.

Hoping that the fire is mainly contained so I can get the hell out of here, I take the stairs three at a time. The doorknob that separates my studio from the stairwell is warm, not scorching, so I think... maybe. Maybe it's a small electrical fire that's only so bad because of the smoke.

The smoke is definitely something. As I pull open the door, I throw my hand up over my face, choking on the thick, black smoke.

The fire is *everywhere*. It looks like someone flitted around my space, leaving a trail behind them, and the fire is following that exact path. It hasn't consumed every-thing yet, but give it a few more minutes, and the entire place will be engulfed in flames.

That means I have one shot to get out of here, and I'd feel a whole better if most of the fire didn't cut me off from the front door.

The window, I think, stumbling toward it. There's a clearer path to the shop's glass window, and I'm thinking of ways to break it when I see the familiar face staring back at me through it.

For a heartbeat, I'm back in Hamilton. There's the

thick glass wall of our cage, and the leering bastard on the other side.

Only I'm in Springfield again, and someone is standing in front of my window, mesmerized by the flames.

Mickey fucking Kelly.

Oh, hell, no.

He sees me. He sees me bursting out of the smoke, trying my best to avoid the fire as I move toward him. He sees me, and he *waves*.

Later, I'll realize that I never even thought about what I was going to do. As if on instinct, I whirled around, searching for the rolling stool I use for tattooing my clients. It has a padded leather seat—and thick metal legs that end in wheels.

Grabbing it by the seat, avoiding the hot metal legs, I start hitting the glass window as hard as I can.

The fire must've done enough damage to weaken the structure of the glass. After three hits, it splinters. Mickey's amused expression dies, and the prick takes off down the street before the fourth strike has the glass raining down on me. I don't even hesitate. Closing my eyes only long enough to make sure I don't get any glass shards in them, I shake the glittering glass off the best I can, toss the seat behind me, and climb through the open frame.

I've inhaled smoke. I don't know where the flames touched me, only that the adrenaline coursing through me is enough to postpone the pain wherever they licked at my skin. The glass could've torn my flesh to ribbons and it doesn't matter. I take off running the second my feet hit the sidewalk.

Mickey had a head start. No doubt about that. But this is my turf, I'm at least a decade younger, and I'm *furious*. I catch up to him in no time, throwing all of my weight at him to tackle him to the sidewalk.

He's gotta weigh at least two hundred pounds, but when he face-plants on the rough ground with me on top of him, I roll off, then flip him over before straddling his gut.

He smirks. His chin is split and his nose is already bleeding from the fall, and still he smirks. "Knew you were a fag. Just can't wait to get on top of me, huh? Guess it's better than you wanting my cock up your ass."

Mickey thinks he can distract me with his homo-phobia bullshit? "You lit my fucking place on fire?"

He shrugs, and I lose any self control I might've had left.

I whale on him. Pinning him with my legs, I go for the face to stun him, then lower my aim to his chest when he starts bucking his hips, trying to shake me off of him.

I'll give him credit. He takes the beating, only grunting as each hit lands, and when I take a second's pause to see how he'll respond, he sucks in a breath and asks me in a strangled voice, "Did you really think I was going to let what you did to me go?"

I hit him again, going for the gut. If he can still talk, I haven't made enough of an impact on him yet. "If you were smart, you would've. And you wouldn't have stuck around after you struck a match."

He grunts, but refuses to lose that mocking glare. "Can you blame me? I wanted a front-row seat to see you burn."

"Well, I didn't." I tighten my fingers so that the next punch to his jaw hurts both of us. My fingers scream, but Mickey doesn't. Not yet, at least.

He grins, his mouth bloody this time. I got a good, square hit and he thinks it's *funny*. "For as much as that cost me, I'll be asking for a refund then."

I don't understand. Is he insane? I plow my fist into his cheek, his head snaps, and as soon as he shakes off the hit, he's talking nonsense about refunds. A refund on what? The accelerant he used that failed to catch?

"Winter lost, you dick. Even he hasn't come after me yet. If *he's* smart, he's written off Springfield and moved on. But you had to come back with *fire*?"

"Got your attention, didn't I? Besides, you're the fucking moron who slipped up. You really think this is still about a job? Fuck, no. This is personal. And I'm going to make it personal if it's the last thing I do."

Oh, trust me. *That* was the last thing he did.

As though he really believes he's getting out of this confrontation alive, Mickey laughs. His face is covered in blood, one eye already swelling shut from my fists, and he laughs.

"Beat the shit out of me if you want. That won't stop what's coming. You were only the first target. I'm gunning for that Libellula bitch next." He spits in my face, the glob hitting me right in the cheek. "For Noah."

Genevieve.

Bracing his shoulders with my hands, ignoring the spit dribbling down my cheek, I lower my face until we're almost nose to nose. "I'll kill you before I ever let you get near her."

Mickey's eyes are insane. That's the only way to describe them, and he has to be because no one sane would taunt a Sinner while he's at his mercy.

But that's exactly what he does. "What you did to my cock was reflex. I was so big, you couldn't help but bite down, da Silva. But killing anyone? You're a fucking pansy. You ain't got the balls. That's why that cunt took out Noah. *You* couldn't. *Cocksucker.*"

Throwing my trauma in my face would've been enough to earn him a death sentence. But threatening Genevieve?

I take two fistfuls of Mickey's hair. Rearing back, I grab his head as I move, then shift forward, cracking the back of his skull against the asphalt. There's a sickening crunch as his eyes flutter and roll back, showing off the whites.

My chest is heaving. Adrenaline has me smashing his head again once more for good measure before climbing off of him. I don't know if he's dead yet. He might be, but if he isn't? He will be soon.

But I can't leave him here to die. The cops in Springfield are crooked as hell. Devil has half the force on his payroll, with Damien owning the other. Sinners and Dragonflies can get away with a lot, but murdering a man in cold blood and leaving the body out for civilians to stumble over? Even a guy like Officer Burns, one of Devil's most bought beat cops, would have to call that in.

No. I've got to deal with this.

Besides, it's not like I can save my studio. I'm the only one on this strip who lives in an apartment over their shop, so the street's empty. I hate to think that my neighboring stores might go up in flames because they have the misfortune to be built next to mine, but they have smoke alarms to go with their burglary ones. I do, too. I wouldn't be surprised if the SFD is already on their way to battle the blaze.

And that means I need to get Mickey out of here *now*.

My bike's out of the question. My keys are still in the apartment upstairs, and I couldn't leave Springfield with an unconscious body strapped to my back. I don't own a car, and without my phone, I can't call any of my fellow Sinners to help me with this. Rolls would drop everything in a heartbeat to help me fix this mess, but he's all the way at Paradise Suites with his wife.

And this fucker made it a point to threaten the woman I mean to make mine.

Growing up in Springfield, a kid can pick up quite a few skills. Especially when he graduates high school and, following after his friend, falls in with the wrong crowd. Rolls idolized Devil when he was a brawler fighting for cash, and he ended up using his quick fingers as both a pickpocket and the best three-card monte player on the streets. Me? In between doodles and the odd piece of graffiti before I met my mentor and got into ink, I stole more than my fair share of cars.

Chop shops paid enough for me to survive after I got kicked out of foster care. I stopped once I got my own studio and my career started to take off, but there are some things you never forget how to do.

I grab Mickey by the feet, hauling him into the nearest alley. Once he's out of sight, I go jogging up and down the row of parked cars that cover the street no matter what time of night it is. This is one of the only parts of Springfield where parking is always free, so even if the Third Avenue shops are shut-up, someone's always gonna park out this way to avoid congestion pricing.

The first thing I learned when it came to stealing cars? Some people make it just so *easy* to do. All it takes is one idiot to forget to lock their door and I'm in. I don't have a screwdriver to remove the panel of wires, so that might be a problem, but my faith in the sheer stupidity of civilians is proven once again when—after only hitting eight cars and not triggering a single alarm—I find an old ass two-door Hyundai with the key still in the ignition.

Yes.

I slip into the seat, starting the car right up. I peel out of the spot, adding the stench of burning rubber to the overwhelming fire in the air, and back up to the alley where I left Mickey's body.

He's still out. Obviously. The dead weight makes it a

bitch to heft him up, but I'm particularly motivated. Plus, I didn't really care if he gets banged up as I toss his top half into the open trunk, then shove in his legs until he's folded up like a pretzel in there.

That done, I slam the trunk down and get back into the still running car. In the distance, I can make out the scream of a fire engine's siren. Just before they appear in my rear view mirror, I shift the car into drive and take off into the night.

mariposa

TWENTY-SIX

PIT STOP

CROSS

I make one pit stop on the way out of Springfield.

It's quarter after two in the morning. The only store I could find that might have what I need is this rundown big box knock-off that has bars on its windows, three cars in the lot, and a maybe eighteen- or nineteen-year-old manning the only cashier lane that's open.

He was scrolling his phone when I jogged through the door, my bare feet slapping against the sticky tile. I can't tell if it's the noise that startled him, or a lack of usual customers coming in at this hour, but he glances up with a sneer—and quickly loses it when he meets my eye.

The poor kid gulps. "Hey. Um, You need any help?"

A ton of it, I'm sure.

I shake my head. "Nope. Know exactly what I came in here for."

"Oh. Cool. Well... if you need anything, I'll be over here."

As far away from me as he can get, I bet.

I nod, then look around. I've never been here before, but these stores are basically the same. Ducking down the aisle of men's clothing, I keep going until I hit the shoe section. I find the first pair of boots in my size I can find, rip off the price tag, and tug them on. I do up the laces so I don't trip, then go jogging for housewares.

In less than five minutes, I have everything I need—and no way to pay for any of it. So instead of heading toward the check-out, I go right for the exit.

I know what I must look like. I definitely smell like smoke. I walked into this store without any shoes on, only to have a pair on my feet now. My knuckles are swollen. I've got blood spatter dotting my face, my arms, my neck. It's hard to pick it up on my inked skin or my black t-shirt, but you can't miss it on my face.

I look like a deranged guy who just might have an unconscious man in the trunk of his stolen car—which is exactly what I am.

The kid from before gets this expression on his face like he's going to shit his pants as I bear down on him. I almost regret it, but then I remember the way Mickey threatened Genevieve. He tried to burn down my place, and that would've earned him an early grave as it is, but for threatening my butterfly?

I'm not going to make it quick.

For so long, I've kept my trauma behind a cage inside

my chest. What happened to me as a kid fucked me up. It fucked me up so bad, I've spent twenty years pretending it didn't happen. I don't know if it was Mickey's intention or not, but by setting that fire, by trying to *burn me alive* just like what happened to my family... he's unlocked that cage, and now he has to deal with *me*.

I buried Carlos when all that was left of Ana Lucia, Rafe, and my poor mother were scattered ashes and bones. He was a scared, angry little boy who became a guarded, impassive man who only found any hint of joy in the art he created with a little ink and a tattoo needle.

Until Genevieve. Until her flames thawed out the icy remains of a battered and bruised heart.

If I had lost her, well and truly lost her and her love, I would've let the flames consume me tonight. I know that. After what happened in Hamilton, I was on a collision course with the death I narrowly escaped when I left home after the last time my stepfather hurt me. Having known what it was like to be loved by Genevieve Libellula once, I don't think I could've survived much longer without her.

But she's mine now. And there isn't anything I won't do to keep her.

So, yeah. I regret that I'm probably scaring the shit out of this poor overnight clerk, but it can't be helped.

I show him the rope I picked up. The knife I snagged from the housewares section of the store. The shovel I have tucked under my arm. The price tag from the shoes I shoved my feet into.

"It's an emergency," I tell him. "I forgot my wallet, but I can come back and pay for these in the morning if that's cool."

Then, just in case he missed it on my way in, I not-so-discreetly tap the devil on my arm.

Either he thinks I'm some insane man trying to steal from his shop, or he'll recognize the devil and know I'm a Sinner. I'm leaving with this shit regardless. I just hope he has the good sense not to get in my way.

"Yeah, no. Don't worry about it. It's fine." He gulps again. "Besides, we don't, like, have cameras or anything. So, uh, you can just go and it's like you were never here."

Smart kid. "Thanks. Appreciate it, man."

"You, too," he says quickly, and I swear I can hear his knees knocking from where I'm standing by the open door. "Have a good rest of your night."

I grin, and he blanches. "Oh. I *will*."

IT'S A SHAME. I SCREWED UP THAT POOR KID FOR NOTHING.

Well. Not really. I needed the boots to go marching off into the woods where I planned on burying Mickey Kelly when I was done with him. Same thing with the shovel since I wasn't about to dig up the dirt with my hands. But the knife and the rope? Damn it. I had *plans* for those.

Too bad that Mickey had the indecency to die before I could get to them. He made a hell of a mess in the trunk of the car, too, which I feel a little bad about; the owners are gonna be in for a surprise when I return the car and they see the dried blood in the back. If I hadn't just watched my life's work go up in smoke, plus everything I own, I might feel worse, but as I glare down at Mickey's corpse, I only wish I could've gotten more information about what exactly he planned to do to Genevieve if he'd managed to off me first.

He'll never get the chance now. Dumb fuck wanted revenge for what I did, then to go after my butterfly because she had no choice but to take out that other prick who lorded over us the entire time we were held as Winter's prisoner.

Mickey's dead. Noah's dead. I don't know about Baker, and between Devil and Damien, Winter's days are definitely numbered. The leader of his gang of Snowflakes seems to be a pro at hiding—especially since he technically doesn't even *exist* as he and his brother were playing the part of one man before Johnny took over the operation on his own—but I have faith that he'll get what's coming to him, too.

Just like this asshole did.

At least I know that there's one target off of Genevieve's back. Underestimating Mickey was my mistake; after he left the compound to get his cock reattached, I figured I'd never have to worry about him anymore. I'm just grateful that he decided to come for me first, but I know I won't be able to end this night until I have Genevieve in my arms again, assuring myself that she's alright.

After that, this staying apart shit is *done*. Her brother doesn't want me staying at her place, and because of her studio, there are times she can't stay at mine, but keeping us apart at all? No fucking way. My place is gone now. Sinners & Saints? Destroyed. I had to leave the fire behind me after I took off to go after Mickey, but that's just stuff. I can replace it.

If anything happens to Genevieve... there's no replacing *her*.

I need to see her. To hold her. To see that she's okay. I can't call her. Like everything else I owned, I left my phone in the fire. My keys. My wallet. None of that mattered before, but that just means I have a stolen car, stolen shoes, and a dead man I need to get rid of.

But once I've got Mickey Kelly in a shallow grave, I'm taking one more joyride before I return the car where I found it. It's the middle of the damn night. So long as I bring it back before dawn, I should be fine, especially since there's gotta be firetrucks blocking the street by now, dealing with the inferno I ran away from.

Hmm. In that case, maybe I'll abandon the car a couple of miles out and hoof it. Let the cops deal with the missing car and the blood in the trunk, and I'll just stroll up to the charred remains of my old life after the fire's gone.

Who needs the past when I have a future with my butterfly to look forward to?

mariposa

TWENTY-SEVEN
THREE A.M.

GENEVIEVE

I can't sleep.

I got spoiled. Assuming I already wasn't, ever since the night I slept over at Cross's apartment a week ago, I've gotten used to snuggling up against him, sleeping in his arms. There was something different about it, too. When we were being held captive by Winter, we were clinging to each other because we were all each other had.

Now? It's still so new, knowing that Cross is mine and that I'm his, but when we're in the same bed—whether we're sleeping or fucking—there's such a beauty in the fact that we don't *have* to do this. We *get* to do this. We're free to choose each other.

Damien still won't budge when it comes to letting Cross stay over, and since he's more than happy to host me, I've spent every night in his apartment this past week —until tonight.

I knew better than to try and convince myself that I could sleep with Cross, then get up bright and early to prepare for my meet with Director Adamson of the Riverside Ballet Corps. I need to be in top form, stretched out, limber, and ready to shine in case he auditions me for a place in his company on the spot. Cross offered to drive me in the morning if I stayed over, but I had to refuse.

I have a routine. It's the same one I've done for every performance, every audition, every competition since I turned ballet from a hobby to a career. I know me. Cross would inevitably point out how sexy I am in the splits while I'm stretching, and I'll end up showing him just how flexible I am in a way that'll only leave me too tired to be at my best for the meeting.

Part of that routine? I'm in bed by nine-thirty. Asleep by ten. With Orion curled up by my pillow, I managed it, though my sleep was fitful at best. I kept waking up, checking my phone to see the time, and rolling over again.

It's three in the morning when something pulls me out of my slumber.

I scowl when I see the time. Three a.m.? Seriously? I don't have to be up for three more hours to shower, stretch, and do my hair and makeup.

I'm on my back now, the weight of Orion pressed against my chest while he lays on top of me. As I toss my phone again, shifting my body enough to disturb the cat, he gets up, pressing down on my tits.

"Ow," I mumble. "Get off, you butt."

Orion stretches, his big, furry behind in my face. I shove his rump, and he turns, giving me a baleful look.

"You weigh, like, twenty pounds, Orion. You're squishing my tit. Go."

He pads down to the end of the bed, but right as I'm ready to move onto my side so I can get those three hours of sleep, I go still.

I hear voices.

My heart lodges in my throat. For a hot second, I'm back in the cell, only it's dark instead of the constant bright lights that tortured us. Listening for footsteps, dreading that I would hear voices, hoping they would leave us alone...

Wait. I *know* those voices.

Damien. Savannah.

Why are they arguing in the hall outside of my room when they both know damn well that I *need* to *sleep*?

I give them a couple of seconds to shut the fuck up, and when they don't? I throw my comforter back, storm across my room until I've reached the door, and fling it open.

"Are you serious?" I demand. "This is the first role I'm looking to land in *months*, and you two decide to have a stupid lovers quarrel outside of *my* room? What's wrong with yours?"

Damien thins his lips. At first, I think it's because I

yelled at him, but he should be used to that by now. But then I notice the way that Savannah is glaring at him, Damien jutting his chin just so as if in defiance, and I know... I *know* that something's wrong.

Savannah crosses her arms over her chest. "Tell her. Tell her now, Damien. Because, if you don't, I will, and when Gen never forgives you for treating her like a kid about *this*... I won't blame her."

My stomach drops. "Dame? What's going on?"

Damien takes a deep breath. "There's nothing you can do now. Let me say that plain: I wanted to wait until the morning when we might know more, but as you see, my wife obviously disagrees. And..." he sighs. "Savannah is right. If it was her, I'd want to know."

If it was her, I'd want to know...

I reach out, digging my nails in his arm. The fact that he's wearing a button-down shirt and a pair of suit pants, like he was ready to head out on Family biz at three a.m. should've been my first clue that something wasn't right. Savannah is wearing an oversized t-shirt that she either slept in or must've just pulled on, but Damien is only missing his shoes.

And without him telling me, I *know*.

"Cross," I whisper. "What happened to Cross?"

My brother takes another, deeper breath, then says the four words that have my knees going weak beneath me as I fall into his arms:

"There's been a fire."

Cross isn't dead. He *can't be*.

So he's not answering his phone. So Devil called Damien after the Springfield Fire Department got the blaze partway under control. As of three o'clock, when Damien got the call and debated with Savannah all the way up to my room whether or not he should tell me that Sinners & Saints was gone, there were still a few hot spots. The fire burned long enough, though, that if Cross was asleep in his bed when the fire broke out and couldn't escape, there's no reason for anyone to check for survivors.

Which is fine. Because he's not dead.

I know that man. The only time he sleeps, it's when I'm with him. No way in hell did he miraculously beat his insomnia in time to die the same sort of death that's haunted him since he was twelve. He had to have gotten out.

Does that explain why no one has heard from him? As the man who technically owns Sinners & Saints since it's a Sinners Syndicate property, when the fire alarm went off, the company called Cross first, then Devil.

The mafia leader got in touch with Rolls McIntyre, Cross's friend I haven't met just yet. I still haven't. As the boss, Devil decided to come down to look at the fire himself. Rolls stayed back at the luxury apartment building where both he and Devil live with their families. He's with his wife, plus Devil's wife and kid, in case this is the next stage in a continued battle between the Spring-field mafias and Winter's Snowflakes.

Damien didn't even try to get me to go back to bed. There was a perfectly good reason why he got dressed before he came upstairs: because he knew damn well that I would insist on heading across Springfield the second I heard the news about the fire.

Five minutes after I pulled myself together, I was dressed, he had his shoes on, and we were on the way.

Time crawled. I must've dialed Cross's phone at least a hundred time before we arrived at the end of his street. Two firetrucks blocked Damien from getting any closer, but before he even killed the engine, I was out of the car, running as close to the smoldering remains of the tattoo parlor as I could.

Damien left his door open, racing after me. Smart man. He knew what I was about to do, and if he hadn't caught up to me, wrapping his arms around me to keep me from running inside, I would've done just that.

The fire's out. Hours after it was set, it's finally died—and I absolutely refuse to believe that Cross died first.

I fought Damien's hold, of course. I needed to check for myself. If he was in there... I don't know what I would do, but at least it would be better than not knowing.

Right?

Devil is standing with his back against his car, glaring at the ruined remains as if it owes him money. Damien keeps his voice low, saying something to the other leader, but over the roar of blood in my ears and devastation in my soul, I'm not listening to them. I'm just waiting for my brother to lose his concentration so that I can stomp on his instep, escape his hold, and get in that place.

And then the only sound I think could've made it through the noise filters its way through my consciousness. Even if Damien was a fucking anaconda, he wouldn't have been able to hold me any longer—

"Butterfly."

Cross.

I break free of Damien, spin on my heel, and there he is.

He's a fucking mess. One of his tatted arms has a long, raw burn on it. His black shirt is singed in places. His hair is sticking up, his face is dotted with... blood? Shit. Is that *blood*? He's flexing his right hand as he stalks toward me, and all I notice is that his knuckles are split before realization slams into me and relief nearly knocks me on my ass.

I knew it. I *knew* it.

He's *alive.*

I throw myself at him, laughing and sobbing at the same time as I run my hands over his hair, his neck, his back. I kiss every inch of skin I can reach because, if I'm being real, I knew he wasn't dead but could I really have been sure?

He's murmuring my nickname over and over again, clutching me to him. He smells like smoke and oil, but he's here, and he's alive, and I almost want to throttle him for scaring the shit out of me.

Damien clears his throat. I nearly kick out behind me at him to shut him up, but because he brought me here—and because he's my brother and I do love him—I refrain from unleashing one of my arabesques straight to his nuts.

Instead, I pull back enough so that both Cross and I can see that Devil and Damien are right there.

Cross straightens up. Whether it's because he's facing my brother or his boss, I don't know, but he throws an arm over my shoulder, tethering me to him, as he nods at the two men.

"So," Devil rumbles, "you got out. I'd hoped so when the firefighters said the window was smashed and they didn't do it. It didn't look like it was from the fire."

"No, boss," Cross answers. "Someone jammed my window. I couldn't go for the fire escape, so I threw my stool through the glass to keep from roasting in there."

Okay. I get that... kinda. Maybe not the window being jammed part—because, damn, that's suspicious—but smashing the glass to escape? Cross tried the same thing when we were being held captive, and I'm so fucking glad it worked this time.

So, yeah, I get that... but where the hell has he been since then? And why did he only just show up *now*?

Before I can demand that he tell me, Devil has another question for Cross:

"What do you think? Was it Winter?"

In the car, Damien said as much to me. That when he spoke to Devil, they came to the agreement that Winter had decided to get revenge on us for escaping him by targeting the easiest one of us to get to. Cross's apartment was the perfect target over my brother's man, but if I'd been on Third Avenue with Cross... well, two birds with one stone, right?

I squeeze Cross's side, needing to feel him warm and alive and here with me as I gasp in horror, "Winter tried to burn your place down with you in it?"

He shocks me by shaking his head. "No. But Mickey Kelly sure as hell nearly managed to pull it off."

Wait—*what*?

I'm so stunned to hear that name again that I just gape up at him.

Damien, however, looks at Cross and says: "Explain."

He does. About how he was barely asleep when he woke up to the smell of smoke, just like I figured he would. He went right for the fire escape, and when he saw that the window leading outside was glued shut or locked or something, he didn't waste time with it. He ran downstairs, saw the fire, and noticed Mickey Kelly smirking at him from the other side of the shop glass.

That's when he grabbed his stool, smashed the glass, and, to put it bluntly, beat Mickey to death with his bare hands and the help of the cement sidewalk.

Cross gives me a sideways glance as he goes on to admit that, when he thought Mickey was still alive, he stole a car, threw Mickey in the trunk, drove him out of Springfield while only stopping long enough to steal some rope, a shovel, and a pair of shoes. By the time he arrived at the dumping point where he planned on torturing Mickey to find out what his plans were if he accomplished killing Cross—because seems like I was that sick fuck's next target, whee—he was dead. Cross buried him, then—

He rubs my bicep. "I had to make sure you were okay. My phone burned up in the fire. It was the middle of the night. I drove all the way to the East End to assure myself you were still sleeping soundly. When I saw your light was on, I got worried, because I knew you needed to sleep for your meet this morning."

"Screw my meeting," I say—and I mean it. I can always reschedule or audition for another company. But there's only one Cross, and I don't know what I would've done if I lost him. I squeeze him again. "I'm so fucking happy you're okay."

Cross kisses the top of my head. "You, too, butterfly. I came all the way back here since I really didn't want to break into your place and scare the shit out of you. Besides, what if you decided you got a taste for sleeping with the light on after Winter fucked with us?" I snort at that, and he gives me his first grin since I saw his approach a few minutes ago. "See. Made you laugh."

I know what he's doing. I can only imagine how freaked out I looked when he showed up and proved he survived the fire, and even though I understand better what happened now, that doesn't excuse the fact that I spent the last hour or so losing my mind because I didn't know where he was.

All along, Cross was afraid to treat me like my brother did. I guess he shouldn't have worried after all because, of the two of us, I'm the Libellula here. Which is why, now that I know my love is safe now, I'm going to do everything possible to make sure I *always* know that.

Moving out from under his arm, I jab Cross in his butterfly-covered chest. "You're getting a tracker."

He raises his eyebrows. "What was that?"

"You heard me."

From behind me, Devil makes an amused noise. "You want to give me one reason why I should let you track my artist?"

Crap. I forgot he was there.

Oh, well.

"Why?" I ask, whirling on him. My hands go straight to my hips. "The truce."

Devil scratches his stubble-covered jaw. "I'm listening."

"Springfield runs better when the Sinners and the Dragonflies work together," I tell him.

"That so? It seems to me like we've had nothing but fucking trouble since your brother put a gun to my wife's head."

Oh, come *on*. I resist the urge to turn around and give Damien a dirty look. You'd think that, after all I've seen and done and learned since I broke free from my cage, I wouldn't be surprised hearing more about my brother's ruthlessness.

And then one of his former rivals-turned-allies lets

slip that Damien held a gun to Devil's wife's head. Or I remember that my first meeting with *Damien's* wife came after she stabbed him in the side with his own knife, then he forced her to marry him in return—before 'convincing' her to blow him that very same night.

I shake my head. "Think that if you want. But you have to admit, Winter is still out there. He's still a pain in our ass. Damien might've put a gun to your wife's head, but he didn't pull the trigger—and that's when you were still considered rivals. Can you say the same about the head Snowflake freak?"

Devil's expression turns murderous, and I finally think I understand why they call him by that name. If he sprouted a forked tail or horns right now, I wouldn't be surprised at all.

"I will never let anyone get close enough to Ava again," he growls in obvious warning.

A warning, sure, but it also proves my point.

"Because you track her, don't you?" I glance at Damien who has his features twisted in a haughty yet slightly innocent expression that tells me that everything Devil accused my brother of was true. "I know you and Savannah can find each other. Why can't I find the man who means everything to me?" Back to Devil, and I amaze myself by not quailing under his stare. Damien doesn't scare me. Devil? He's *terrifying*. "You can track me if you want."

"You wouldn't let me," my brother points out.

Yeah, well, obviously. If Damien could track my every

move, I would've never had any freedom. He would've kept me locked up, safe and sound, and it wouldn't have been necessary to have a tracker at all if I never left the third floor.

"I love him," I say simply. "I love you, too, Dame, but not like I do Cross." I turn, searching for Cross, unwilling to look away from him for too long in case he disappears again. When I see the love and affection and worry in his dark eyes... I fling myself at him, wrapping my arms around his waist, burying my face against his chest. "You're mine."

His arms close around me. Cross rests his chin on the top of my hair, giving me a squeeze as he whispers, "From the moment I drew that butterfly, I've been yours. Track me if you want. If I have it my way, I'll never be apart from you again."

Know what? I don't care if it's crazy. I don't care if it's possessive. I don't care if he decides that I'm too much to handle and he wants to get rid of me after all.

Good luck, babe.

Forever?

I'm going to hold him to it.

mariposa

EPILOGUE

CROSS

THREE MONTHS LATER

I knock on the door to Genevieve's private studio. "Butterfly? You ready for me yet?"

She lowers the music so that I can hear her call back, "Almost. I'm just getting my new costume on. Then I'll show you the piece I plan on auditioning with tomorrow."

Leaning with my shoulder against the wood, I smile. "You don't have to get dressed up for me for that. You know I love you in anything. Especially when I get to watch you dance."

"Who are you kidding, Cross? You love me in *nothing* best."

"Mm," I agree. "And that's because, when you're gloriously naked, I get to see just who you belong to."

Genevieve laughs. "That's on you, babe. You told me not to get a tattoo that represents someone until you're sure they're a permanent fixture in your life. You covered your whole damn heart with a butterfly for me. You knew I had to one-up you." Fabric rustles, and I can only imagine the delicious leotard that's wrapping its way up Genevieve's delectable body. "And I did, didn't I?"

"Your cross is barely two inches tall," I remind her.

She squealed the entire time, too, gripping the armrests so tightly as I tattooed her, she left fingernail dips in the leather. It wasn't from pain, though, but because her tat is in an area very sensitive to vibrations. I refused to hurt her, and if I overdid it with the numbing cream, that was because I wanted her first experience with my needle to replace the questionable memories of her first time with my cock.

Genevieve is a fucking angel. She knows how much I still struggle with the aftermath of our time being held by Winter, and it's so much worse that that sick fuck seems to have fallen off the face of the planet. Not even Tanner can find him, and if the Sinner's tech expert hasn't found any sign of Johnny Winter since our rescue—and Tanner's been locked-in after being so pissed to find out that he existed in the first place—there's a good chance another one of his victims caught up to Winter before we could.

And if I try to convince myself of that so that I don't

pull a Damien and lock Genevieve up in our new home in the hopes that no one could ever get to her again, that works, too.

I refuse to see my butterfly caged again. She deserves to be free, and I'm glad she's not worried about Winter and his goons coming after her. She shouldn't be. Between her brother and me, anyone who puts her in their sights will end up in a shallow grave, and that's if they're lucky and they're not kept alive and tortured instead...

"So?" she retorts. "It might not be as elaborate as some of your tattoos, but isn't it the placement that counts?"

"You're right. And that's why I have your butterfly covering my heart."

Genevieve snorts. "Big deal. I let you tattoo a cross on my pussy."

I laugh. Something about Genevieve's blunt way of getting straight to the point... I fucking love it.

Almost as much as I love *her*.

"Okay. You win." I rap my knuckles against the wood, then push away from the door. "Ready now?"

"Five minutes. I just want to stretch a little first, make sure I'm loose and limber before I show you the piece."

"I can help you out with that," I offer, meaning every word.

I think about just how flexible my butterfly is, and how she let me massage her last night in particular after another long training session in her studio. I don't know what I enjoyed more: the feel of her soft skin under my calloused, rough hands, the gentle moans that escaped her when I rubbed out a particularly tense muscle on her back or her calf, or how she was so relaxed by the time I was done, she just laid there as I buried my face in her pussy, capping off her pleasure with an orgasm that had her yanking my hair and screaming.

Good thing our new home is far enough away from our neighbors. Genevieve's screams of pleasure belong to me, especially when she's coming all over my face...

Too bad she doesn't take me up on my offer now. She warned me when we were first talking that while art is my life, dance is hers. After she missed that audition while we were being held captive, part of Genevieve died; when she was forced to shoot Noah, so did another part. I can't bring her back to the woman she was before she pulled the trigger, though I would if I could.

When it comes to ballet?

She wasn't ready to move on from it. I knew that, even when I was torturing myself by staying away. Damien knew it, too. That's why, when her controlling older brother ceded the tiniest bit of it by picking out a house that would work for both my needs and Genevieve's, he made sure there was a front room to serve as my sterilized tattoo parlor, a back room that was a duplicate of Genevieve's dance studio at her brother's home, and an upstairs where we can build our life together.

Just like how I've been scouring the internet for local dance companies that were accepting new dancers, or performing centers hosting auditions for upcoming ballets.

I found one. It's a small theater in Springfield, and they're putting on a month-long showing of *Romeo and Juliet* in the new year. In so many ways, it's the perfect opportunity for Genevieve to dance professionally again, after she couldn't reschedule the meeting she was supposed to have the day after the fire.

She was so disappointed to miss out on Riverside's Christmas ballet, but if she can get a lead part in *Romeo and Juliet*...

Another snort. "I'm sure you could. Now, go. The longer you distract me, the longer until I'm ready to let you in."

"I'll be down here, so just shout when you are."

"Will do!"

Genevieve's private dance studio is at the back of the first floor. Down the hall, past the bathroom, there's another door that separates my studio from her half. I open it, and because I closed my shop up for the night earlier, I don't bother shutting it so that I can hear Genevieve when she calls for me.

Instead, I sit down at my desk, anxiously tapping my fingertips against the top. Normally, I would reach for my iPad or a notebook or something to distract myself with, but since I don't want to get *too* distracted in case I miss it when Genevieve is ready to invite me into her studio, I pull open my drawer instead.

And there it is.

I take out the tiny crystalline figure, holding it lightly between both my pointer fingers and my thumbs. It's about an inch or so high, and depending which way I turn it, the colors shift from different shades of purples and pinks.

I know what it is, too. It's a hummingbird. One of those small birds with the fast wings and a long needle-like beak. I know what it is… I'm just not sure what it was doing in my old studio.

To make it even more mysterious, after the arson investigators came and combed through the ashes of Sinners & Saints—paired up with two guys in Rolls's clean-up crew—this was one of the only things that survived the heat of the blast on the ground floor.

It's a trinket. Cheap. It should've imploded in the flames, and the reason it didn't… the reason why I'm staring at it now, trying to make sense of it… is because of how it was found. Tucked just inside my studio, positioned in a fireproof box that definitely wasn't mine, both Rolls and Devil came to the consensus that whoever poured the gasoline and lit my place on fire left the box behind for someone to find.

As if we had any doubts, the arson investigators confirmed Mickey's babbling confession. That fire was set to kill, and since someone—and odds are it's the same someone—glued my window shut so that I couldn't use the fire escape, it's pretty obvious that I was the intended victim even without Mickey's gloating before I took care of him.

So what's up with the hummingbird? After Rolls had a couple of guys sweep through my old place to make sure they recovered anything I might need, they recovered the small fireproof box and that was about it. I didn't recognize it, but I took it—then almost immediately forgot about it.

Can you blame me? In the same night, I was technically jobless, homeless, and terrified that Genevieve would realize that choosing me as her partner would only put her in *more* danger. The fire triggered my childhood trauma, and though I've accepted I'll never be free of it—or ever get over surviving when my family didn't—it was a bit of a blessing, finally killing off the ghost of my stepfather at the same time as I eliminated Mickey.

That was three months ago. Since then, things have completely turned around.

As his way of showing he accepts our relationship, Damien bought Genevieve the narrow, two-floor house that she accepted as a space of her own. It's a toe over the line into Dragonfly territory, but as long as I can ride my bike to the Playground and get there in no time, Devil was gracious enough to look the other way when it came to one of his top Sinners shacking up with a Dragonfly on their turf.

And if anyone thinks that Devil's gone soft since becoming a girl dad? Just think about what he did to Dave Saunders after he tracked the traitor down—and what he plans to do to Johnny Winter once he gets his hands on him—and you won't have to worry about the Devil of Springfield losing his edge anytime soon.

But the hummingbird...

Someone went through a lot of trouble to plant the figure in a fireproof box so that, after my old place burned down, it would still be there for someone to locate. Obviously, that someone wasn't meant to be *me*, but because it was my shop, Devil decided to give the box to me without even opening it first.

I didn't want it. It was Genevieve who took it, and though I spent a few nights on Rolls's couch because Damien has his limits—and letting his baby sister's lover stay in the manor, plowing her under his roof was definitely one of them—until Genevieve threatened to go no-contact with him if he didn't let her come stay with me, I wasn't sure what ended up happening to it.

Once the initial furor over the fire died down, Devil arranged for Genevieve and me to spend a few weeks in a Sinners-owned hotel on the West End, all while Damien pushed his people to get our joint studios completed. We eventually moved in about a week ago, and as Damien's Dragonflies—led by Genevieve's scowly cousin, Vincent—moved her entire wardrobe into our rooms upstairs, she handed me the fireproof box and told me to open it when I felt ready to.

Because it was important to her, I used a pair of scissors to jimmy it open. Neither one of us could understand what the significance behind the hummingbird was, but I told Rolls and she told her brother, just in case.

That was supposed to be the end of it. Still, barely a week later, I can't keep myself from taking it out, looking it over, and wondering why it's so damn important—

"Babe? I'm ready."

I palm the hummingbird, then place it securely back into the open drawer so that I don't accidentally smash it. Later, I tell myself. I'll figure out the mystery of the hummingbird later.

Rising up, I use my hip to bump the drawer closed. "Coming."

Well, no. That would be great if I was, but since Genevieve made it quite clear that she needs to concentrate on her big audition tomorrow, and it'll be impossible for her to do that if I get her under me, I won't be coming tonight.

Damn it.

I swear, though, that woman is more than just my addiction. She's the air that I breathe, the rhythm of my heart beating, the fire that keeps me going. I went years in between finding someone to lose myself into before forgetting about them once I finished, but since that night outside of the Playground, I consider it time wasted if I don't have her snug pussy wrapped around my cock at least once a day.

She wants this part, I tell myself. She deserves this part.

She's been dancing her ass off for days, proving that she still hasn't lost her talent and her grace. My dick can wait—

—though, I have to admit, the poor thing doesn't quite get *why* when I let myself into Genevieve's studio and see what she's wearing.

It's a costume alright, but my first impression is of those harem girls from old cartoons. Or Jeannie, right? That television show my mom watched on re-runs growing up, with the blondie in the gauzy costume. Only Genevieve's is white fabric so incredibly sheer, I can make out the curves of her hips, the swells of her tits, and, mi amor, the black cross peeking out from the top of her freshly shaved pussy.

I run the back of my hand over my mouth, sure I'm fucking drooling.

She preens, running her hands down the swoopy, draped fabric that covers her from tits to ass. Going up on the balls of her dancer's feet, showing off her pretty pink toenails—and her immaculately shaped body—she gives me a daring look as she pointedly asks, "What do you think?"

That I'm about to jack off to the vision of you in this costume.

No, Cross. That would be fucked-up. She wants you to watch her perform the piece she's going to audition with tomorrow, not yank your cock all because she's the most stunning creature you've ever seen before.

So, swallowing the lump of obvious arousal lodged in my throat, I tell her honestly, "I think if you show up at the audition like that, it doesn't matter if you're a little rusty. When they're looking at you in this, they won't notice if your toes aren't pointed as much as you want. They'll be mesmerized, mi mariposa."

And that's if I can resist the urge to drape her in my leather jacket so that no one else can glimpse this monumental beauty that I'm lucky enough to call *mine*.

Her lips curve upward, a daring smile. "You'd actually let me leave the house like this?"

"Could I stop you?"

She moves into me, patting my chest. "Good answer, babe. But this isn't what I'm wearing to my audition tomorrow."

Thank fucking God. "It's not?"

"No. That one is *way* more see-through."

I grab Genevieve by her hips, pulling her up against my chest as I bend my knees a little. "You're killing me, butterfly. You know that, right?"

Oh, she does. And she *loves* it.

My butterfly drapes her arms over my shoulders, our faces on the same level as she leans in, nipping my bottom lip. "Just wait until you see me move in it."

My cock twitches. "I'm dying to."

She grabs my face, clutching my cheeks as she gives me a quick peck. Letting me go before I can place my hands on the small of her back and deepen her teasing kiss into something that'll get the both of us into trouble, she dances over to the other side of the room.

"Stand over there," she orders, squatting down gracefully so that she can turn the music on—and give me a perfect view of the cleft of her ass through the fabric.

I hate to move, but if that's what Genevieve wants...

"Here?"

"Perfect."

The music starts, she strikes her opening pose, and I stand in one place as my Genevieve, my lover, my muse, *my butterfly* starts to dance.

Usually, Genevieve has her hair up in a tight bun when she's practicing. For some reason, she's left her golden hair down in soft waves. As she spins, it whips around her, a stunning contrast to the sheer white fabric that seems to float all around her.

It's beautiful. Everything about this woman, from her body to her talent to her inexplicable ability to forgive... *she* is beautiful. I've already accepted that I can't exist without her. To do so would be madness, and I've had enough of that to last me a lifetime. For as long as she's content to be mine, I'm going to keep her.

But when I look at her, I still see flames, but I *feel* hope. I feel *love*.

And, like always when Genevieve dances, I'm *inspired*.

I don't know how long she's actually dancing for. She makes it look so effortless, and I could watch her forever, but it seems like no time at all before she goes down on one knee, the other folded to the grand beneath her in her final pose before she pops back up, sweeps her hair over her shoulder, and asks me expectantly, "So? What do you think?"

Honestly?

"I need my pen." I pat my pockets, reaching up to my

ear to check if I've kept one there. Shit. I'm empty-handed. "Let me go grab my iPad. I have to sketch something real quick."

Genevieve knows that that's the highest compliment I can pay her. This sudden need to draw my butterfly swaddled in clouds, wrapped up in a cyclone made up of golden threads... I have the image in my head, one I'm suddenly desperate to get down.

I have room on my thigh. It would be a perfect spot to ink it once I have the design just right—

"Wait."

I'm sure my eyes are wide and frantic. My fingers are twitching like they used to when I overdid the caffeine. I need to draw—

Genevieve wraps her arms around my neck again, pressing her tits against my chest, taking all of my need to draw and, just like that, transferring it straight into a need for *her*.

"What's the rush?" she asks. "Stay here. With me. Draw later."

If I stay in the studio with her, I'll fuck her, and we both know it.

"Genevieve," I groan.

"What's the matter, babe?" she whispers against my lips.

"I'm trying so hard to behave, mi amor," I whisper back, brushing mine against hers. They're so lush and plump, and her taste... God, her fucking *taste*... "You have an audition tomorrow. You need to eat, to hydrate, and then get a good night's sleep."

"Do you know how often people tell me to behave?" Her eyes twinkle mischievously. I never thought I'd see that spark again, but then it came back the night I bent her over my motorcycle—and I'm so incredibly grateful it never left again. "Well?"

"Just as often as you tell them to fuck off?"

Her chuckle is warm on my skin. "Exactly. And speaking of fucking…" She drops her hand, cupping my cock possessively before letting out a sound of pure approval. "I think you're more than ready for me."

I squirm under her forceful hold, doing everything I can not to buck up against her palm as I grate out, "I mean this with all my love, Genevieve, when I tell you that I don't think anyone is ever truly ready for you."

"Maybe not," she says, a hint of a tease in her voice, "but it's always fun to see you try."

Such a tempting minx. I shake my head, hair falling in my face. Genevieve likes it long, and I've been growing it out these last couple of months. It's nowhere near the length it was before I cut off most of it last winter, but when she can't keep her hands away from it, it's *perfect*.

She runs her fingers through the strands, pushing it out of my eyes so that I can look dead into hers.

I see the lust there. The desire. The temptation…

"You need to prepare for your audition," I tell her, not sure if I'm trying to remind her—or convince me.

"No, I don't."

"Genevieve..."

"No. Really. Wait." She bites down on her bottom lip for a second, hiding a teasing smile. "Did I forget to mention that my audition was canceled tomorrow—"

My stomach goes tight. After all her hard work this past week, it was canceled? Or did she cancel it? "Butterfly, no—"

"—because I already got the part."

My stomach lurches, then calms. "What?"

She nods. Then, a wide grin on her gorgeous face, she uses her hands on my shoulders to brace herself before jumping up. Her long legs wrap around my waist, and though she has phenomenal core strength and can hold herself up, I'll never miss the opportunity to get my hands on her ass.

I kiss her quickly, then nuzzle her neck. "I'm so fucking happy for you. But, wait..." I lift my head, searching her face. "Without having to audition?"

She shrugs, still holding tightly to me as she does. "Of course. I mean, I am Genevieve Libellula, after all."

I've never forgotten that for a minute.

I squeeze her ass cheeks. "Don't tell me your brother used his pull to get you in."

Though, if I'm being honest, I wouldn't blame him if he did. Hell, if I could use my Sinners brand to make life easier for Genevieve in Springfield instead of the opposite, I would. I just... I never thought she'd accept that.

And I'm right.

"Please. This is the ballet world. When they hear 'Libellula', it's not Damien they think of. It's me."

I raise my eyebrows at her. Hearing that pride and cockiness in her voice... I palm her ass a second time, pressing her against the noticeable bulge in my jeans. Everything about this woman revs my engine, but Genevieve knowing her worth... if I wasn't afraid of tearing the delicate material that probably cost an arm and a leg, I'd undress her in a heartbeat so that I could get inside of her.

She knows, too. Even though we're both dressed, she arches her back, riding me, making it seem like we're fucking in the mirror surrounding us. I get distracted by the sight of her lithe and graceful body, anything to keep from coming in my jeans like an inexperienced fool, as she does everything she can to make me lose control.

Believe me. She doesn't have to try too hard, only she did, didn't she? If she knew she didn't have the audition tomorrow after all...

"So why did you put on a show for me tonight? The dancing... unh... and the costume?"

"Two reasons, Cross, baby. One: because you love to watch me dance—"

I do. I always will. "Mi mariposa..."

Genevieve grins, then releases me. Just her arms, though, as the strength of her legs and her core keep her wrapped around me as she bends her back far enough that the ends of her hair skim the studio floor.

I don't know what it is that she does exactly, but she

reaches behind her, tugging one of the sweeping pieces of see-through fabric, before shaking her entire top.

Suddenly, to my surprise—and the downfall of my self control—the fabric falls apart. What I thought was a complete costume seems to have really been fabric wrapped all around her, falling like a cocoon as she pulls herself back up, her tits right in my face.

"And two," she adds, "because I couldn't wait to see your face when I did that."

The fabric has pooled at her waist. No longer giving a shit at all if I rip it to shreds, I grab a handful, tugging it until I have a gloriously naked Genevieve Libellula in my arms.

"Like it, babe?"

My answer is to hoist her up with one arm, giving me enough room to unbutton my jeans, yank the zipper down, and get my cock out before positioning her right on top of me.

Forever ready for me, Genevieve is so hot, so wet, so slick, her pussy so hungry for her man, I barely get the head in before her greedy little cunt is swallowing me whole.

She knows that I'm the guy for her. She proved it when she invited me to fuck her the fist time, the second time, and now, every time I work myself into her tight snatch, I revel in it while knowing that there will never be a last time.

Not for my muse and her artist.

This isn't the first time we've fucked in her studio. The

night we moved into the place, she insisted on chris-tening every space—except for my part of the business floor—but while I wasn't about to get come all over the surface where I plan on inking my clients, Genevieve absolutely insisted on watching me fuck her in the room full of mirrors.

And that's what we do right now.

"Yes." Her groan of pleasure is thick and throaty as I jerk my hips, seating myself inside of her. Her nails dig into the material of my shirt, her pussy squeezing me so tightly, I just about nut then and there.

I send another silent thank you over to Savannah, who was the one who insisted on taking Genevieve to get an IUD after she decided she was nowhere near ready enough to get pregnant. We're on the same page there. Devil will go to war to protect baby Clare, and if Rolls and Nicolette have a kid next, good for them, but I just found my muse. She inspires me. She *chose* me. I have no inten-tion of sharing her anytime soon, and with birth control, I don't even have to think about stopping until I've given her every drop of come that I have.

And my dainty ballerina will take it all because she's mine, I'm hers, and no one will ever separate us again.

Not her brother.

Not my own trauma.

Not anyone in the goddamn world.

This is my butterfly, and like the ink on my chest, we're fucking *permanent*.

CROSS
THE ARTIST

Dance with the Devil

GENEVIEVE
THE BUTTERFLY

AUTHOR'S NOTE

Thanks for reading *Dance with the Devil*!

While this book quite clearly ties in to the events of *Dragonfly*—specifically because Damien is Genevieve's overprotective older brother, and because we first meet one of the Winter brothers and his goons in that book—I really wanted to give Genevieve a chance to come into her own, and to explore the quiet artist who joked around with Royce and deferred to Lincoln in previous stories. I love Cross and Gen together, and I can't wait to introduce you to the final couple in the series: Kylie and Luca. Luca, of course, is the driver who risked his safety by returning to Hamilton and working for Winter. As for Kylie... you might not have known she was there, but that's because the Hummingbird is just that fast—and that vicious!

Keep reading/scrolling/clicking to see the cover for the final book in the series—and an insight to these two!

And keep an eye out for two new books, coming soon: *Oubliette* (Haven's story, the mute captive mentioned before she was 'relocated') and *Bloody Wedding* (introducing you to the Order of the Owed).

Also, as always, if you purchase a physical copy of this book—paperback, discreet paperback, or hardcover—send me your name and mailing address via email (carin@carinhart.com) and I'll mail you a free bookmark and a signed bookplate!

xoxo,
Carin

A woman with a secret. A man trying to avoid his past. A case of mistaken identity that changes everything. In this explosive finale, the city of Springfield will never be the same...

KYLIE

It was supposed to be a quick job. I had a name, an address, and a means—and right as I walked on the scene, I watched as the Devil of Springfield himself blew away the vice mayor.

My first instinct is to wash my hands of the whole thing, but before I can get out of there, I'm caught and, well, *caught.*

I've had some wild experiences in my line of work, but being grabbed and tossed in the back of a trunk? That takes the cake, and by the time I'm brought to a small hideaway, I'm kind of just wondering what's going to happen next.

To be honest, I'm expecting a bullet in my skull, and I'm kind of welcoming it—and that's when I meet Luca, a member of the Sinners Syndicate... and my new babysitter.

He tells me this is just to keep me safe. That his boss wants me dead, and even if he didn't, there's a new threat in the city: a faceless assassin who goes by the Hummingbird. So long as I do what I'm told and stay where he put me, I might actually make it out of this alive.

And for the first time in years, I'm digging that idea.

Only Luca... he doesn't know what to make of me. He expected tears; I give him a flirty smile. He expected me to beg; I ask him if he wants to play checkers. I'm having the time of my life, and the sparks flying between us have me close to igniting.

And then he discovers that *I* am the Hummingbird—and, whoops, things aren't as much fun anymore...

LUCA

When the pretty brunette saw something she shouldn't have, I had no choice. Devil gives the orders, and he told me to put the girl in the trunk.

I put the girl in the trunk.

Rumors run that becoming a dad changed Devil. Made him soft. Anyone in the life knows that's BS, especially when he decides he's going to eliminate the threat to the Sinners. Only I... I can't let him.

So I ask to keep her instead. If I make her mine, if I win her loyalty, then she won't snitch.

It's easier than I thought it would be. Kylie is the strangest yet most intoxicating woman I've ever met, and the more time I spend with her, the more my obsession for her grows. I want to *save* her—but when I learn the secrets she's been hiding, I have no choice.

The Hummingbird is supposedly a threat to Springfield. But if anything happens to Kylie... I might just lose my cool.

And ask anyone in Hamilton: bad things happen when Luca St. James loses his cool.

I want Kylie. I'm going to keep her.

And if anyone tries to take her from me, I'll show them everything I've learned from the man I've spent the last three years driving around the city...

---

*This is the fifth and final book in the **Deal with the Devil** series. It tells the story of a cheeky assassin and the man behind the wheel who will do anything for her—before realizing he enjoys letting her take care of him.

And I believed that for more than a decade—until I received an invitation to my own wedding.

I thought it was a joke. No way was I going to be forced into marrying one of Owed. It wasn't going to happen—

—and, yet, there I was, dressed in white, about to get married to a man I didn't know.

Whoops. Wrong again.

Because the man who walked in on the ceremony, calmly shooting my 'fiancé' before taking his place?

I know *him*.

Adrian Heller. My biggest tormentor... and my biggest secret.

ADRIAN

For too long, I had to hide how I felt about Loni Dougherty. Considering my obsession with her was the biggest open secret in all of Harmony Heights, I didn't do that great of a job.

Everyone knew—except *her*.

She thought I was her high school bully. And maybe I was, but I also made her untouchable. No one could have her, and I wouldn't let anyone hurt her more than I had to.

But once I became one of the Owed, I could make her mine. I held onto that, too, until she disappeared and my new loyalties meant I couldn't chase her out of town.

That doesn't mean I gave up on her, though. And

when she gets dragged back to Harmony Heights to be given away to another Owed, I make sure the whole order knows that I claimed her first.

She looks so pretty with blood on her wedding dress and my name on her lips, even if her eyes are filled with hate as she vows to be my bride.

But I don't care about that. Loni is mine, and I'll end anyone who tries to take her away from me again.

* *Bloody Wedding* is a dual-POV dark romance that begins the new **The Order of the Owed** series. With the same possessive dark heroes you've met in the **Deal with the Devil** series, and a secret society twist, it gives new meaning to the phrase: *'til death do us part.*

coming in 2025
ARIN HART
PLEASE
THEY LOCKED YOU AWAY.
BUT THEY COULD NEVER MAKE
HIM FORGET...
oubliette

KEEP IN TOUCH

Stay tuned for what's coming up next! Follow me at any of these places—or sign up for my newsletter—for news, promotions, upcoming releases, and more:

CarinHart.com
Carin's Newsletter
Carin's Signed Book Store

facebook.com/carinhartbooks
amazon.com/author/carinhart
instagram.com/carinhartbooks

ALSO BY CARIN HART

Deal with the Devil series

No One Has To Know *standalone

Silhouette *standalone

He Sees You *standalone

The Devil's Bargain

The Devil's Bride *newsletter exclusive

The Devil's Playground

Dragonfly

Dance with the Devil

Ride with the Devil

Reed Twins

Close to Midnight

Really Should Stay

The Order of the Owed

Oubliette

Bloody Wedding

Standalone

My Wife